I0525205

Cirsova®

P. ALEXANDER, Ed.
Xavier L., Copy Ed.
Mark Thompson, Copy Ed.

Novels

Novelettes

Strange Short Stories of Thrilling Suspense

Fall Issue
2023

Vol.2, No 16
$15.00 per copy

Dead Men Do Tell Tales

By TEEL JAMES GLENN

A gangster with vampire thugs is on the warpath, and Dead Fred's still-talking head may hold the key as to why! Will Ghostmaker Jack Silence get answers or the bite?!

Chapter One:
Heads Up!

"You gotta help me, Silence, they're gonna kill me."

"You're already dead, Fred," I said into the talking crystal. "Remember? I went to your funeral five years ago." He'd overdosed on heroin, then some Necromancer looking for business had brought him back as an advertising stunt. Fred went back to his old habits, though now he could inject bleach directly if he wanted to get high. I swear it's true—zombies have no brains.

"I'm serious, Silence."

"Okay, okay," I was lying in bed after a late-night job of fighting an infestation of para-unicorns; those freaking horns are sharp. "Come on over, I'll have Grondo whip me up some eggs and hunt up some sheep's intestines for you."

"No, no," he desperately whined. The effect of the talking crystal, unlike when cell phones used to work, was to have the voice come from all around you. "You have to come to me; too dangerous to go out."

"Jeeze, man. It will take me a while to get to Potter's Field."

"No, I'm not at my place in the cemetery," he said.

"Where then?" *I should have put my crystal in the drawer by the bed to block the signal.*

"The haunt."

"The haunt?" *Oh, man, that's at the edge of no man's land.*

I knew Fred from the haunted house I used to work in as an actor before The Convergence when the land of the Fey and my mundane world reintegrated seven years ago. The irony is that he *played* a zombie then as a promoter for the haunt selling discount tickets.

The haunt was on the edge of Hell's Kitchen in Manhattan. These days I hated to even go near there. It had earned its old nickname in the recent past when real hell-mouths actually opened there.

"Can't you—" I started, but he cut in.

"Gotta go, they might be close."

I started to say, "What the hell is this about?" when the signal went as dead as he was.

I levered my sore, fifty-year-old body out of bed and yelled downstairs to my aide-de-camp and all-around assistant.

"Hey, rock pants," I called. "Fry me up a couple of eggs and reload my shotgun. I'll be heading into The Kitchen." *Jack Silence, Ghostmaker, was on the job again. I make the parafey go away!*

I took a quick shower and suited up.

By the time I got down to the kitchen on the second floor of the townhouse, Grondo had a full meal on the table and had laid out my firearms. He was a gnome of the garden variety, made of living stone and about three feet tall with a neat little white beard. He always had a corncob pipe clenched in his mouth. He also wore a ridiculous red cone-shaped hat.

"I did bacon, eggs, and blueberry pancakes, boss," Grondo said. "And fresh-squeezed orange juice."

"If you were the right species, I'd marry you, Grondo." I plunked my two hundred and sixty pounds at the table and ate like I had never seen food before.

"You couldn't afford to keep me in the style I need, boss," he said with a grin. "I loaded the Mossburg with the usual, two slugs and then bird shot, boss, but I didn't know which sword you wanted."

"Thanks, buddy." I washed the meal down with the OJ. "I think I'll use the naval cutlass. I'm going into the haunt to meet Dead Fred, and it can be tight in there if things get wonky."

"Why're you meeting that walking meatcicle? He's such a drama queen."

"But he also sends a lot of business our way, buddy, and I did know him when he was still breathing, so I kind of feel obligated to listen to him."

"You're too soft."

"And you're all stone, your point?" I donned the purple Inverness cloak that was good at allowing me to hide the sawed-off shotgun and my sword. I was licensed to be a walking arsenal, but no need to show off.

"Miranda is handling the phones today," Grondo said as he stepped up on the little platform that allowed him to wash the dishes in the sink. "I have to go over to the weigh-in for the Minotaur/Troll fight over at Citi Field."

"You got money on the troll?" He would gamble on the sun rising and was always chasing a lucky streak.

"I've sworn off gambling till I catch up on what I owe you."

"Really?"

"You can bet on it!"

Incorrigible!

"*Sim, Sim, Salabim!*" I ordered one of our company flying carpets to rise to about shoulder height once I was on it, and then gave it the directions. "Across Fourteenth to Seventh, then up to Forty-Second Street."

The carpet obeyed my command, and we zoomed out to Fourteenth Street and headed crosstown. Flying just about shoulder level, it weaved in and out of the pre-lunchtime traffic with its own intelligence. The street was just as busy as in pre-Convergence times.

The carpet maneuvered me around centaurs, horses, griffins (with clipped wings), a few tame unicorns, and some other things I wasn't sure what to call, as well as other carpets. It was still a strange feeling with my memories of the old city superimposed over this new one.

Back then I was a working actor and

fight choreographer, just middle of the pack. Then, *bam!*—the Fey were here, things went wonky, and I discovered an ability I didn't know I had—or maybe never had before. EOP—Extra-Olfactory Perception! I could smell the parafey—those creatures of the Fey realm below sentience that seemed to suddenly spring up when the worlds combined.

Not real smell, in the sense of smelling old fish, or the griffin and centaur dung that was making NY smell old-timey—no, I could smell them often just before they came through into our realm, which allowed me to stop them and kill them—hence the Ghostmaker title.

I was able to market the hell out of myself with that, and suddenly I was a successful guy who created my own niche market before anyone else realized we needed it. Once, I went toe-to-toe with a paragargoyle clan who took over a country estate; it made the papers, and I had more jobs than I could shake a boomstick at.

At Forty-Second Street and Times Square, the carpet turned left, and I coasted down the new Duce. This new one had echoes of the old one, for sure, having slipped back from the Disney/family-friendly tourist trap of a decade before to the red-light district for the city. It attracted the lowlifes and outcasts from a dozen species—which meant that bestiality rules were a grey area of law now.

Sirens were singing half-heartedly on the corner, and I wondered if they were still up from last night or getting an early start on the weekend's bridge and carpet traffic. In either case, they looked like the lower end of the temptress scale.

A lone satyr was leaning against a wall under one of the marquees that proclaimed the double feature: *Lord of the G-Strings* and *The Medium Was Very Large.* By his state of undress—he wore only a backward baseball cap with his horns sticking out from it—it was clear what he was selling to johns who might wander by.

I carpeted past a centaur cop clopping down the street with a conventionally mounted human on a regular horse beside him. Things were to the point where even the cops traveled in pairs on The Duce. At night, if they were brave enough to come here at all, they moved in a larger pack.

There were also a couple of Elf-walkers waving to and chatting at the cops, looking golden in the sunlight, but their golden skin was clearly mostly make-up, not natural glimmer. Dream-weed users for sure.

The year-round Haunted House I used to work at was on Forty-Second Street and Eighth Avenue, right on the edge of Hell's Kitchen. The Crossroads Crypt!

It was the second and third floor of a skyscraper accessed from a marquee at street level, but when people could see horned monstrosities lumbering along the daylight streets, why pay to be scared of fake monsters? It had been shuttered for years now.

The haunt building itself had the ground floor all boarded up with plywood nailed over the windows and doors, but it was not a problem to find one that was loose over one of the side doors.

I sent the carpet up to hover at the twenty-foot height till I summoned it and slipped in through the boarded-up exit.

Inside, the emergency lighting high up on the walls was still working, but I had a flashlight clipped to my shotgun, and I used it to sweep the area ahead of me. The reason I was still alive was that I am paranoid.

The steps at the entrance led me up to the second floor, and I found myself in the faux hotel lobby set that had been the entrance to the actual haunt itself. It was now genuinely creepy after years of neglect.

The place also now had fast food wrappers, used condoms, chicken and other sorts of bones (there were lots of species to choose from these days) scattered all over the place. Not to mention enough empty beer cans and wine bottles to stock a store.

Beyond the inner entrance to the faux hotel lobby was what had been the waiting line area and entrance to the bar area. I could see shapes moving around in there, some human and some clearly not. But I sensed—smelled—no parafey that might be a problem.

Dead Fred would not be there, however. I knew he'd be in the haunt itself. It would allow him a number of escape routes if one of the different crime factions he did errands for really was after him.

The haunt was a rabbit warren of corridors divided into four 'sets'—maze, asylum, circus, and butcher's shop. The gate to the stairs that led to the haunt was still locked because there was no percentage in struggling with it for the scavengers who could make easy use of the second floor. Fred and I both had keys from when I worked securi-

ty in the haunt, and he used to come in early to get promo tickets.

I locked the gate after me, then went up into the musty-smelling darkness, all the more alert now. If I met anything up there, it would not be some casual street stray.

I could have switched off my flashlight since I knew every foot of the haunt by feel and was used to running through it at full speed in the dark to get ahead of customers; some sense memories don't fade.

I figured Fred would be in the butcher's shop—the last set—since it had an old meat storage locker in it that Fred had gotten working awhile ago to sleep in when his own mausoleum out on Potter's Field was too far to travel to.

I went through the maze and the asylum set, where I waved hello to the rubber dummy sitting in the electric chair. We used to call it "Jazzy Jaime," though he was looking worse for wear. Some fallen debris covered him and the chair in plaster dust and chunks of ceiling.

I made my way through the set easily but paused at the circus. I called out, "Fred?"

The circus set was garishly painted in red and white stripes, clown masks hung along the walls, a couple of dilapidated clown dummies and a sad, ratty-looking stuffed camel in one corner that used to 'spit' at customers with a fine mist of water.

There was no answer from up ahead, but the smell of the place—the real smell, not the paranormal smell—got worse as I approached the faux butcher shop. It was the smell of death, fresh death.

I entered the next room with my flashlight sweeping the space, ready for some kind of trouble. I got a shock that equaled any in my life when I did. There on the counter of the butcher's shop was Fred's severed head. When my light hit it, his eyes popped open!

Chapter Two:
Button Down

I really should not have been that freaked out—I mean, he had been dead for a while, but as a whole zombie—this modular Fred was a new wrinkle. He saw me and blinked his eyes at the light, then began to move his lips, as if to speak.

There were no lungs to push sound through his mouth, but I'd done a production of *Children of a Lesser God* years before. When I learned Sign Language, I'd also learned lip reading, so I was able to understand him.

"Hi, Jack," his head said. "Thanks for coming."

"Jeez, Fred, what the hell happened?" It's not like he was the most put-together guy to begin with, but this was extreme.

"Ha, the jerk thought he could torture the info out of me by cutting me up." The head gave a silent laugh. "Guess he didn't realize revenants don't feel pain like live folks; but I didn't let him know that. I screamed like anything, should have gotten me a Tony Award for it."

"Why? What the hell was he torturing you for, and who was 'he'?"

"That's a funny story," the head began, "So I was about to climb in the case here and—"

"Fred, just tell me why someone was torturing you and why you called me."

As he started to open his mouth, the wall of the set suddenly exploded. A body hurtled through it and slammed into me like a freight train.

I went down hard, cursing myself for getting distracted by Fred's noggin. I hit the floor with my attacker bear-hugging me, so I couldn't get at any of the weapons I had festooned all over myself.

The attacker tried to squeeze the breath out of me, pinning my arms to my side. It was dark, but he was big, over my six-foot-six and felt like he was twice as wide. He also smelled like garlic and liverwurst and was trying to bite my face off.

I was able to roll over while dodging the teeth of the attacker by swinging my head back and forth. I hard-smacked the guy in the nose with my forehead several times.

I felt the arms slacken a bit, and it was enough for me to snap the sleeve gun into my palm. I jammed the double-barrel derringer into my attacker's groin and let him have both silver-coated bullets. It was a waste of my anti-werewolf capabilities, but I didn't have much choice.

He levitated off me with a squeal to wake the dead—well, the ones still in coffins, anyway.

I rolled to my knees, swung the shotgun up on its carry strap, and blasted away with the first shot, which was a slug.

The solid chunk of lead slammed into the attacker and drove him back through the canvas set wall where he fell on the clown set and didn't move.

I sat on the floor for a minute, chambered another round, and waited.

After a couple of minutes, I heard no other noise and smelled no parafey, so I climbed to my feet—man, my back hurt— and stumbled over to look at the goon who had attacked me.

He was a big puppy, easily four hundred pounds, and clearly half orc. His never-not-ugly face was even more so in death with twisted tusks and wide-open, bloodshot eyes. He had light grey, pebbled skin, and was bald as a very grotesque baby. He wore a yellow tracksuit and a pair of red *Sidhe-He* high-top sneakers.

Just to be sure, I kicked the corpse and jumped back. Nothing.

"Okay," I said out loud, then turned back to Fred's head. "Now, what the hell is going on? Why didn't you warn me about that?"

"Hey, I didn't know he was still here," he said. "I can't exactly look around."

"I gotta call the cops on this one," I said, more to myself than to Fred as I searched the attacker for some I.D. "I have a license to keep, and I can't just kill Fey willy-nilly."

I used my crystal ball necklace to call Morgan O'Flynn with the Major Fey Division of the NYPD. "Hey, Morgan," I said with as cheery a tone as I could summon. "How's it going?"

"Don't pull my hind leg, Silence," she said. "You never call me unless you want a favor or did something bad." I was silent for a moment, and she shot back, "What did you do?"

"Just bring a bag and tag unit to the old Crossroads Crypt, Morgan. I'll explain when you get here. Up in the haunt."

"Wait, what—" I cut off the connection and stuck the crystal in a shielded pocket so she couldn't call me back.

"Damn," I said, "you better have a good explanation for this, Fred." When I turned back to him, his eyes were frantic and his lips were flapping full speed.

"You can't bring the cops into this, Silence."

"I have to. I can't just go around shooting sentient Fey any more than I could legally shoot humans." I heard a siren getting closer and figured that was probably Morgan; she would love to chew my head off for hanging up on her, and I had to just hope it wasn't literally—she was half-Fey and a werewolf.

"You will get yourself killed, and me, too—again—if you get the cops in this, Silence."

"Then tell me what—" I heard the heavy tread of John Law feet down below, and the derelicts squatting there started to yell in chaos.

"Damn!" No time to quiz the freaking zombie, so I grabbed his head and dodged into the circus set. Grabbing one of the clown masks off the wall, I slapped it on Fred and set him on a shelf.

"Stay there, Fred; I'll come back for you tomorrow—if they don't throw me in jail!"

It's a good thing he could not make noise 'cause he was probably cursing me and my entire ancestral line.

I ran down the stairs and got to the

locked gate just as the blue wave got there.

"Hi, Morgy," I said as I opened the gate. "Welcome to my parlor."

"You don't get to call me that, Silence," she said as she pushed past me leading three uniforms from three species up the stairs. "Tell me what happened, and don't lie, or I'll give you rabies."

Morgan O'Flynn, sweetheart of the detective division, was six foot, redheaded, square-jawed, green-eyed—with the ability to go full-on Lon Chaney Junior on command. She had thrown parafey work my way, and I'd helped her on some cases when an official investigator couldn't go someplace. Problem was, I couldn't lie to a woman who could literally smell my pheromone level change. So I had to dance around the truth.

I told her about the call from Fred and about arriving and being jumped, but simply didn't mention finding his head. I hoped sticking as close to the truth as possible would not trip me up.

"Well, you found Fred," she said when we entered the butcher's shop after her guys had gotten the lights turned on. I was about to wonder how she knew when I realized she was not talking about his head—in the cold fluorescence I could see the new decorations that had been added to the shop's rubber arms and legs. Fred's arms, legs, and torso were scattered around the room.

"Damn!" I said with real surprise.

"Looks like this skell literally tore Dead Fred apart," Morgan said, with disgust in her tone. "And joint by joint. He must have really hated the little jerk." Well, she did

know Fred—not the most likable little jerk, it's true.

What could make someone hate you this much, Fred? The fact that I could not run into the next room to ask his head was driving me nuts.

"You have no idea why he called you?" she asked.

"Honestly," I said, honestly, "I have zero idea." She seemed to accept that and set her guys—a Satyr, an Elf, and a human—to photographing the scene, then gathering up the pieces of Fred. Turns out the smell was from a bucket of entrails and calf brains since zombies don't decay. Fred must have brought them with him for a snack. Quite the epicure, our Fred.

"You get a pass on this one, Silence," she said, to my surprise. When she saw that reflected on my face, she laughed. "You don't know who this big thing is, do you?"

"No, I swear I never saw him before at all."

"I'd be surprised if you had. This is Burton the Button, an enforcer for Mark Van Patten, major player in the artifact smuggling business. Need a wand with pedigree but without a curse? A scrying mirror? A Hand of Glory from Haiti? He can get it all."

"Wow, I'd heard the name but"—I shrugged—"not in my social circle."

"Well, water finds its level, Silence." The way she said it was not a compliment. "I'm thinking this might have to do with the slaughterhouse we found in Spanish Harlem."

"Slaughterhouse?"

"Marco Herrera and his whole crew were shot, chopped up, and drained last night. Somebody wanted something he had and they weren't in a talking mood."

"Clues?"

"Why the hell would I tell you?"

Her human uniformed cop came up to her.

"We found all of him in the room but his head, Detective," he said. She looked at me.

"Must have had a partner," I ventured, "maybe took it for a ritual or souvenir?"

"Could be," she said thoughtfully. "Button works with Waters and Brooks, two neck biters."

"So I can go?"

She gave me a side-eye. "Surrender the two guns—they are evidence now—and I expect you in my office tomorrow with a full statement."

I handed over the shotgun and the derringer. She handled them gingerly.

"This the one with the silver bullets?" She knew it was. "You think your ass is worth that much silver?"

"Love you too, Detective O'Flynn. Till tomorrow." I turned and headed out, trying not to make it look like I was running, worried she would change her mind.

I jumped on the carpet and shot across to the East Side, where I went to a sporting goods store and made a purchase.

When I figured enough time had lapsed for O'Flynn to have fled back to the station and piles of paperwork, I went back to the haunt. I slipped into the place from the floor above instead of entering from the ground floor.

I snuck in and went straight to the circus set. Fred was still there where I put him and as angry as a severed head could be.

"What the hell did you do, Silence?" he silently yelled at me. "You left me here in a freaking clown mask!"

"I had to wait for the cops to quit the place, dead boy. At least I came back."

"That female cop didn't really believe you, you know?"

"I never really think she believes any of my bull, but the paperwork of taking me in isn't worth it most of the time."

"But she likes you."

"Really?" I probably sounded more eager than I should have.

"No," he laughed. "She cursed you out six ways to Sunday as a two-face man."

"I could just stick you in a sock and sell you to a soccer team, Fred, so shut up."

I was about to question him when there was a noise from down below, and I heard the gate open.

"I forgot to tell you," Fred mouthed. "They left a cop to keep an eye on the scene—he just went to the john."

Damn! I grabbed the jerk and shoved him in the bowling ball bag I'd bought at the sports store and raced back upstairs then down another staircase to my carpet.

Once we were in the air heading south, I called the office.

"Silence, the Ghostmaker," Miranda answered the talking crystal. "We make parafey go away! How can I help you?"

"Hi, M," I said. She was a college student doing post-graduate work in comparative mythologies who did research for me and occasionally filled in at the office when Grondo was busy losing his paycheck elsewhere. "On the way in, any news?"

"Nothing new," she said. "Uh, when are you coming back?"

"On the way," I said, then realized she had never asked me that. "Oh—at my usual Thursday bowling league tournament," I said. She knew I didn't go bowling, and the smart girl picked up on that.

"Hope you scored a split for me again like last week," she said.

"I tried, kiddo," I said. "But maybe next time. I'll be there in about a half hour, see you then." In fact, I was only ten minutes away, and now I knew something was up. The only question was, what it was and what was I gonna do about it?

Chapter Three: Double Header

Something was wrong at the office, and with my life as it was, it could be any level of danger from a crazy ex-girlfriend to a pissed-off dragon, so I unzipped the bowling ball bag as I cruised toward my townhouse.

"I'm gonna drop you off with a friend in the bodega on the corner near my place till I find out what is going on."

"No," Fred mouthed at me, giving me puppy dog eyes. "Don't leave me again; I'll take my chances with you. Please."

Who could turn down a zombie with those pleading eyes?

So I zipped up, and we carpeted to my place. I wished Morgan hadn't taken my sleeve gun and the Mossburg, but at least I still had my Broomhandle Mauser pistol. I loosened it in my holster and hoped I had enough notice if things went south.

Turns out I didn't.

The second I walked into the door, I found myself pinned against the wall by a hand the size of a snowshoe. The arm on the other side of that hand belonged to the largest woman I have ever seen, sumo big, with a lot of muscle, and a head like a cinderblock.

She was as white as flour, had jet-black hair, wide cheekbones, and vaguely almond-shaped eyes. She also had a wide smile that showed off her two-inch fangs.

I hate Vampires, freaking mosquitoes!

She was wearing a long blue leather coat with a fur collar and had glitter on her cheeks, like she was late for a rave.

"Don't damage him, Brooks, darling," a cultured voice came from around the corner. "At least not for now, we might have use for Mister Silence."

The delicate damsel grabbed me by the vest with both hands and carried me into the office with my feet dangling off the floor.

The office was a large room with a window looking out onto Gramercy Park. There were two desks on either side of the room and a leather couch between them on which sat an outrageous figure.

He was a handsome black man, wearing a powder-blue double-breasted suit, a red shirt, white tie and spats. He had his arms around Miranda, who was sitting stiffly and looked terrified.

"I'm sorry, Mister Silence," Miranda said. "They just barged in."

"Tut, tut, little sister," the black man said. His voice was like a muted clarinet. "Mister Ghostmaker here knows you tried to warn him, but he was all about checking out the danger, am I right, Mister S?"

Brooks set me down, and a second figure appeared from behind me suddenly, and before I realized it had stripped off my cloak, taking my pistol and cutlass with it. This new arrival was a rail-thin figure dressed in his own long blue leather coat and with pale skin and sharp features, including fangs.

"Thank you, Waters," I said, trying hard to be nonchalant. "To what do I owe this visit, Mister Van Patten?"

"So you know who I am," Dapper said.

I took notice that his two bloodsuckers bracketed me, both watching me from beneath lidded eyes, like cats, still, but with tremendous potential for movement. I knew that while real vampires were weakened in direct sunlight, they were no more susceptible to bursting into flames than any other albinos.

"What can I do for you?" I said. I sauntered over to the corner of Grondo's desk to sit casually on the edge. I set the bowling ball case to the side in a clear space among the piles of files.

Van Patten laughed, a soft gentle laugh that sent a chill up my spine. "You are a funny man, Ghostmaker. You kill my button man and ask me what I want?"

"You are well-informed."

"Key to success." He smiled, and I was reminded of a televangelist in his smooth manner. "Also focus." He let the fingers of his right hand idly toy with Miranda's cornrows, and she shuddered at the touch.

"Focus?" I caught Miranda's eye and tried to give her a reassuring look. "So, if you are focused on me, there is no reason to keep the young lady here."

"Burton was a moron, but he was my moron." Van Patten said. "With him dead, I am not happy."

"Self-defense," I said. "Your goon tried to make me into a snack. I dare say you would have done the same."

"Maybe, but I didn't, you did. And actions have consequences." He suddenly clenched his fist in Miranda's hair, and she gasped.

"Leave her alone!" I started to move but in an eyeblink, Waters was right at my side, his long thin, claw-like fingers lightly touching my cheek.

"Easy, bloodsack," Waters hissed. His touch was like ice.

"Yes, easy, Ghostmaker," Van Patten said. "I want my property. I get that, I just might forget about the Orc."

"What property?" I should have found a quiet spot and quizzed the zombie. Fred was a weasel but not an outright thief. And to steal from Van Patten meant he was a thief and an idiot.

"Don't play dumb. That cold case intercepted a delivery for me and then called you. So—"

"Hey, look, I'm not playing dumb, I'm the real thing."

"Don't be smart with me."

"Which is it, dumb or smart? Either way I don't know about—"

"Waters!"

DEAD MEN DO TELL TALES

The bloodsucker slapped me hard on the side of the head, so I fell over on the desk. My face landed in a pile of the colored pencils that Grondo used in the coloring books he used when things were slow. I noticed he was not good at keeping in the lines.

"I suppose you expect me to say you hit like a wimp, Dracula," I said when I stopped seeing stars, "but actually, you have a nice follow-through."

Waters hissed.

"My patience is wearing thin, Ghostmaker." The clarinet voice was a very minor key now. "I want that throne."

"Throne? You constipated?"

Waters demonstrated his backhand on my other cheek.

"I want the Throne of Solomon, Silence." He rose to his feet and took a step toward me, his eyes narrowing, and he was all a predator. "I paid a lot of money and had to have several people and two elves killed to get that. The creeping corpse friend of yours diverted the delivery to Marco Herrera, and then when me and the twins here went calling, Marco drew down on us."

I was beginning to see why Fred had been scared. Van Patten was a stone-cold killer. He walked up to stare me in the face with Brooks and Waters standing on either side to intimidate me. It worked.

"The haunt," I blurted out. "I swear. He hid it in the haunted house." All my years of acting went into that lie. I figured Jazzy Jaime was in an electric chair, and a chair is close enough to a throne.

"The haunted house?" Van Patten did not sound very convinced.

"The guy in the electric chair in the Asylum set. Perfect place to hide it."

He looked like he was about to sic the dogs on me when my savior came from the most unexpected source.

"I remember that electric chair guy," Brooks said. We all looked at the giant vampire woman, who shrugged. "I went there on a date once before it closed."

Van Patten looked at her with his head cocked to the side.

"I used to date," she said defensively. "How do you think I ended up crossing over? A bad date."

"Hey!" Waters said.

I do not want to know their story.

"You lie to me, Silence, and I will feed you to these two."

"Cross my heart," I said. *Hope not to die.*

"Okay, Brooks, you take me there," Van Patten ordered. "Waters, hold these two until I know he was telling the truth. I'll crystal you."

"And then?" the skinny bloodsucker asked.

Van Patten looked me and Miranda up and down like he was checking out livestock. "We will see." He smiled a shark smile. "Sometimes you have to leave people around as examples, right Ghostmaker? Sort of like advertising, so other people know who you are."

"Good business strategy," I said. "Word of mouth is all we got with no Instagram anymore."

"You better be telling the truth."

"Fey Scout's honor!" I held up my hand in a Scout salute.

"Don't make light of that," Waters hissed. "I was an Eagle Scout."

I just can't win.

The smuggler and the giant vampire left on their griffin carriage while Waters, Miranda, and I settled in to wait for the axe to fall. I'd bought a little time, but when they found a cheaply made prop chair instead of their ancient artifact, they'd call the lithe leech and he'd suck us dry.

Miranda stayed on the couch while I stayed perched on the desk. Waters just sort of lurked, unmoving, by the window like he was a desiccated statue of a person, his eyes focused directly at me. Creepy!

"So, Miranda, tell me about this Throne of Solomon." I might as well know what I was dying for, and it just might keep the girl's mind off our impending doom.

She looked at me as if to say, *are you kidding?* but to her credit she just reached into her memory and spouted. "The legend says that the Hebrew King who could control demons and married the Queen of the Djinn invested his powers into his great seal that was placed in the back of the throne. It disappeared when the Temple at Jerusalem was looted—at the same time that the Ark of the Covenant was taken. If that guy gets his hand on the throne and the seal, he will have almost unlimited power over summoning demons!"

"Pretty fancy butt rest, eh?" I noticed that the tall mosquito was interested in the topic, and it gave me an idea. "So, you think you'd recognize this seal if you saw it?"

"I've seen engravings that more or less guess at what it looked like from descriptions. Why?" She was looking at me oddly, but I could see she was catching on that I had some sort of half-assed plan.

"Well, I picked up this thing that I think Dead Fred must have dropped. I guess he pried it off the chair, if it is real." I twisted on the desk and started to unzip the bowling ball bag. This got Vlad's attention, and he flowed over to stand near the desk.

"Here," I said as I reached into the bag. I yanked Fred out as I screamed, "Get 'em, Fred!" and threw the zombie head at Waters's throat.

The head clamped his teeth on the vampire's neck, the best irony I could hope for, and actually freaked the vampire out. Waters squealed and backpedaled as he tried to dislodge the chomping creep.

Before the bloodsucker could get a handle on things, I grabbed a pencil off the desk and stuck it between the ring and screw-you finger of my right hand as I made a fist.

True fact, you can drive a straw through a potato with enough velocity or a pencil into a heart with a well-launched karate twisting punch.

Also true fact, a wooden stake, even a thin one, driven into the heart of a vampire will kill it. Also, a stake driven through the heart of any living animal will kill it, as well, just in case you're not sure.

Waters dropped to the floor stiff as a board, and I was glad vampires don't bleed 'cause it was an expensive rug.

Fred was still chewing hard on the thin throat of the monster, so I had to grab him by the hair and yank him off.

"Okay, Fred, he's done!"

I went eye to eye with him, and he mouthed, "Tastes like turkey."

"What the hell is that?" Miranda asked as I stood up with the zombie head in my hand. She didn't waste any time waiting for an answer but grabbed my cutlass and proceeded to lop Waters's head off.

"I guess I have a matched set now." I explained to her quickly whose head I was holding.

"Just have to call Morgan to come get this two-piece thug, and we are set." I put Fred on the desk and realized he was staring at me urgently and flapping his lips again.

"What have you done, Silence!" he mouthed.

"What do you mean, Fred, I saved my and Miranda's lives and set up Van Patten for the cops."

"You sent them straight to the Throne."

"What?"

"I hid the throne by disguising it as Jazzy Jaime's electric chair!"

I just can't win!

Chapter Four:
Chair Today, Gone Tomorrow

I grabbed Fred in his bowling ball bag and some special armament and leapt on my fastest carpet. I was gambling that the griffin carriage would be slow enough for me to beat them to the haunt.

"Morgan, I'll explain it all when you get there," I yelled into the talking crystal, trying not to be blown off as the flying carpet zoomed at dangerous speed up Eighth Avenue. "Send a bag and tag group to my of-fice, and please be gentle with Miranda."

I gotta give Miranda a raise and send her to free therapy.

"I am gonna neuter you, Silence," Morgan's voice screamed around me.

"I may deserve it for sending that stuffed shirt to get the most powerful weapon on the planet since the Convergence."

"What the hell are you talking about?"

I jumped off the carpet as we looped into Forty-Second Street to race up the stairs without answering the wolf-cop.

The emergency lights were still, so everything had a ghostly blue cast to the haunt.

I came into it just beyond the butcher's set at the same time I heard a grunt, and the gate down below being broken into.

Opening the bag, I locked eyes with Fred. "Stick to the plan," I said.

"What the hell else can I do, I'm just a head?"

Heavy footsteps of his queen-sized neck-biter came up the stairs followed by Van Patten's own softer tread. "If that jerk lied to me about this Throne," Van Patten said, "I will eat his liver."

"As long as I get the heart and the juicy parts," Brooks said, with obvious glee.

I hustled through the circus to the Asylum, well aware that my home-court advantage was pretty much neutralized by the vampire's own night vision and reflexes, but I planned to use that against her.

"Wait for me, Brooks," Van Patten said. I heard him blundering around.

I made it to the electric chair set. Knowing what it was, I could see that the rubber figure, covered with the debris, was not sitting on the prop chair.

You're clever, Fred, I'll give you that.

We used to hide in a little setback and pop out to terrify the customers, and I was hoping that would help me against Brooks's preternatural reactions.

Fighting parafey was a hell of a lot easier than the undead. Give me a gibbering, unthinking paragoblin over a calculating vampire—or a human crook—any day. Gibbering is more my speed, or so my second-grade teacher used to say.

I took Fred out of his carry case, holding him in my right hand. In my left, I cocked the air rifle that was the center of my plan.

Van Patten and his minion came into the electric chair room. He stood there for a moment, staring at the prop prisoner, then seemed to shake himself and said, "Okay, get the doll out of the chair and uncover my throne."

The giant vampire stepped forward and lifted the rubber dummy out of the chair in a cloud of debris to throw it aside.

That was when I tossed Fred and hit the UV light. It was a 25,000 Lux light that I had duct-taped to my chest.

The vampire screamed as the blinding pseudo-sunlight hit her then threw her arms up to protect her eyes. That was when I fired the air rifle with the horse tranquilizer in it. The dart struck her right in the neck and staggered her.

Meanwhile, my throw with Fred had been good, and he'd latched his teeth onto Van Patten's leg. The smuggler started to scream like a Girl Scout on fire and swatted at the head, but Fred went to town chowing down.

The vampire flung the rubber dummy at me and charged. I'd been prepared for that and whipped up my shotgun and fired. Instead of slugs, I had loaded shells with dimes. About twenty dollars of whirling coins slammed into her like beanbag rounds, but with more punch.

This staggered her further, which made her roar with anger. She closed her eyes against the light and surged at me again.

Crap!

I chambered and fired a second barrage, but she was so angry she ignored it and kept coming, slamming me against the wall like a pickup truck.

She got her hands around my throat. I tried to get my cutlass into play, but she was crushing my windpipe and I started to black out.

Suddenly there was a howling sound louder than even Van Patten's screaming and a red ball of fur and fury rocketed across the space to land on Brooks's back. It was Morgan in full werewolf form!

The vampire forgot all about me and there was a full-on catfight—or wolf fight—as the two of them danced around the room with Morgan sinking her jaws into the vampire's neck.

I got my breath back just as the tranq took effect and the giant undead thug suddenly fell over. Morgan deftly jumped off the giant and was back to full human form just as half a dozen uniforms swarmed into the room.

One of the cops pulled a gun and was about to shoot Fred. "Don't!" I yelled and ran over to pull the chomping creep off of Van Patten's leg. The pant leg of the immaculate suit was a bloody mess halfway up the thigh and the smuggler was hysterical.

"What the hell is this all about, Silence?" Morgan licked her chops but otherwise was her own charming self.

I held up Fred who started to flap his lips. I translated. "Fred here saw Van Patten and his flunkies go into Marco's before the shootout as he was delivering Solomon's Throne and then hightailed it here with it. That is when Fred called me."

She stared at me like I really had grown a second head. "What is this, a mime ventriloquist act?"

I explained to her about my lip reading while Fred smiled and said, "Van Patten really tastes like chicken."

"You mean this—this head can pin the Herrera massacre on Van Patten?"

"That's the full story, Morgan. Fred is a star witness."

She looked like she wanted to curse but just said, "You really annoy me. Okay, bring the dead head."

He flapped his gums at me, and I relayed it to Morgan. "He'd like to know if you guys kept his parts. He's got an itch on his nose."

It might have been the wrong thing to say; Morgan punched me.

I really can't win.

Teel James Glenn has published dozens of novels and his poetry and stories have been printed in over two hundred magazines including Weird Tales, Mystery, Heroic Fantasy, Blazing Adventures and Sherlock Holmes Mystery. His novel A Cowboy in Carpathia: A Bob Howard Adventure *won best novel 2021 in the Pulp Factory Award. His website is: TheUrbanSwashbuckler.com*

The Dusk Next Door

By MARK PELLEGRINI

Every year, the children draw doodles for the Duskmen! And every year, one high-schooler must deliver them to the town of Dusk to keep them over there!

Scott drummed his fingers nervously upon the leather satchel resting on his lap and then held his breath in anticipation of the electric lights. The lonely train car—of which he was the sole passenger—had just plunged into the darkness of the Duskway Tunnel, so it would take a moment for the automatic lights to hum and ignite. Scott slid the strap of the satchel back onto his shoulder and clutched his precious cargo in the vise-grip of his armpit. The lazy lights were taking too long.

For 364 days of the year, the tunnel could not reach the neighboring town of Dusk. This was the one day on which it could, and Scott pondered what strange mechanisms must be operating in the blackness beyond the window glass to accommodate this annual occasion. The train rumbled in a way that flipped his stomach and forced the bad air out of his lungs, leaving Scott with the impression that he probably wasn't meant to see what was going on in the darkness. Anxiously, he slid the strap off his shoulder, set his satchel onto the empty seat to his right, and began picking at the brass buttons with his fingernail. Breathing again, he elected to ponder something more productive.

Every year, his high school had a lottery. And every year, a senior was Appointed to make the delivery to Dusk. It wasn't a big deal. In the 17 years Scott had been alive, only *once* had the Appointed failed to return. And that was so long ago, he was too young to remember it. The administrators at town hall had given him three months to prepare, which was plenty of time to interview the previously Appointed and commit their advice to memory. It was a lot of strange stories from a lot of strange people. Fidgeting, Scott snatched his satchel from the seat and held it to his chest. The strangeness of the stories hadn't disturbed him half as much as the strangeness of the people.

The previously Appointed were respected, but always from a distance. Everyone who had been to Dusk had come back odd, and that was what jittered Scott's nerves the most. He could steel himself for seeing and doing strange things, but the thought of being forever changed by the experience was a consequence he could not ready himself for. "It's not too different from enlisting in the Army, if you think about it," Mr. Carver had told him during his interview, hoping to ease his apprehensions. Mr.

Carver was a kind old man, but he would only talk to people when their heads were turned in profile—an odd habit he brought home with him from Dusk, his contemporaries whispered. Scott tried to imagine what odd habits he'd bring home with him and unconsciously bent his satchel down the middle with both hands.

The sound of the construction paper crinkling within the leather folds snapped his mind to the present. Carefully, Scott unbent his satchel and tucked it safely back into his armpit, lest he absentmindedly damaged its irreplaceable contents. He hadn't dared to unsnap the buttons and take a peek inside, but he didn't have to. Scott already knew what the contents looked like: "Doodles for the Duskmen."

Every year, every first grader in town would make a drawing in class. It was a simple sort of portrait in crayon: themselves, their families, their pets, and their house. He'd drawn one himself when he was in first grade. "Doodles for the Duskmen," his teacher had called it. Scott hadn't given the assignment much thought at the time. It was what the men from Dusk—the Duskmen—wanted, his class had been told. And it was "what kept them over there." The Appointed would take the train to Dusk on that day each year, deliver the Doodles to their post office, and that would make the Duskmen happy. That would keep them over there.

Scott had asked why the Duskmen wanted drawings from children—of themselves and their families and their pets and where they lived—but none of his interviews had yielded a firm answer. "It's what keeps them over there," replied the previously Appointed, both young and old alike. "And we don't want them coming over here," they would always say next. Standing up, Scott began to pace around in the dark, his right hand raised and fingers sliding along the upper handrails to keep him steady as his left hand gripped his satchel until his fingertips went numb. He could feel the train gradually dropping speed, which meant he would be "over there" very soon.

A sickly light, hued somewhere between red and purple, seeped in from the front of the car and oozed steadily in Scott's direction. The electric lights had never come on, not that it mattered, as the train was exiting the opposite end of the Duskway Tunnel. Scott ceased his blind pacing and clutched the handrail as tightly as he could with his sweaty, slippery palm. The creaking whine of the slowing gears pierced his eardrums. The ugly, dim light flooded the rest of the car. The doors slid open, and a voice in lieu of a whistle growled for him to disembark. It was the voice of the engineer, and Scott knew better than to keep him waiting.

The engineer was a weathered man named Mr. Richards, who had declined Scott's request to be interviewed. Mr. Richards had never been Appointed to deliver but had instead been served what many in town considered a *worse* fate. It was Mr. Richards who drove the train to Dusk and back each year; even the years before Scott had been born, and even the years when the Appointed had not come home. Those whom Scott had been able to interview confidently suggested that Mr. Richards's distant demeanor and distinct "weathering" were the result of having to make this annual excursion.

Though he wouldn't speak to Scott, Mr. Richards had evidently been keeping an eye on him through one of the mirrors in his engine. No sooner had both of Scott's feet found the Dusk Station platform than the train began lurching and screeching along the rails once again, headed determinedly toward the darkened recesses of a nearby roundhouse. Scott didn't need to exert much brainpower to deduce that Mr. Richards was eager to reorient his vehicle and ready himself for a hasty departure (with or without his passenger). One glance around the outskirts of Dusk, and Scott sympathized well with the man who wouldn't speak to him.

"We call the town 'Dusk' for a reason," Colonel Weatherby, a greyish retiree, had told him in his interview. "We don't know what *they* call it, of course, but *we* started calling it Dusk because the sun is always hiding just beyond the foothills and the moons never set." Scott hadn't been sure what to make of this story at the time, seeing as how "Colonel" Weatherby did not start identifying himself by that rank or boasting of his expansive war record until after he'd fulfilled his duties as Appointed. His compulsive lying was semi-tolerated in town, albeit only due to the circumstances which changed him. Scott had been hoping the Colonel's answers were just another one of his tall tales, but the landscape and sky

corroborated every word.

The town looked to be nestled in a valley with the Duskway Tunnel perforating the granite face of a sheer wall to his left. Stretching out beyond the platform and tracks were trees that grew into each other rather than beside each other, looping like a chain-link mesh. In the distance were the foothills, visible only as dark, bumpy silhouettes, because concealed behind them was the sun that serviced the town. Or what the previously Appointed had *assumed* was a sun; one couldn't be certain since whatever it was, it never budged from its hiding place behind the hills. The dampened glow drizzled and cascaded its murky purple ooze through every nook and cranny of Dusk, leaving the town suspended in a moment that would never know the serenity of a starlit night sky.

As for the sky, the only thing up there aside from dismal colors were the moons. There were several of them, but Scott did not waste time trying to count them. In fact, he did his best to keep his line of sight as level as possible. "I know it's tempting," Jacob Matthews had told him through the keyhole of a locked bathroom door, "but whatever you do, don't look at the moons. You might see something walking around up there. And if it catches you gawking at it, it'll try to reach down and grab you." Jacob, who was a senior when Scott was a freshman, began to laugh after that. "Worse, they might try to follow you home! And trust me, we want whatever's in Dusk to stay over there." When no other sounds had come out of the keyhole for ten minutes, Scott deduced that the interview was over and left. It was good advice, he figured, although he did not like the prospect of *anything* following him home.

Scott turned his back to the ugly trees and ugly glow so that he could face the station gate and the town beyond it. Dusk was unsightly, ancient, and forebodingly gloomy. He could see the scope of the town even without leaving the station, as its winding, lamp-lit streets and dirty buildings crept up the other slope of the valley. Scott craned his neck upward to survey the extent of the place, but recoiled when the rim of a moon snuck into sight and he thought he saw a dark thing roving about the cratered disk.

It didn't bother Scott that the town looked deserted. What bothered him was that he could tell by the noises creeping toward him from around distant corners and through the cracks of splintered fences that Dusk was very much *occupied*. The window of the ticket booth looked out at the exit gate, and Scott could hear busy movements coming from inside. The sound of someone—a Duskman—stamping and shuffling paperwork with the occasional scratch of pencil lead in between. The Appointed did not require tickets to arrive and depart, so Scott clutched his satchel tightly and passed in front of the ticket window without stopping. As soon as the interior of the booth came into view, the busy noises were silenced. Scott did not stop to investigate, but from his passing glance, he could see that the booth was empty, though the glistening of wet ink and the flutter of pencil

shavings informed him that someone had been in there as recently as a second ago. Upon passing through the exit gate, he could hear the work resume within the booth. But Scott did not look back.

There were footsteps in the baggage room, but Scott kept walking. They stopped as he passed and resumed once his back was to the station and everything in it. He knew something was peeking around the corner to get a look at him; he could *feel* it. But he also knew it would be pointless to turn and check; he would "just miss them." He didn't want to know what a Duskman looked like, anyway, so he hurried along.

The asphalt of the main thoroughfare looked black and fresh under the lamplights, but the stalks of pigweed clutching skyward from widening cracks suggested that these streets hadn't felt a wheel in a very long time. "They try to keep up appearances," Old Man Desmond had muttered during his interview, a sympathetic nurse stroking the back of his hand all the while. "They try to keep up appearances, but we've been over here and they've been over there for so long, they can't quite remember what those appearances look like. But they try, oh, they try. I guess you could call it hospitality. *They* don't need over there to look like over here. They make it that way for *us*. *Hospitality*. Sure."

Old Man Desmond (less politely known as "Demented Desmond" in town) had been one of Scott's least pleasant interviews. The codger was geriatric enough to be harmless to others, so the tension instead came from the damage he could do to himself if he worked up his blood pressure. "You don't see them. The Duskmen are always *there*, but you don't *see* them. Always *just* out of sight. Always *just* miss them." The nurse had continued stroking the back of Desmond's hand as it gripped the armrest of his easy chair to the point of tearing the upholstery.

"*I* saw them, though," Desmond had whispered, and Scott recollected the beads of sweat that those words had suckled from the glands in his forehead. "The others will tell you they're harmless. They're *liars*. *They* didn't *see* them. But *I* saw them. And the Duskmen didn't *like* that. They almost *got* me." It was at that moment, Scott recalled, that the nurse's soothing fingers recoiled with a jolt. She had stroked an inch too far down Desmond's wrist, touching the end of a series of winding scars that looked like someone had stapled pink spaghetti strands to the old man's wrinkly arm.

"They almost got me," Desmond had continued, his heart beating loud enough for Scott to hear it. "But I kept them over there. Better that they're over there and we're over here, you know. I kept them over there. Look for that sign I carved. They say it's still there. And don't. *Don't.* Don't let the Unkinders spot you in their headlights."

It was about then that Desmond's heartbeat slowed, his body went limp, and he began to snore. The nurse had told Scott that the old man would be all right and would rest easier now that the interview was over. The babble of "insight" had still been lingering in Scott's head as he left, but what he recalled most vividly from the encounter

was the way the nurse had stuck her recoiling fingertips in her mouth like she had just touched a hot stove. If touching where the Duskmen had touched someone *else* hurt that badly, then Scott resolved not to be touched directly by the Duskmen. Better yet, he'd endeavor not to see them at all.

Scott proceeded up the incline of the street, the stillness and silence around him broken only by the occasional clattering of a Duskman behind a shuttered window. Uphill seemed as good a direction as any. In fact, once he found what he was looking for, it would mean that gravity would be on his side as he fled back toward the station and his eager escape engine. Scott looked forward to that moment, after he'd found his destination. A shame he didn't know how to get there, though.

"No sense drawing you a map," nearly every interviewee had said in so many words. "Dusk is different every time. Different streets. Different buildings. Nothing is ever in the same place twice. You'll have to find it yourself," the chorus of voices reminded him. "But you'll know it when you see it."

Scott knew what a post office looked like. What worried him was if the Duskmen knew it. Then again, "they keep up appearances," so his destination should at least look semi-recognizable. And once he got there, all he had to do was—

The momentum of Scott's thoughts came to a screeching halt, along with his heartbeat, as he saw a yellow beam of light pass languidly over the toes of his shoes. Scott didn't breathe again until he'd taken cover behind the crumbling stoop of a mossy brick tenement. Keeping his head down, he swallowed a fugitive scream as the streets shivered with the violent echo of a hungry crowing noise.

He spied the thing, perched atop a wireless telephone pole, talons carving deep grooves into the pinewood as it screeched another rallying cry to its less conspicuous cousins. It was a bird, as big as a German shepherd, covered all over in black feathers that dripped something thick and sticky from their moistened tips. It had the neck of a turkey, though violently angled in all the most painful places, and the beak through which it crowed was rimmed like the edge of a steak knife. When it opened its eyes, urine-colored beams of light shot out and rolled like theater spotlights along a stage, searching for the star of the show.

That bird must have been one of the "Unkinders" Demented Desmond had warned about, Scott deduced, ducking down so as to avoid another strobe of the mangled avian's headlights. Scott waited motionlessly as the beam passed him by two more times.

A few more passes and then, content that the landscape was unoccupied, the Unkinder let out a hideous caw that rattled the shuttered windows. Dousing the sickly lights in its eyes, it spread its dripping wings.

Globules of steaming tar spattered all over the street and sidewalk, narrowly missing Scott's shoes. As its wings expanded to their limits, their feathers and flesh oozed off the bones, dribbling in piping-hot blobs down the telephone pole. With a single flap of its desiccated sticks, the Unkinder propelled itself into the purple sky, held aloft not by currents of air but by some other force that was equally invisible. Scott watched it depart toward the forested end of the valley, careful to keep his eyes off the moons.

Scott hadn't cared for that particular bird, but he liked the *others* even less. Because once the leader had crowed and taken flight, a dozen other Unkinders revealed themselves, launching in a similar fashion from shadowy corners and crevices overlooking the street, the stoop, and even Scott. Had any one of the creatures opened their eyes, they'd have caught him in their headlights. Scott swallowed a trembling breath and contemplated what might have happened to him then.

The violet of the sky reflected off their wet, fluttering forms in shimmering strips as they hovered over the knotted woods, their headlights probing the dense tangle. At times, one of the birds would suddenly plunge straight down like a boulder, crashing destructively into the gnarled trees, only to emerge skyward an instant later. The lights of its eyes would then flicker, as if rapidly blinking while chewing. Scott squinted and thought he saw the nearest bird's beak chomping on something writhing and stringy, but the light was too low and the target too distant for him to identify the meal. Scott didn't really want to know what the bird-thing was eating, anyway. Wobbling out from the questionable safety of the stoop's shadowed corner, he at least now knew why the creatures were called "Unkinders."

Scott continued his trek up the potholed incline with increased trepidation, his eyes searching for terrible poultry in every overhanging hiding place. Eventually, he reached the first U-curve at the hillside's edge, which looked to him like an incorrectly zoned fishing district. The squat and squalid wooden houses were decked with nets and harpoons on exterior racks, along with rowboats left to dry out on their porches. Their rotting timbers were thoroughly damp and crusted at the low-points with barnacles that pulsed like ripe pimples. There was no body of water to service this decaying marina; the network of creaking piers jutted off the hillside to overlook a distressingly deep oblivion that plunged into the space where Scott knew the Duskway Tunnel should have been.

There was movement along the pier and the pit that Scott recognized, encouraging him to sidle flat along the wall of moist buildings as he carefully followed the street's inner curve. A trio of Unkinders was going about their strange business, perched on the planks that could barely support their weight, and splitting the bad wood with the clutch of their talons. Two of the Unkinders rested at the edge overlooking the chasm, eyes closed and lights off. They coughed like sick cats, vomiting a stringy substance, dyed black by their saliva, into the lightless abyss. The fibrous blobs fluttered like cotton balls caught in a breeze, though their strands warped and writhed on their descent into the darkness as if a con-

sciousness motivated them to suffer uncouthly.

The third Unkinder was pecking and popping the masses of barnacles, releasing their treasures all over the pier. Things that looked like roly-poly bugs as big as hand-grenades wriggled from the slimy cavities and scurried madly along the planks. The Unkinder peeked with a quick flash of yellow light, then spat up a net of black, sticky fibers toward the scuttling bugs. It caught most of them in one cast, then slurped the bulging wad back into its beak to be chewed with a crunchy potato chip sound. The rest of the glistening newborns fled over the edge of the pier, falling into space to join the masses of pulsing black cotton wherever they might land.

No one Scott had interviewed had warned him about this scenario. He grimaced silently and secretly as he sidled away. There were always fresh horrors to be encountered in Dusk. That was why the interviews were so important.

Something tickled his thigh. Scott shot a glance down in time to see that it was one of the ugly bugs. With its oh-so-many legs, it was scurrying up his thigh, and several of its broodmates were close behind. These bugs looked much bigger than the hatchlings he'd spotted a moment earlier. Either the perspective was deceiving, or the creatures grew *very* quickly. Whatever the case, Scott shrieked and stumbled out into the open street, madly swatting at the clinging nuisances.

The legs of the things pinched like hairclips, securing them tightly to his clothes in spite of Scott's frenzied slapping. They were moving steadily upward, finding their way onto his swinging satchel. Loathe as he was to touch the slimy, wiggling monsters, Scott had no recourse. Barely able to get his fingers all the way around their wide carapaces, Scott began yanking them off his clothing with little mind to how much fabric went with them. Five or six slippery tosses eliminated his infestation, sending the bugs plopping and rolling at the precipice of the pier. He was satisfied to see the famished Unkinder spread its black net across them, reeling them in for a well-deserved fate. Scott trembled, patted himself all over for about a minute to ensure the bugs were all gone, and then made his position less conspicuous.

Rounding the U-turn, he put the dripping locale and all of its grotesque fauna behind him, though the fishy odor clung to his clothing for many paranoid steps.

Buildings towered to his left and right, obscuring the view of Dusk's adjacent landscape. Scott didn't mourn for the view, though the windows of the rickety tenements that corralled him flickered with lights that extinguished and reignited as he approached and departed their direct observance. Doors slammed shut as he neared them, while the unwelcoming hands that propelled them remained obscured and unseen. He could hear low whispers drifting through the cracks of the locked doors and darkened windows. Their hushed words were foreign to his ears, sounding less like language and more like many hands riffled through piles of shredded paper. Scott was

eager to round the next U-curve, despite knowing that the next stretch of street would prove no more inviting.

Winding behind the line of tenements on his upward trek, Scott watched the buildings sink as he climbed until he'd scaled five stories and their rooftops were no longer in sight. He'd ascended to what looked like a dead suburb; half-collapsed houses, yards of yellowed hay, and picket fences shedding carpets of off-white paint chips.

One particular picket stake, cordoning off a gravel lot that shifted and roiled with something underneath, captured his attention. At first glance, it was no better or worse than any of its decaying neighbors. But upon a second glance, Scott noticed lines carved deep into the crumbling wood. It didn't say much, merely: "I saw them."

Scott supposed it was the message Demented Desmond had mumbled about during his fit. While the note did not provide him with any new insights, it did instill Scott with a meager notion of comfort. If Demented Desmond had been in this exact place and made it home alive, then it was entirely possible that *he* could manage the same feat.

Scott shaded his eyes with one hand so as to obscure the moons and what walked on them. Feeling slightly less prone, he began scoping about the desolate neighborhood. When it came to his destination, he was told he would know it when he saw it. But he wasn't going to see it if he didn't try to *look*. His gaze searched along the parallel rows of condemned houses, seeing nothing but gaping punctures in shingled roofs and fragments of doors swinging on rusted hinges. The derelict domiciles were silent, devoid of the "just around the corner" noises of the voyeuristic Duskmen. Evidently, even *they* did not want to live in such squalor—a squalor Scott was eager to isolate them within for another year. Projecting his gaze to the top of the street, he spotted something that would have made his heart skip a beat if he hadn't recognized it so quickly.

It was a gigantic bird, but not a *real* one. It was a flat, iron-cast eagle mounted atop the handless clock tower of what could only be Dusk's post office. Scott knew it as soon as he saw it and immediately charged uphill at an uneasy pace.

The steps leading to the entrance were littered with papers and envelopes, all of which were decorated in squiggles and zigzags. Pages clung to the bottoms of his shoes, as the ink was still fresh, leading Scott to scrape them off on the edges of the steps. Through the doors, he could hear the commotion of a lively post office; the thud of stamp pads, the squeaking of cartwheels, the crackle of tape being stretched from its spool. Emboldened, Scott did not hesitate to pull open the door, confident that the Duskmen would have fled before he could catch a glimpse of them.

The lobby was empty; he had *just* missed them. The floor was canvased in the same wet, scribbled papers. A teetering tower of packages collapsed on the service counter, as though a Duskman had abandoned it in mid-stack so as not to be seen. The crashing noise failed to startle Scott, as the boxes were empty and hardly made a sound as they plopped onto the floor. None of those details meant a thing to him, anyway. He was in a hurry to find what he was looking for.

"They don't use any kind of language, so far as I know," Mr. Miller had said during his interview. He was a middle-aged former Appointed who was normal enough, though recognized as a terror among the local restauranteurs for his habit of only ever taking a single bite of his meal before ordering seconds, thirds, and so on, then discarding the rest without taking it home. He didn't trust second bites. "So when you get to the post office, don't look for any kind of sign that says 'Outgoing Mail' or what have you," he had continued. "There'll be a big arrow above a slot in the wall. Just deliver the doodles, and you're home free. And they'll stay over there..." Mr. Miller had paused as he took a sip from a fresh bottle of cola, then set it on the table with the other three dozen mostly full bottles he'd sipped from during the interview (he didn't trust second *sips*, either). "They'll stay over there. And it's better that they stay over there and we stay over here," Mr. Miller had concluded.

The arrow was easy to find, even if the red paint had faded and chipped with years of exposure. It still pointed to the mail slot in the wall nearest the cashier counter. There it was. That was it. His Appointed task was almost over. Further emboldened, he charged his way across the lobby, lifted the bronze cover of the slot, and reached into his satchel to collect his burden for deposit.

Scott recalled his hand as soon as he felt

the touch of something smooth, wet, and wiggling. It crawled out of his open satchel, one of the ugly bugs from the pier, and then plopped down into the pile of loose papers before scurrying out of sight. Scott didn't have time to be frightened by the bug, as the next thing his hand felt within the satchel was entirely *more* alarming. It felt like *confetti.* And as Scott pulled his hand back out, he found that's *exactly* what it was.

The bug had devoured the Doodles for the Duskmen. All that remained were nibbled scraps; scarcely a handful. Scott's heart began to race, and his breaths shrunk shorter with each puff. Desperately, he flattened the bits of shredded crayon drawings and tried feeding them a fragment at a time into the slot. It wasn't his fault. No one had warned him about the bugs. No one had told him they might eat paper. And he was *still* delivering the Doodles for the Duskmen. No one said they *had* to be intact. He was *still* fulfilling his Appointed task! He was *still* honoring the arrangement!

Pat.

Scott felt it rest quietly and gently on his right shoulder. It was so light, it was practically weightless, but the five points of pressure beginning to clutch assured him that it was a hand. If the sudden jolt of distress hadn't paralyzed him, the lack of preparation for this predicament certainly would have. He'd been assured that the Duskmen never showed themselves, so none of the previously Appointed had told him what to do or say if he was ever approached by one. The pressure of the fingertips began to

change; trembling and wriggling and writhing in too many directions at once. With no wisdom to guide him in the moment, Scott glanced down toward his shoulder. If the appendage touching him had started out as a hand, it wasn't one anymore.

Five twisted, wet, red ropes extended from a beige sleeve. They were already beginning to unravel into threads that spread along the arm and collar of Scott's shirt, prodding the wrinkles of the fabric. Unfreezing, Scott turned around with a jerk, and the red strands ripped free with the sound of peeling duct tape, taking small swatches of his shirt with them.

A set of clothes stood close behind Scott, though the vague shape of humanity that filled the shirt, slacks, and shoes was already coming undone. The Duskman was nothing but a collection of thin red veins, knotted and twisted and bundled together to imitate a headless, four-limbed torso. It had tried to maintain appearances but was retiring the façade, as its clothing burst at the buttons and split at the seams. A wad of throbbing fibers rolled in violent coils toward Scott, who instinctively threw out a hand to catch the strange mass.

The tips of the fibers were as sharp as hypodermic needles, and they found the currents in his arm as soon as they touched it. Fire surged through Scott's bloodstream, and he screamed so hard he nearly vomited. He stumbled backward along the lobby, slipping on the loose papers as the Duskman spiraled its threads back into shaggy lengths of rope. Scott pulled his arm away, and the strands of Duskman exited his veins almost cleanly, leaving only a few strings behind with a tearing sound. Scott plucked the wiggling fibers from his arm before they could work themselves all the way in, though they burned his fingertips at the touch. He discarded the bits on the floor where they slithered promptly back toward the rest of the Duskman, which was already bounding in strange strides toward him.

And more were on the way. All the Duskmen Scott had "just missed." All the Duskmen that had been "just out of sight." Scott could hear them coming. They were on the other sides of the walls. They were *in* the walls. They were coming *through* the walls. Scott turned and fled, shoving the door to the post office open with the paralyzed meat of his right arm dangling at the shoulder.

As he hurried onto the street, Scott let gravity guide him back the way he had come since his eyes and ears weren't going to be of much use. The Unkinders were engaged in a feeding frenzy, their headlights strobing and clashing along the landscape, and their gluttonous cawing thickening the air with seismic vibrations. The Duskmen were squirming through the cracks and crevices of their world, displeased that their "hospitality" had been so disrespected by an Appointed.

If Scott was deemed edible by the mammoth birds, he was judged less so than the Duskmen. The Unkinders dropped from the sky and began to gobble the exposed tangles up, gumming them into helpless blobs with the black tar of their saliva; their fate to be used as nets for catching weird insects be-

fore being discarded into the dark chasm.

As Scott raced around the first curve and found himself between the towers of tenements again, all he could think about was what he was going to say. How would he apologize for failing in his Appointed task? He didn't even know what the punishment for failure was. No one had ever told him, and he had never thought to ask.

Scott careened from the street and into the brick façade of a building on his right. The Unkinders were quieting, evidently satiated for the moment, and Scott spotted a small gap between buildings beside him. Hardly four feet across, it was more a crevice than an alley, but it was a potential shortcut. The sooner he made it to the bottom of the valley, the better, and best to sneak away from the obvious path while the birds still had the Duskmen distracted. Scott began to slink through the crack, greased by the wet mold on the bricks, and hoped that his pursuers wouldn't cut him off before he emerged on the other side.

The Duskmen did not assault him from either end of the alley, nor did they squeeze their way through the bricks that sandwiched him, and he escaped the shortcut unharmed. Searching for his next steps, Scott found he was standing on the crest of a hill of dead grass that overlooked the bottom-most street he'd come in on. The train station, platform and tracks, were visible from this vantage point, and he could see with clarity that his train had been reoriented and was ready to head home, its engine rumbling anxiously. It would have been manageable to reach it; he could just slide down the hill, dart across the street, leap into the loitering train car, and be off. Scott didn't bother, though. Not when he'd have had to make the return trip with so much *company*.

The platform was crowded with Duskmen, some still crumpled inside lopsided clothing and others striding along tangled processions in their natural states. They were boarding the train car and filling it fast, eager to exploit Scott's failure. Mr. Richards was sounding the whistle, also eager to depart, though Scott could tell from a distance that it wasn't Mr. Richards *anymore*. His veins were bulging in hideous splintered paths all over his half-nude body, and his head hung sideways at the neck, flopping and superfluous. Something *else* had gotten into his body and was now driving it in a manner similar to how Mr. Richards drove his train.

When the platform was empty and the car was full, the train chugged forward toward the Duskway Tunnel. Scott wasn't sorry to see it go. And he wasn't sorry that he wouldn't be going home with it, either. After all, it was better that *they* were over *there* and *he* was over *here*.

Mark Pellegrini is a native of Bunnyman Country in Northern Virginia, though he currently lives just East of Boggy Creek Country in Central Arkansas. Mark is a prolific comic author, having written the war-action-rabbit **Black Hops: U.S.A.-*-G.I.**, *the tokusatsu send-up* **Kamen America**, *and the political parody* **Wall-Might**. *His horror-fantasy novel,* **They'll Get You** *is currently available on Amazon.*

Fossils of Truth and Grace

By E.E. KING

A young grad student staying on the Cornish coast discovers a witch's pit! Is the mystery connected to her past? Her mother had been a guest at Trelawny Manor!

Note: The trials of the Pendle Witches are factual. Only the names have been changed to protect the guilty.

It was a grand old place. The kind you read about in Victorian romances or gothic novels, all curving mahogany staircases and domed glass ceilings. My room even had a quilted reading seat nestled into the bay window that looked out over Cornwall's shaggy moorland and cold, raging sea.

I'd come for peace—peace and time. Time to breathe. Time to think. Time to wander the moors. And time to finish the damn thesis that had been dangling over my head like some literary sword of Damocles.

It was "perfectly normal," they said.

"Many of our most brilliant students suffer from stress and even issues with completion," they comforted. But I could hear the whispers, or rather I could feel them, creeping out of night corners like phantom rats to gnaw at my fragile sense of purpose and belief.

My mother had been haunted by similar demons, as had my two aunts, my grandmother, and her sisters before her. My lineage reached backward into a pedigree of despair. They were all gone now. All dead by their own hand before age thirty-three.

My mother had received her medical degree from Harvard at twenty-five. She only practiced for a year before going to Oxford to study history, where she'd met my father, who was finishing his doctorate in Physics. They had fallen madly in love, married, and had me.

Two years later, on a vacation to the Cornish coast not far from here, she had waded into the cold North Sea, never to return.

I thought I'd escaped. I'd been a quiet, calm, studious child, reaching for nothing more emotionally challenging than stones and bones. I had few friends. I was taunted for my thick black eyebrows and unruly dark hair, though now I realize it was not so much my appearance as my bookish introspection that made me an outcast.

At nineteen, I entered the Earth Sciences

department at Oxford, and at twenty, I waded into the pond at Island Wood, my pockets weighed down with samples of limestone fossils purloined from the lab.

I don't remember who saw me or pulled me out, just a shooting pain that ran up my leg as large, strong arms enfolded me, pulling me up out of the pond's muddy clutch, the hard press of rough lips against mine, sucking water out and pushing air in, and a faint scent of winter nights and ageing pub fires that was somehow familiar.

My father, now a Physics professor at Oxford, was called. Rest and medication were prescribed. And so, after a month of mind-numbing boredom, I'd been sent to write and recuperate at Trelawny Manor, the oldest and largest estate in Cornwall.

I packed a sketchpad, some charcoal, and a panoply of medicines. Antidepressants that kept me from feeling joy. Mood stabilizers that fogged my brain. Painkillers to soothe my aching ankle, which I'd broken in my wade toward eternity. The grey cloud that had enveloped my world had lifted slightly, but only because I was too numb to feel anything as strong as despair.

Trelawny Manor was managed by the Kernow Trust. During the summer, it was a popular high tea and luncheon stop for tourists and academics. But during the winter, it was mostly deserted. Though rooms were available for scholars of Cornish history who wanted to immerse themselves in study.

I had not focused on Cornwall, which was not particularly rich in fossils, though the coast does hold a special place in paleonto-logical history. In 1676, in the limestone cliffs that line the strand, Reverend Robert Plot, Professor of Chemistry at Oxford and curator of the Ashmolean Museum, unearthed the first dinosaur bone ever discovered, though he believed it belonged to ancient species of giants, possibly Goliath.

I'd taken a train to Cornwall and a cab to the manor. The driver was a large, red-faced man with inquisitive blue eyes that missed nothing. My small bag, which he tossed in the trunk, was dwarfed by his huge, meaty hands. I wondered if he would speed away with my belongings, leaving me alone and without clothes, shoes, or medication.

I should keep my medicine in my purse, I thought, as he slapped me on the shoulder, genially, but with such force as to propel me forward into the highly polished black leather back seat. I knew he was just being affable and welcoming, but my spirit shrank from the contact.

"Welcome to Cornwall, little lady," he said. His warm breath smelled faintly of ale, corned beef, and long winter nights spent by ageing pub fires. "It's just about the best little county in Great Britain.

"Me name's Charlie. Lived here all me life, I have, and I can tell you just about anything you want to know." He started the cab without even asking where I was going.

"Are you hungry, Miss? Because Cornwall has hundreds of pasty shops, and we'll be passing the Horse and Jockey, and Anne's, and Philp's, which are ranked among the best on offer. They make proper pasties, they do. Probably aren't permitted on no Weight Watchers diet, but, begging me pardon, Miss, you look like you could do with putting on some.

"Not many people come here in winter." He peered at me in the mirror, his keen blue eyes kindly but curious. "You may fear you're in for nothing but bad weather, but that ain't at'll true. The mornings can be a tad dreary, but those crisp winter days on the beach are to die for. No crowds, no tourists (sorry Miss), fresh sea air, plenty of room for dogs to run around, and, when the wind does decide to blow, there's something about grabbing a safe spot and watching Mother Nature batter our sea walls from a distance, as long as you're not a fisherman worried about your boat rag-dolling around in the harbor.

"Well now, I haven't even asked your name or where you're headed? Me missus always said I talk more than I think. But there's only one direction from the station into town."

"I'm going to Trelawny Manor," I whispered.

There was no sound from the front. I cautiously looked up, fearful that a glance might unleash another torrent of unwanted chatter, but the man was mute. A look at his face shocked me. All the color had drained from the ruddy cheeks, leaving him pale as a peeled potato.

"Do you know the place?" I asked.

"'Course I do," he said. "And a mighty fine place it is… in the summer… but in winter…" His voice drifted into silence like a fading wind.

I thought of asking what was wrong with the Manor in winter, but I dreaded conversation more than mystery. These rural types were often superstitious, believing in omens and cyphers rather than evidence and proof, and I wanted none of it.

Trelawny's roots reached back to the 1200's, though it had been revamped in the late Victorian era. It stood on the top of a grassy hill that sloped down to a ridge above the sea, four stories of plaster, stone, and thatch that rose from the land like an enormous ammonite. The coast seemed miles away, but to my left it curved sharply inland like a giant wave and looked to be an easy walk from the Manor.

Charlie pulled up to the grand circular flagstone entrance and handed me my bag.

"If you don't like it here, Miss," he said, pressing a card into my hand, "just give me a call. There's many another place in town that'd be happy for lodgers in winter."

I twisted my mouth into what I hoped was a smile. My face felt stiff, the muscles unused and exhausted from staring into the void. I paid him and turned to the large wooden doors which opened surprisingly quietly and easily considering their mass.

The entryway, carpeted in thick red plush, led to an arched alcove of vines and banana trees awash with intricately detailed bees, butterflies, and frogs, carved by a master from some dark, probably extinct, hardwood. Below the arch, behind a large walnut desk, sat a woman. An almost unruly halo of slightly bluish-gray curls encircled her tight-lipped, pale, doughy face. It was the only free, even slightly wild, aspect of her person. In back of her, the cubbies of a hotel key box gaped like empty mouths, each holding a long brass key dangling from a long brass hook. The keys twisted and turned, catching stray light beams and flashing up out of the darkness like metallic eels.

The corners of the woman's mouth turned upward as she handed me the only key that had managed to wriggle free, but the smile didn't quite reach her eyes, which were a cold, curious blue.

"I'm Mrs. Molchany," she said. "You're the only one stayin' here now, and I'll be the one seeing to your comfort and needs. I attend the scholars that come here to finish their—projects." She paused before the word "projects," and sniffed as if the word were somehow unclean. "I serve meals in the dining room; breakfast at eight, elevenses at 11:30, luncheon at one, tea at four, and dinner at six, but I do not stay on site overnight." She paused, as if expecting me to protest, but I said nothing. In the silence, I heard the ticking of some unseen clock.

"There are many paths along the sea and through the moorland that you're welcome to explore." She narrowed her eyes, as if she disapproved of exploration in general and mine in particular.

"Just don't use the track on the left, Miss. It leads most directly to the sea, but it's boggy and dangerous. Many a sheep and more than one child have been lost in the marshlands. And once the black mud gets hold of you, you'll never escape." She said this with an odd satisfaction, as if she approved of her land punishing wayward wanders. "Also, the coast is 'specially treacherous there."

She waited. I said nothing. Somewhere behind me, the clock continued counting away the minutes, hours, and years. I wondered how old it was and how long it had been there. I wondered if Mrs. Molchany was even aware of it or if time and custom had made it as inaudible to her as her heartbeat.

"And you'll be wanting to look at this," she said, pushing a long, faded, red-leather book toward me. It was engraved with gold, some of which had worn away and left rough grooves in the cover, making it resemble the bed of a dried riverbank.

"All of our scholars do. It's been our guest book, since 1602, signed by each and every one of our guests." She said this as smugly, as if she had personally supervised the inking of each and every signature. "And which part of our rich history will you be investigating while you're with us?"

"Ancient times," I said. "Precambrian Serpentine."

She didn't reply, just stared at me out of those probing cool eyes, as if I were a not-very-interesting relic from another time, something which she needed to file away and keep safe even if she doubted its purpose. Or perhaps it was me, mistrusting my own drive and commitment, floundering in a sea of suspicion and finding it, even where there was none. My medications made everything seem distant and out of focus, as if mind and memory were trapped in a clinging fog. I took the key and turned away.

"You'll be wanting to sign the book," she said, "even if it's not your time period." Was I imagining her disapproval? Did she prefer students of the sixteen or seventeen hundreds?

"And I'll need to show you the dining room as well as your room; it's on the third floor, next to the library. Not easy to find if you don't know the floor plan."

"Of-of course," I stammered. "Thank you. I'm just tired after a long day of traveling."

"Why sure you are," she said, laying a hand on my arm. "Why don't I show you up to your room, and when you're rested, after you unpack, I'll bring you up a nice cup of tea?" Her voice was sympathetic, motherly even. I felt ashamed and paranoid. I followed her mutely up the wide curving staircase.

My room, which was large and light-filled, had a white iron bedstead, a gigantic dark wooden dresser, and a small white desk and chair. It smelled faintly, not unpleasantly, of old lavender, mothballs, and the rough, slightly fermented, scent of salt and kelp.

It didn't take me long to unpack. I had few clothes. Mrs. Molchany brought me up a strong, slightly bitter cup of tea. I left it cooling on the desk, where its refined astringent odor mixed with the lavender, mothballs, and sea.

Despite my fatigue, I couldn't sleep. I took the one sleeping pill I was allowed each night and waited. Perhaps a tiny exploration would exhaust me? Mrs. Molchany had mentioned a library. I could never resist a library.

The hall, lit only by the light of my phone, was like the inside of a giant, chambered nautilus, a creature whose relatives date back to the Early Pleistocene. From my room on the third floor, swirling mahogany balusters curled down two levels and swept upward to a crystal cupola. Tiny pieces of stained glass dotted the dome. Rays of moonlight stroked them, making them sparkle and dance like brightly colored constellations.

I followed the curve around to the first open door. It was the dining room, bare and uninviting. Six backless benches flanked three long wooden tables, like some Dickensian orphanage or monastery. As I turned to leave, a light flashed out of the darkness at the back of the room. I inhaled sharply, my whole body tensing, but it was only the phone light's reflection from a silver tea service hiding in a cupboard, waiting for breakfast.

I pressed one hand against the middle of my chest, and the other on my stomach. I slowly inhaled, filling out my abdomen with air and counting to three, as I'd been taught.

Calm, I thought. *Calm*.

Next door was the library. I smelled it before I saw it. The fragrance of vanilla and almonds seeped out of the old books into the corridor. Father said that the smell was caused by the breakdown of chemicals in the paper, which also made it yellow. Odd that decay should smell so sweet. Perhaps there is a heaven for books that people never dream of, where deterioration is lovely and ideas live on.

The idea made me uncomfortable. I liked facts, fossils, the hard clarity of science. I resented these fanciful notions that drifted through my mind like stray clouds, obscuring the bright, hard, unwavering light of reality. Could this be another side effect of my medications? Not only blurring the edges of experience, but also filling my mind with fictions and fancies?

What would happen if I cut down on the mood stabilizers? Would I be clearer? Or was it the combination that made me feel as if I wandered through a fog?

A powdering of stars twinkled through the three-quarter bay window. Magnificent wooden shelves entwined by a jungle of hardwood vines that had been carved by the same master hand evident in the foyer. The shelves, however, were disappointingly bare.

There were a dozen musty old treatises on the Church of England, a few shelves of paperback romances, an almost complete collection of the Encyclopedia Britannica from 1925, a Bible, and a dictionary.

I turned to leave, the pills and the journey having finally wearied me beyond my ever-present anxiety. I could sleep now. I was almost certain of it, when a slim leather volume caught my eye. It lay horizontal on a bottom shelf as if hoping to escape from view. It had no legible title on the cover or spine, only the indentations of some worn-away script and a flash of golden flakes embedded in the grooves of vanished text. The scent of rosemary and lavender seeped out from between the covers. It made me think of long-ago gardens, forgotten promises, and the bitter sweetness of the old powdered lemon drops I'd found in my mother's purse when I was five.

The purse had been hidden away in a drawer, escaping my father's organization and the maid's cleaning. It was the first tangible piece of evidence I'd found that my mother had actually existed. I'd rubbed the faded satin lining and sucked on the ancient hard candies, my lips dusted with powdered sugar. I'd closed my eyes and tried to reach through that long-forgotten sweetness back into my mother's soul. I had tried so hard, it made me ill. To this day, I will refuse lemon drops, although until this moment I'd forgotten why.

I shrugged, trying to shake away this unwanted memory, and squinted at the purpled calligraphy on the frontispiece. "The Complete and Truthful History of the Tragedy at Trelawny" was inscribed in curling letters that made me think of many-limbed sea creatures scuttling through night waters. Again, I shook my head, trying to dispel these ideas that were not mine, and these recollections which were. I took the book back to bed with me and began to read, but I remember nothing.

I was deep in some dark dream when a light or a sound awakened me. I sat up, knocking *The Complete and Truthful History of the Tragedy at Trelawny* off my chest onto the floor.

I rose and went to the window, pulling aside the translucent white gauze curtain that hung over the glass like milk. The moors were illuminated by a bright, full moon. Every blade of grass and mound seemed etched into the land. For the first time in months, my mind was equally sharp and clear.

As I watched, clouds drifted across the moon's surface, diffusing the light, throwing everything into soft focus. The world became an old black-and-white photo with misty edges. There were no shadows, but to the left, at the edge of land, where the coast bent closest toward Trelawny and the shaggy grass fell away to the cold, foaming sea, I could make out a few dark huddled figures bent over the ground. I saw the flames of small fires. The acrid scent of burning hair filled my room. It was odd that anyone should venture there, where Mrs. Molchany had said the cliffs were the weakest, but perhaps my bearings had been confused by the wandering clouds and flat light.

One of the figures straightened up and began walking toward my window. It was a woman, as small as I am, but so slender and well-formed, she gave the impression of great height. There was something ominous about the intensity of her focus. She seemed so fixated on me, or at least on my lighted window, as to be ignoring her surroundings, though she walked along the very edge of the roaring waves.

A mist rose up from the sea, engulfing everything in a fog so thick, even the bright, white moon was blotted out. A damp breeze blew through my window, chilling me and scenting my room with the heavy, acrid smell of damp earth, dark places and burning hair.

I returned to bed but couldn't sleep. I took another pill, even though one was the accepted dosage. Sometimes sleep was more important than directions. I suppose I drifted off, but I got no repose. My night was filled with dreams that woke me often, leaving me disturbed and unsettled, though I couldn't remember any of them.

I awakened late and only left my room at 6:00 pm. Mrs. Molchany was waiting for me in the preposterously large dining room with a plate of overcooked greens, a desiccated pot roast, and a mountain of mashed potatoes rich with butter and cream.

"Well, you must have needed your sleep then?" she asked. I couldn't decide if her voice was kind or disapproving. She smiled, but there was a sharpness in those cold blue eyes that made me feel small and unimportant.

"I—I've been ill," I stammered.

"So I've been told," she nodded.

I felt the blood rush to my face. I tried not to think about what she'd been told.

Depression was nothing to be ashamed of, they'd said.

"And—and the moon was so bright," I added.

"Moon?" she said. "T'was a new moon last night, black as a Newgate knocker out there."

"New?"

"You must have dreamed it," she said, shaking her head. Her blushish-grey curls bobbed about her cheeks like cumulus clouds.

But despite the logic of that, I could not shake the memory of light, and the scent of burning.

I spent my days lazily at first, resting by the window, studying *The Complete and Truthful History of the Tragedy at Trelawny* and looking through the venerated guest book, trying to ignore the hollow in my heart and the Precambrian paper waiting for completion.

Both books were truly extraordinary. One for what is said, the other for what it implied.

The Complete and Truthful History of the Tragedy at Trelawny was an account of the trial of Truth Singleton, the first guest at the manor. Accused of witchcraft by her six-year-old daughter Grace, Truth had been convicted and burned at the cliff's edge, right where the coast curled toward Trelawny Manor. The history was written by some ancient hand, a list of dates, prosecution, and death, brutal and horrible.

The guest book was different. Its swirls of signature, individual as fingerprints, were open to interpretation. I liked tracing my fingers over the slightly indented curves of each moniker.

It was categorized by year. Each section containing names and comments in various shades of yellowing ink. The penmanship was impressive, the early pages filled before the typewriter had destroyed the art of calligraphy. There was true artistry in the beautifully shaped letters and the personality evident in each signature, like essence in ink. The more I scanned the pages, the more I became convinced that handwriting was a mirror of the soul.

I had never much been interested in souls, or philosophy either. Those things seemed less real to me than science and mathematics. If you learned a formula or the properties of a stone, you had data that would never change, but beliefs, opinions, and even history were fragile things that could alter with knowledge. A plant that was edible was always edible, but a theory about the soul or mind or God was as malleable as wet tissue. And history, always recounted by the winners, looked very different depending upon which version you read. Now, though, sitting on the window seat, looking over the moors and the frothing sea below, I studied the names in the book, ran my finger over the old signatures, and imagined the people who had written them.

The Manor had been built as a private estate for the Trelawnys sometime in the 1200's and opened as an inn in 1602. The first few years saw only a few summer visitors, most likely families seeking a respite from plague, fire, or one of England's many religious or civil wars.

Queen Elizabeth I was dead. James I was king. The Virginia Company was establishing settlements in North America. And on July twenty-sixth, 1609, English scientist Thomas Harriot looked through a telescope and drew a map of the Moon, preceding Galileo by several months.

It was what I both loved and hated about science. The map of the moon was unchanging, but the men, and especially the women, who received credit for their discoveries were as variable as planetary phases.

That same year a Truth Singleton and her four-year-old daughter Grace moved into the manor. Unlike most, she had started her stay at Trelawny in the winter. Truth's signature, in purpled ink, which took up a whole page, had blotted in many places. She must have been bearing down hard as she wrote because the words were actually engraved into the creamy vellum pages. When I closed my eyes and ran my fingertips over the letters, it was like reading Braille.

When I opened them, the blotched page looked like bloody footsteps floundering in snow.

True to her word, Mrs. Molchany had a huge, largely indigestible breakfast set on the sideboard at eight, which gave way to stale granola bars at 11:30, followed by tea at four and dinner at six. Tea was the only meal I enjoyed, not the dry, hard scones, but the rich, slightly grainy, clotted cream served with strawberry jam that filled all the corners in my hungry heart.

Slowly I began feeling better. I began to cut the dose of the antidepressants and to bring up and down the mood stabilizers, trying to find the perfect balance. The doctors didn't know; they were merely guessing. I knew my brain better than they did. I took the painkillers. They didn't dull my perceptions but made them sharper and slightly more focused. I began to take them more frequently when I needed some insight or understanding. Amazing that you could bottle clarity.

I awoke early and wandered the moors, loving the shaggy rough grass that seemed the coat of some prehistoric beast. Craggy rocks rose out of the green land, some jagged as giant canines, others smooth and pressed tightly together, possibly the remnants of a Roman wall.

I avoided the shale and serpentine cliffs, those parts of stone that held both the fossil past and my own unfinished thesis. Instead, I followed narrow paths of mud and moss till I was tired, and then returned to my window seat, running my fingers over the rough penmanship of Truth Singleton, as if I could conjure the woman by her trail of ink. I couldn't say why her signature had such power over me, just that it drew me to wonder about its origin as before I had only wondered about fossils and bones.

Then the rain began. The sky opened, and it poured for two days straight. I should have worked on my paper. I could have written letters detailing my progress and health, but instead I sat in my window above the sea, reading the guest book, inhaling the fragrance of vanilla and almonds that drifted up from its yellowed sheets.

The guest book in my lap fell open, or had I turned the pages without realizing it? I didn't know; all I could be certain of was the signature at the bottom of the page, Nicole Stevens. It was my mother's. I stared at the name as though it might vanish before my eyes. It was dated 1998, twenty-one years ago, the same year she had marched off into the sea, never to return.

I closed my eyes, seeing in that inner darkness the scene I tried never to think about. The slender form of a woman I had never known, leaving me her only child without a backward glance. What had driven her into those cold, unfeeling waters? What had driven me? Nothing solid, nothing specific, just an unbearable sadness, a dark, suffocating curtain I could not see beyond. It was written into my genes, engraved by maternal hands so deeply into my being that there was no escape. But I had no children, not even a pet to anchor me to this life. If I'd had, would it have made a difference?

I pressed one hand on the middle of my chest, the other on my stomach. I inhaled slowly and deeply, breathing into my abdomen and counting to three.

Calm, I thought. *Calm*.

I began to leaf back through the pages. Each name a dark house, concealing lives behind ink walls. And there—just fifteen years before my mother's visit, I found another familiar name: Alice Turner, my grandmother.

So, my mother had been here, and her mother before her, which was as far back as I could trace. With a family tree like mine, you don't look for ancestors. You're afraid of what you might find. Death had been engraved in my bones—and not in the way it's engraved into all creatures—an undetermined conclusion to happen at an unknown time. Perhaps that's why I didn't like philosophy, with all its talk of free will. Perhaps that's why I never was interested in history, when my own seemed destined to have such a bleak and definite ending.

I took three pain pills. It was incredible how they could ease spirit as well as body. I preferred dosing the pain, rather than dulling everything with anti-this and stabilizing-that.

That night I drifted into sleep as smoothly as twilight turns to night. I was deep in dreams when some noise startled me awake. I rose and looked out the window. There along the wavering edge of land where the coast bent inward, a small fire blazed, tended by a single dark figure. A curl of inky smoke rose from the flames swirling like the dancing curves of old signatures. I should not have been able to smell the fire, as it was distant and there was no wind, but the odd metallic scent of scorching flesh and the ammonia of singed feathers filled my room. And as it did so, the delicate lace curtains blew across my face. I tried to pull the drapes back, but they were sticky and clung to my skin like spiderwebs. I tried to yank them off, but they wound tighter and tighter around me. I began to claw at my face and awoke, standing above the open window. My face bleeding, remnants of skin and blood beneath my nails.

The next day, the weather, which had been cold and damp, usual for that part of the country at that time of the year, gave way to a sudden, unexpected burst of warmth and sun. The moors glittered a brilliant emerald green. There was something almost transcendent in their vast loneliness. Steam rose up from the grassland like the departing spirits of birds. This phenomenon, not uncommon when pouring rain is followed by hot sun is called "summer geese," a phrase so exquisitely apposite, I shall never see fog rising from soaked earth and not think of it.

I packed a small bag with water, a few stale, purloined granola bars, my sketchpad, my painkillers, a small spade and pick, and set out toward the cliff, where I had twice seen small night fires burning, though whether in reality or in dreams, I did not know.

I dared not take the most direct route. It looked an easy walk, but I remembered Mrs. Molchany's warning that the land there was marshy, and the headlands especially treacherous.

The ledge was farther away from Trelawny than it had looked. Without trees as signposts, land and sea flattened into an endless perspectiveless swath of green, grey, and blue. It took me more than an hour to reach the cliff. The earth, sodden with rain, was marshy. At every step, my feet sank into the spongy soil, and the mud sucked at my shoes as if to pull me down beneath the emerald carpet.

At the bluff's edge, overlooking the battering waves, a small path wound above the shore like a ribbon of dirt and stone. I had gone just a little way when the ground gave way. My leg sank into the mud up to my knee. I lay on the wet, wet grass and slowly pulled myself backward. The field slurped at my leg like an earthbound lamprey. After I had extracted myself, I remained prone, exhausted, drenched, and covered in sludge. I hoped I could sneak into my room without Mrs. Molchany seeing me and without leaving a trail of filth.

The sun was bright, but the day was winter brisk, and I began to shiver. Still, having come this far and found this… whatever it was I had found… I opened my bag, pulled out spade and pick, and began to dig.

I peeled layers of turf from the earth. They sounded like dry skin being pulled from the bones of the dead. Beneath the grass was a hole—could it be a posthole from some long-ago fence? But no, it was too large, almost a meter deep and about half again as wide.

I began to enlarge the sides. The dense webs of roots of the rushes wrapped around my hands like the sensitive tentacles of some blind earth-dwelling creature. The soil was heavy and ladened with water.

I could see now that the bottom of the hole was covered in black clay and lined with white feathers. It might have been a bird-plucking hollow, such pits were common at the turn of the 19th century. But no—what I had thought was dark clay was really a charred body. As my eyes grew accustomed to the dimness, I could just make out small, outstretched limbs, a long sinuous neck and a tiny, delicate head that was mostly just orbital lobes. The feathers were still attached to the skin. It was a carbonized swan, lacking only its beak.

The Queen of the United Kingdom has many titles: Head of the Commonwealth; Defender of the Faith; Commander in Chief of the British Armed Forces; Sovereign of the Most Noble Order of the Garter; Sovereign of the Most Ancient, Most Noble Order of the Thistle; and Seigneur of the Swans.

There is a legend that swans were introduced to Britain in the 12th century by Richard I, but the bird is native. Swans were luxury goods in Europe, the medieval equivalent of a Lamborghini. Ownership was recorded by marks nicked into the beak. These marks were restricted, and any swan that didn't bear one was the property of the crown.

The penalties for ignoring or defacing swan marks were harsh. "If any person do raze out, counterfeit, or alter the mark of any swan [they...] shall suffer one year's imprisonment." There were similar sentences for stealing eggs or killing birds.

If this skin was as old as I suspected it was, someone had risked at least a year of freedom to bury this here, probably a lot more.

On top of the swan skin were a small circle of bird claws and a pile of colorful stones that I recognized as coming from a section of the coast at least thirty kilometers distant. Who had brought them so far, and why?

Around the stones were nestled fifty-five eggs, seven of which contained chicks that were close to hatching. I could tell because though the shells of the eggs had dissolved, the moist environment had preserved their membranes. There was something unutterably sad about the dried, yellow embryos, curled in on themselves like pictures of despair.

As little as I liked to admit it, this seemed like a witch pit. Swans, long a symbol of true love, had often been used in marriage or fertility spells.

Uncover a nest or discover a den, and there will be a reason for everything, every twig or dropping or bone, essential to the story of life and death. But in witch pits, nothing made sense. These objects were the product of delusion, the human drama that made no sense. I'd been trying to avoid it my whole life.

The killing of swans has been illegal since the 11th century, and the witchcraft laws were only scrapped in 1951. A shiver snaked up my spine as I imagined someone coming here in the dead of night, digging a hole, and carefully laying in these offerings. What made them desperate enough to risk death if caught?

The remains of two other large birds, possibly magpies, were arranged on either side of the eggs and stones. As I gingerly turned the bones over in my hands, I realized they were bound together. Though worn and faded, the cord was unmistakably orange— a synthetic twine that could not have been manufactured before the 1960's and was probably not used in Cornwall until even later.

Something thin and brittle was stuck to the twine. It was a scrap of newsprint, worn and yellowed, but I could just make out a faint headline. "Dr. Nicole Stevens, to join the History department at Oxford." My mother, again.

I imagined generations of women coming here to ask favors of their gods, devotees reaching back into the 1600's in an unbroken chain, but surely my doctor mother had not been among them? I leaned back, hoping for support, needing to feel something solid. As my sweater touched the cold, wet mud, I gasped. The anguish of the body superseding the torments of the heart, as it always does.

I snipped the string on either side of the paper, not an approved collection practice, but the cold had seeped through my skin into my bones. I needed to get back, and I wanted—no, I needed this paper. It was proof, verification that I was not going mad.

I pulled myself out of the hole. The sun, huge and orange, had already begun sinking into the waves. The wind howled, warning of the coming night. Mounds of gray clouds blew in like an advancing army, blotting out sea, shore, and sky, encasing me in pervasive twilight. I pulled out the pocket flashlight I always kept on me for checking under rocks and beneath ledges. It offered only a faint, yellowish glow. I looked for new batteries but had none. I, who'd been taught to be prepared for every outing, had in the course of a few endless months, let my supplies go untested like any ordinary idiot. I could see the disappointment in my father's eyes, staring at me through the directionless gloom.

A few ice-cold raindrops slapped my face. I hunched my shoulders against the wind and began to slough my shivering way back to the manor. The squall whipped around me, howling the sharp, high, mournful cry of a lonely hound. My hair blew against my eyes, blinding me. The sky had turned into a grey sheet of slanting water. The feeble beam from my flashlight transformed the deluge into tiny golden comets. I didn't know how far I had gone or even if I was headed in the right direction. I might be walking straight toward the cliff and the sea

below. For the first time in what seemed forever, I didn't want that, a cold and hopefully sudden end to pain and despair. No, I wanted to live, at least long enough to discover why my mother's name had been buried in a witch pit on the Cornish coast and why my mother and grandmother had visited Trelawny Manor. But neither the yearning to live, nor the desire to die are enough to make it happen. I stumbled and lay on the wet grass, unable to rise as the rain pelted me, driving me down into the earth. I imagined my body dissolving in the bog, my bones turning to fossils for some later archeologist to discover.

The small, eager faces of children bent over a glass case containing a grinning skull. Attached to the jawbone by a loop of white cotton twill tape was a beige tag, with the words: "Remains of female found on the Cornish Moors, circa 2018," neatly printed on it in graphite pencil. The children's mouths opened and closed, laughing, chattering, whispering, but though I saw the movement, a low, wild keening in my ears made hearing impossible.

When I awakened, Father was sitting by my bed reading. His pale grey eyes peered at me over the wire reading glasses perched on his nose.

"You were found on the moors." His voice was dispassionate, as cool, calm, and detached as if he were explaining a simple equation to a slow but eager undergraduate.

I looked down at my hands. They were clean and empty. Someone, probably Mrs. Molchany, must have removed my clothes and bathed me. "Did you see the paper?"

He shook his head, "All they found on you was your pack, a dead flashlight, and an empty bottle of pain pills." His eyes narrowed slightly. I flushed, realizing he must have examined my neglected supplies and found me wanting.

"I was told that your fist was closed as if clutching something, but nothing was in your hand."

No, I thought. It would have disintegrated. My proof of sanity had dissolved in the rain.

"Did you know Mother was here?" I asked. "I found her signature in the guest book."

He shook his head. "I didn't know, but she was studying the history of Cornwall and the coast. It's logical she might have visited."

His face was locked, proof against necromancy. I would not tell him that my grandmother had also been here. I would not tell him of the witch pit with my mother's name bound up in twine. He liked human drama and mystery as little as I. He loved me, but he loved order more. The systematic diagrams of chemicals and compounds, the compulsory, unaltering connection of base pairings. The first mistake of his life had been to fall in love with my mother; the second, to have had me. He did not believe in miracles or even coincidences. He had faith only in probabilities and outcomes. The fact that my mother had stayed here meant nothing to him. And I knew, if I told him that I had found my grandmother's signature too, he would have an expla-

nation for it. As for the newspaper, he might have believed it to be a delusion of my fevered mind. It sounded reasonable, more logical than anything I could conjure. As for the figures in the mist and the scent of burning? I had no explanation.

My father never spoke of Mother, nor did he now. Instead, he stayed quietly by my side for a week, each involved in our own worlds. I drifted in and out of fevered dreams while he studied equations more arcane than the bones of ancient sea creatures.

Did I remember my mother? A measure of song, light falling on a face, the scent of milk and comfort. Who knows when first impressions take root?

A dim recollection surfaced in the back corridors of my mind, probably the first of my life. It washed into my consciousness with a clatter and a whoosh. I must have been about a year and a half old.

My mother was kneeling on the kitchen floor, head submerged in a bucket.

I hadn't known what I was seeing, just that it was disturbing in the way misery and violence are.

Her lungs' need for air wrenched her out of the water. The body's necessities ignoring the psyche's desires. The pail overturned.

I can still hear the metal ringing on the tile floor—see the liquid spilling out and mingling with my mother's tears and gasps.

Looking back on it, I wondered how such a brilliant woman could do such a daft thing.

It was almost certainly bound to fail.

"It was a cry for help," they said.

But now I knew better. It was not a cry, it was an honest, albeit unconsidered, attempt to end pain. In the dark of despair, no one is reasonable.

If I'd considered wisely, I'd not have tried to end my misery in a popular waterway near school. I had never understood it, never thought about it before.

When it was obvious I was well, or at least well enough to lie in bed, read, research, and work, he left. He had classes to teach, papers to write, and a life outside of Trelawny and his crazy daughter.

"Be healthy," he said, his slightly chapped lips brushing against my cheek. "Finish your paper when you can, but don't pressure yourself. Call me if you need anything."

My father had made certain I followed the doctor's dosage, and I was feeling foggy again. I needed to think. I needed to work. I halved my dose of the antidepressant and quit the mood stabilizers altogether. But instead of studying the Precambrian shale, which might encompass the fundamentals of evolution and definitely held the key to my doctorate, I delved into the witch pits of Cornwall, which just might contain the secrets to my past.

The guest book was in the foyer. But the history book had disappeared; I searched for it everywhere.

"May I study the guest book again?" I asked Mrs. Molchany. She nodded, unsmiling.

I'd thought to inquire about the other book, but, studying her grim face, I didn't.

One of Cornwall's main tourist attractions was the Museum of Witchcraft in Boscastle. It was only about a forty-minute walk, but I was still too weak to leave my bed. I thought about searching its files online but decided to wait till I could visit in person.

When I punched in the word witchcraft, "Salem" appeared. During the one-year Salem witch trials, though more than two hundred people were accused of witchcraft, only twenty were hanged, and none burned. Impressive, especially as the entire population of Salem was only about six hundred. Still, it wasn't nearly as stunning as the witch trials of Western Europe, which lasted three hundred years and killed more than eighty thousand witches, eighty percent of them women.

Orthodox wisdom attributed the hysteria to a spate of almost supernaturally bad weather. Villages were pelted by freak frosts, floods, and hailstorms. Plagues of mice and caterpillars decimated crops. There were even a couple of rains of frogs. People wanted to blame someone, and old women, anyone over forty and unmarried, were an easy target.

But it wasn't just the ice age that caused the witch hunt. Protestantism had recently emerged as the first truly viable challenger to Catholicism. And what better way to make converts than to combat satanism? The hysteria began in Germany, which was and remained the witch-burning capital of the world. No surprise there.

It began in the 1420s, when two traveling Dominican friars, Heinrich Kramer and Jacob Sprenger began preaching about evil witch women who rode "wooden implements" smeared with a flight-enabling ointment made from the fat of murdered babies.

In 1474 when Kramer was appointed Inquisitor, he immediately accused Helena Scheuberin of witchcraft. However, during her trial, Kramer was so obviously and so disturbingly obsessed with her sexuality, the local bishop ordered him to leave the diocese.

In rebuttal, Kramer wrote the "Malleus Maleficarum"—"The Hammer of Witches,"—a guide on how to identify, hunt, and interrogate witches. Torture and death were the only sure remedy. Women, made from Adam's curved rib, were half-finished, inhuman creatures, a lesser species than even the beasts of the field.

For more than one hundred years, the tome sold more copies than any other book in Europe except the Bible.

With a heaviness in my stomach so dense I felt as if I'd swallowed stones, I followed the trail of notes, from site to site, eventually clicking a promising header: "Witch hunting, the cruelest crime ever." But the site was filled with letters from distraught mothers whose children had been molested by priests. They were not angry, these women, they were heartsick. The faith they believed in, the faith that had given their life meaning, had abused their children. Who could they pray to, or confide in, if not their God? Who could they believe in if not their church?

I clicked away. The reason I studied rocks and stones far older than humans was to avoid these dramas. I had trouble enough dealing with the demons in my DNA.

A man's face is bent over me. His head is shrouded by a black hood. Piercing blue eyes that miss nothing stare out of the darkness.

"Tell me what your mother did last Sabbath night." His breath is so foul I nearly gag as it curls around my face, carrying with it a faint scent of winter nights and ageing fires. I can't say anything. My throat is swollen shut. I can barely breathe.

"Is it not true, Grace Singleton, that your mother, Truth Singleton, is a witch? Is it not true that her spirit can enter the likeness of a brown dog, which kills the livestock of our poor farmers?

"Have you not seen her boiling babies and using their fat and flesh to make a devil's ointment which she smears onto the handle of her broom? Have ye not seen her slipping the wood between her legs like no modest woman, but a common whore, and once astride, using it to fly?"

He takes my fingers in his hand. My bones are small and pliable. He bends them back toward my wrist.

The world is gone. The pain is everything. The ripping of tendons. The breaking of bones. All I want is for it to stop. There is nothing but this.

"My mother, Truth Singleton, is a witch," I cry. "I know this to be true. I have seen her spirit in the likeness of a brown dog…"

"Wake up, Miss, wake up." Someone was shaking me. I pulled back, afraid of what the strange hands might do. It was Mrs. Molchany. Her doughy jowls quivered from her effort. Her chill blue eyes examined me warily.

"You were having a nightmare, Miss."

I glanced around the room. It was still light, but the sun, which was sinking, was hidden behind grey clouds.

"I—I must have drifted off," I stammered. "I was doing some research."

"Not good research," she sniffed. "You're not strong enough, Miss. Perhaps you should read something else. Something good and soothing. I'll bring you up a book and a nice cup of tea."

I wanted to ask Mrs. Molchany if she'd seen *The Complete and Truthful History of the Tragedy at Trelawny*, but the distance of her eyes was a cold stone in my throat.

She looked at me as if trying to make out a vague figure on a far horizon. "A history of Trelawney book? I'm sure I don't know what book you are referring to, Miss."

Had I spoken aloud?

"I don't know of any such history, Miss."

Why was she lying? Was there something in that book she wanted to hide?

She left, returning moments later with the guest book and a mug of steaming Earl Grey.

"That's my mother's signature," I said, turning the pages and pointing to the familiar name.

Mrs. Molchany looked at me as clinically as my father did when he analyzed an unknown element. My mouth filled with the bitter metallic taste of her disbelief. I'd been about to show her my grandmother's name. Instead, I gently shut the book and smiled weakly. I didn't doubt the lists of names would put me to sleep. But I mistrusted it would give me easy dreams.

"Thank you," I said. "I think I'll sleep now."

I spent the next few days resting. My mind was empty, as though still lost in misty night, but I knew that beyond the fog, facts were waiting, lingering in the shadows until I was brave enough to face them.

I leaned over the wooden balcony watching the mourning doves tumble off the railing toward the ground. They didn't glide or dive, they dropped, not as though they were flying, but rather as though they were plummeting to their deaths. Sometimes they almost reached the ground before opening their wings and swooping upwards. It wasn't their power of flight I envied most. It was their fearlessness of falling.

The doves flew toward the cliffs, which curled toward Trelawny like the remnants of a broken conch. Straight ahead, the sea hovered at the very edge of vision, and to my right, the moors expanded outward, obscuring the water completely, but to my left, the coast curved sharply inland. At one point it was only half a mile away. It looked to be but a quick stroll, but I remembered Mrs. Molchany's warning that the way was boggy and perilous. Bits of the golden sandstone slipped regularly and silently into the sea as the waves pounded against shore, slowly wearing away the bluff. Only a desperate person would try to reach the sea that way. Only someone who had no other choices. Yet somebody was there. In the night, I saw a fire burning, flames and smoke reaching toward the stars like a prayer. And sometimes, when the wind was still, I heard screaks. I hoped they were the cries of distant gulls, but something in their urgency and pain made me fear sleep and dread dreams.

I thought to ask Mrs. Molchany about it. Who could be there and why? But when I remembered her distant gaze as I pointed to my mother's signature, the question stuck in my throat like a confession.

It was almost two weeks before I felt well enough to leave Trelawny. And then, almost against my volition, I found myself wandering the rocky green trail toward town and The Museum of Witchcraft.

My ribs were still so sore; I took a second pain pill before I got there.

It was an old two-story structure made of whitewashed brick and thatch built into the gently sloping green hill like a hobbit's dwelling. According to the website, it housed the world's largest collection of folk magic and witchcraft artifacts and acted as a meeting place for Wiccans. In fact, it was "something akin to a site of pilgrimage" for British witches.

How had I ended up here? I who'd always tried to keep my distance from all things unproven and illogical.

The doorway was a rounded arch made of twined willows. As I reached up to knock, it opened. An old woman stood inside. She had more than a few chins and looked like someone I'd expect to see in an Agatha Christie drawing room rather than a witch museum.

She smiled when she saw me, her skin crackling into a million welcoming folds. Keen gray eyes examined me from behind thick wire-framed glasses.

"Come in, me dear, come in. Welcome to The Museum of Witchcraft. We invite ye to explore the deep, ol' history of this place.

"Did you know that a mere three miles away from this spot, a pre-historic maze of stone is carved into the living rock, proof that from ancient times magic making with the world of spirit was active here? The centuries have passed, and times they have a-changed, yet all around us in this wee, quiet corner of England, there's a strange feeling that we are not alone and that the shades of persons passed on and over into the world of spirit are very close. That is why this Museum of Witchcraft is here. Here, one is standing on the edge of the beyond."

She took my hand then, pressing it between her own. A small pulse of electricity raced up my arm like a message being passed from skin to skin. I have read that sea creatures communicate by touch, sending currents through the deep waters. This felt like that, like being probed by another's thoughts.

Her gaze was intense but kind, her eyes huge and blurred behind the thick lenses, though I doubted she missed a thing.

She looked all-knowing and mystic, as though she were privy to secrets beyond the physical. As though she could see further with her myopic eyes than the rest. And yet, and yet I couldn't deny the shock waves, little fingers of current tingling up my arm.

"My mother was here once," I said, not knowing why I spoke. It felt like a confession, like something secret and a little shameful.

"Not here-here, I mean," I stammered, gesturing around at the dusty book-filled shelves and lead-rimmed glass cases packed with straw dolls, whittled bones, and altars of twig and reed.

"I don't know if she was here, in the museum, but in Cornwall." I felt ridiculous, like a child caught in a lie. "She was studying history, I think."

"We can see if you like." She took my hand still tingling at her touch and pulled me toward an old open book.

"What was her name, dear?"

She leafed backward, paging through time. If only I could return through the years with such ease.

My mother's writing scrawled up at me like memory. I rubbed my finger over the line taking comfort in its familiar swirls.

"Did—did you know her?" I whispered.

She shrugged again. "Not in the flesh." She shook her head. The pale, loose skin below her neck wobbled, giving off a faint fragrance of sage and lavender.

"I fear there's things ye need ken to, things only the dead may tell."

She straightened up and smiled. Her teeth were crooked and stained. One of her incisors was missing, leaving a dark hole in her grin. It was a comforting smile nonetheless, as though she'd turned from an uncanny soothsayer into a sweet old lady with the lifting of her lips.

"I'm Mrs. Gypsy Evansleaver, me dear, one of the caretakers of this place."

"I'm Joanna Turner," I replied, wondering if she would take my hand again, curious and slightly dreading the tremor of electricity I feared would follow.

"Come to my house this Wednesnight. We will ask the old women of the village what they may know. Mayhap it will put your soul at peace."

I shook my head weakly, but even as I did, I knew I would go, drawn toward answer I could not find in books, though every fiber of my being pulled away in disbelief.

I had never gone to a séance. While my schoolmates clustered together in darkened rooms over Ouija boards trying to contact the beyond, I stayed in my room, reading about rock substrates and bone density, as far from the supernatural as I could get. I had no desire to talk to the spirits. My dead were already too close, woven into my genes like a warning, waiting to make contact.

Gypsy Evansleaver's cottage was not far from Trelawny, ten miles at most. I could have biked it, if the old cycle had not been permanently rusted to the Yew tree in the back garden. Mrs. Molchany had caught me eyeing it more than once, even though its tires had no air and its chains were the color of a robin's breast.

"You'll not be using that, Miss. You're too weak, and it's in no good shape. Even if it could be gotten freed from the old yew, which I doubt, we've no good pump and no lights. Imagine if you broke down on the moors at night with no one around to be coming to your aid.

"I'll call Charlie to take ye, though I'm sure he'll not be pleased at your going… he's never had a kin fer…" She pinched her lips together as if to keep unwanted words from escaping.

Charles arrived in his old black cab, polished and shiny as a hearse. It was obvious he lavished as much care and attention on it as his progenitors must have on their horses.

"How good it is to see ya, Miss," he cried, his round red face breaking into a smile so wide I could see the darkness where two molars had been. He opened the door, taking my elbow and propelling me in as if I were as fragile as a beam of moonlight.

"I'd heard you'd been ill, Miss. Trapesing all over the moors at night." He shook his head and tisked. "Where are you going?" Keen, and oddly familiar, blue eyes watched me in the mirror.

"To Mrs. Gypsy Evansleaver's," I said.

His eyes grew distant and cold. The jolliness and animation drained away. His face seemed paler and looser. The skin around his jaw drooping as if it had suddenly lost support and structure.

He said not another word but sped through the night, bumping over potholes and ruts as if he were in a hurry to get rid of me.

He stopped so suddenly I slammed forward into the rear of his seat. Reaching back, he lifted the handle, opening my door into darkness.

"It's thata way. Just follow your nose an' don't stray from the road. When you see a slate path on your left, take it."

He gunned the engine, disappearing into the night before I could ask how to reach him.

I stepped down, twisting my left ankle, already weak from its recent break. The hurt was intense.

I lay on the damp cobbles, pain blocking out everything. I pressed one hand against my chest, put the other on my stomach and inhaled. I distended my abdomen, pushing it full of breath. I counted to three.

Calm, I thought. *Calm.*

I washed two pain pills down with a swig of the whiskey I'd begun carrying with me after the witch pit fiasco. I would never be without supplies again. I waited for warmth and clarity to spread from belly to brain.

I arose, and I walked straight ahead, sliding over the slick pavement so as not to trip again. The moon was new, so I had only starlight to see by. Fast-moving clouds sometimes obscured even that dim light. A wind tugged at my sweater, which, even pulled tight, was too thin to shield me from the chill damp.

My ribs ached. I took another pain pill.

I don't know how I found the turnoff, not by sight, but rather by the scent of moist earth and some odd sense of having turned down this way before. The slates were laid flat into the ground, cemented together by moss which looked black in the dim light, as though each stone was set into the dark hole of space. The way was lined by tall narrow trees, poplars or birch that, even in the night, cast the track into a singular obscurity.

After a time, I saw a yellow light divided into fours by lines of lead. The shape of the house itself was hidden, bleeding into the darkness of the night and the shadow of the great old oak behind it.

It wasn't until I got close that I could see that the walls were made of coarse, uneven grey stones that sporadically flashed with color: blue, green, brown, and an occasional touch of copper or gold. From the thatched roof, a slender stream of smoke rose into the sky like a departing spirit.

The door was made from the body of some ancient tree. It opened before I could knock. And there was Gypsy Evansleaver bordered on each side by two old women. Two were plump and two were thin; all were sharp-eyed. Wrinkled by the years yet somehow unfettered to time.

Behind them, six wooden hoop-backed chairs formed a half circle around a small table. They were backlit by the flames in the large brick hearth that gave the only illumination to the space. The dancing fire made the shadows ebb and rise, casting first one face and then another in an orange glow. I could imagine these women digging witch pits on the moors with never a thought to the damp or the mud.

"Come in, my dear, come in," said Gypsy Evansleaver. She took me by the elbow.

Again, I felt that strange flow of current rush through me.

"Eseld Angwin, Jowanet Bligh, Gonetta Carew, Kerensa Angove, meet Joanna Turner." Their names washed over me like water tumbling over rocks, the sounds clear and well-defined, but without meaning. The crones bent around me like an undiscovered country. They fit here, in this room, in this place, somehow made timeless by their obvious belonging. I coveted that sense of rightness. Accident had thrown me here, a stranger, born out of season, haunted by an idea called home.

They'd been sipping tea and perhaps something stronger. On the table sat five china cups, a tea cozy, a crystal carafe half-filled with a golden liquid, and a plate of biscuits topped by candied violets, each petal outlined in crystal, as though touched by the first frost of winter.

Gypsy Evansleaver propelled me toward a chair. It was hard and forced me to sit-up very straight. Again, I wondered at the fortitude of such women who denied even the comfort of cushions to their old bones.

"Take a sip of this, dear," she poured a cup half full of tea, adding in a good shot of the liquid from the crystal carafe. I don't know what it was, but it filled me with golden fire, like warm honey, like tea and sympathy. The room sparkled. The edges were softer, but somehow everything was clearer and more real.

Gypsy Evansleaver took my empty cup. Once again, I felt the flow of energy run through me.

One of the women leaned toward me. I

didn't remember which. She took my hand, too. Her lips moved, but I couldn't hear her words.

Her voice melded into the darkness, the words becoming no more than the crackling of flame.

It is dark and cold. The man in the black cloak bends over me; only the glinting of eyes in the shadow beneath his hood show me that this is a man and not death himself.

"Tell me again what your mother, Truth Singleton, did and what she made ye do."

My thumbs are being squeezed between two boards. The world is only pressure and pain. I will do anything to make it stop.

"I saw her dancing naked under the moonlight," I cry. "She made me naked, too. And then the devil did come and ride her in the shape of a grey wolf."

The caped man lifts his head. He straightens his body. His hood falls back. I see his face clearly. His cold blue eyes are the only light in my cell.

He pulls me outside. My arms are being yanked from their sockets. The sun is blinding, scorching my eyes like flame. How long has it been since I have seen the light?

"Confess," he says. "Confess and be saved."

A crowd surrounds me. It is my neighbors. Them I have known since I was but a wee tacker. There is Sister Kerensa, who used to cradle me in her floury arms and feed me figgy hobbin straight from her fire. And Farmer Angwin, who gave me milk warm from the teat of his cow. And Mother Constance Molchany, who used to care for

me when I was small and let me watch while her ewe birthed five kits. There is a strange man, whose pale grey eyes peer at me over wire glasses. I don't know who he is, but somehow, I know him. All of them gaze on me as if I am a stranger.

In the center of them all, my mother is chained to a pole, her clothes torn, her breasts bare for all to see. I cannot look on her.

"Confess," he says, bending back the thumb of my left hand.

I point a small trembling white finger toward my mother. "I have heard her talking to a brown dog," I whisper.

"Louder," cries the man, twisting my thumb.

"She smears the fat of murdered babes on her broom-end!" I scream. "She flies through the night, across the sky, bringing illness and death."

"Witch," says the man.

"Witch," echoes the crowd. "Cursin' our farmlands an' fornicating with the devil."

"Witch," says the man. "She must burn!"

"Heed the Bishop Bligh! He is blessed by God!" screams Mother Constance.

"Burn the witch! Burn the witch!" The chant rises from the crowd. They close around her. I cannot see, but I hear her voice. The same one that used to sing me lullabies and soothe me to sleep. The same that said she loved me and stroked my hair. But it is not the same. It is harsh and raw as though pulled from her very soul.

"If my flesh and bone accuse me, so it be. And this same curse she be in the blood through all the generations. Not one who's woman of my flesh shall live past my years of twenty-nine. Not one shall live to see her daughter grown. Not one shall dance at her daughter's wedding or cradle her grand babe in her arms. As you have cursed me, I curse you."

"Are you all right, me dear?" The anxious face of Gypsy Evansleaver swam in and out of focus. Old faces bent over me like a hungry crowd.

The same faces as were in the crowd. That can't be possible. But it is. They have returned after all this time, or maybe they never left? And that the stranger in their midst was my father. He was there, too.

"I must go," I cried, struggling to my feet. Hands tried to hold me down. I thrashed out wildly.

"Stay, stay," they begged.

But I would not stay. Withered hands snatched at me. Punching, kicking, I staggered to my feet out into the night, running, sliding down the slate lane.

When I reached the road, an ancient black car was waiting. Charlie's cab. I was saved! I dove, sobbing and laughing, into the back seat, slamming the door behind me. Charlie started up the engine, pulling smoothly away, back to Trelawny, back to sanity.

"You're all right now, Miss. You're safe with me."

His eyes met mine in the mirror. They were the cool, blue eyes of my inquisitor.

The fog had finally cleared. I could see clearly now. The dead had returned, or perhaps they'd always been here, waiting for my return. Waiting for retribution. My father, Charlie, Mrs. Molchany, Gypsy Evansleaver, and the rest.

I pushed the door open and tumbled into the night, rolling off the road into the damp grass.

"Miss! Miss!" His voice called after me, as the car screeched to a halt.

I staggered to my feet and ran as fast as I could. He would not trap me again.

Out on the moors, the air was heavy with the sweet scent of burning flesh. A fire was burning. I heard my mother's cries. I had been given another chance. This time I would not betray her. I can save her. I will save her. But I must hurry. I wash down a couple of pain pills with a warming swig of whiskey and head left, taking the shortest path toward the coast.

I awoke in a bright, white room. The sharp antiseptic of bleach stung my nostrils. I closed my eyes, hoping for a different awakening. One with color and softness and the smell of lavender, but when I opened them, I saw my father. He looked worn and thin, as though he'd been carved in stone.

"It seems you haven't been taking your med," he said, his voice as dry as Mrs. Molchany's scones.

"Interesting reading material," he said, raising an eyebrow and nodding toward a pile of books and news clippings on the bed.

There was *The Wonderful Discoverie of Witches in the Countie of Lancaster*, a small, dog-eared pamphlet. *Daemonologie*, written by King James the First. *Tales of the Witchfinder General*, *The Discovery of Witches*, and *The trials of the Pendle witches*.

My father opened one.

"King James thought that 'Children, women and liars can be witnesses over high treason against God,'" he read.

He leafed through, *The trials of the Pendle witches*.

"The main witness against Truth Device was her daughter, Grace, who was but nine years old," he read. "When Grace was brought into the courtroom, Truth, began to curse and scream at her daughter, making accusations that would lead to her execution. The judges removed Truth from the courtroom so the child could give evidence.

"Grace Device was then placed on a table.

"'My mother is a witch, and that I know to be true.' she cried in a loud, clear voice. 'I have seen her spirit in the likeness of a brown dog, which she calls Ball. The dog did ask what she would have him do, and she answered that she would have him help her to kill.'

"Truth's son, James Device, also gave evidence. 'I have seen my mother making a clay figure and whispering the name John Robinson as she did mold it in her hands. She stuck a pin into its heart, and not but two days later John Robinson was dead.'"

My father looked up. "Truth Device was found guilty and died in horrid conditions at Lancaster Castle while awaiting the assizes. Grace Device disappeared from history until 24 March 1634, when she was one of

I AM WAR

BY EVAN DeSHAIS

twenty tried at Lancaster for the crime of witchcraft, accused of the murder by Edmund Robinson, a ten-year-old boy. Grace ended her days the same way that her mother did, dying in Lancaster Castle, awaiting trial."

"And the tale continues," he said, picking up a newspaper.

Witches of Cornwall Volume 61 Number 6, November/December 2008 by Kate Ravilious

"Archaeologist Jacqui Wood has unearthed evidence of three witch pits beneath her own front yard in Cornwall.

"'We have been uncovering some extraordinary animal pits,' says Wood. 'One was lined with the skin of a black cat and contained 22 eggs, all with chicks close to hatching, in addition to cat claws, teeth, and whiskers. Another held a dog skin, dog teeth, and a baked pig jaw.'

"The biggest shock of all came from the radiocarbon dates for these pits. The cat pit dated to the 18th century, while the dog pit dated to the 1950s. And I doubt it just suddenly stopped in the 1950s.

"'Often when secret rituals are abandoned, people will talk about 'things that were done in me grandmother's day' but there has been no whisper of this,' Wood speculated. 'It makes me wonder whether that is because it is still going on.'"

My father put down the clippings and stared at me as dispassionately as an oddly behaving chemical.

"We pulled you out of the bog, right on the edge of the cliff. It's a wonder you aren't dead. You will stay here for a while," he said. "Where you can be...monitored."

He glanced at the worn books and full bottles of pills. They stared back at me, white and empty as the eyeballs of ghosts.

"Then, when you are better, I shall take you home. And no more reading about witchcraft." He scooped up the books, kissed me on the forehead and left.

The door opened and a tight-lipped, doughy woman, face framed by an almost unruly halo of blueish-gray curls entered.

"I'm Nurse Molchany," she said. "I'll be the one seeing to your needs."

E.E. King is an award-winning painter, performer, writer, and naturalist. Ray Bradbury called her stories, "marvelously inventive, wildly funny, and deeply thought-provoking."
Check out paintings, writing, musings, and books at:
www.elizabetheveking.com and amazon.com/author/eeking

The Gold Exigency (Part 3 of 4)

By MICHAEL TIERNEY

Conrock and Mackstar narrowly escaped the Five-Thousand Fingered Hand! Can they track down the missing Philean with help from Phaedra and her companions?!

Chapter Eleven
"Just lovely"

"What if Genghis didn't make it inside?" Mackstar asked as Conrock prepared to activate the Black Star Reaver tracking device. "What if he's tumbling around somewhere out there in space?"

"Then he'll be glad to see us," Conrock replied. "If he hasn't run out of air, he can probably tell us where Januman went."

He worked the controls as he had watched Januman do, but nothing happened.

"Is it working?" the hulking warrior named Carmdall asked.

"No," Conrock replied, "not yet."

"Now I see why you're C.F.S. certified," Mackstar quipped, but when no one asked, he abandoned the punchline.

"When it's working," said Conrock, "believe me, you'll know it. Then you'll understand why I suggested that we do this down in the hangar and not in the control room."

His fingers felt all around the device. Januman had done something to the connections before he left it behind, but

Conrock was not sure what. The man had been as uncannily quick with his fingers as he was with everything else. Finally, Conrock found a connection that felt loose and tried again. When that did not work, he kept testing the connections until he noticed two components that did not look right to him. Normally Januman's handiwork had a symmetrical pattern to it, but these looked jumbled. He tried switching them about with no luck. Then, on the last combination he could think of, the green light of the hologram began to glow and all the Brudwata all began to howl in pain.

Conrock switched the device off.

"What happened?" Roy Kirk called from the bridge. "That was fairly unpleasant."

"It's over," Conrock replied. "I've got what we're looking for."

The biggest of the Brudwata, Carmdall, had concealed his pain when the others cried out, but his eyes showed his displeasure when he raised a hand that Conrock thought was going for his throat.

"Do not do that again," Carmdall said in a forceful voice as he held the open palm, which displayed a tattoo of a half-lidded eye, in front of Conrock's face.

"Should I be worried about him?" Conrock asked Lonan.

"First that I heard of him," said Lonan, "he was about to eat his youngest son."

"*That's* not a good sign. They're a strange escort for a princess."

"She's no princess," Lonan replied.

"Whatever Phaedra is, those troglodytes treat her like she's one. Where'd you find them?"

"Akara's World. Used to be called…"

"Magus IV to some, Miri to others," Conrock finished his sentence. "That's where Dire Griefs come from. We saw one working with the Madam of the Five-Thousand Fingered Hand."

"What?" Lonan exclaimed. "Phaedra will probably have some questions about about that."

"You saw a Dire Grief with them?" Phaedra appeared from right behind Conrock. But she did not wait for answers as she walked past with a distracted look of concern.

"How does she do that?" Conrock asked when Lonan followed him up the stairs to the bridge.

"Do what?"

"Januman did the same thing—just appeared out of nowhere."

"She was standing behind you the whole time," Lonan replied.

"Lovely," Conrock shook his head, wondering how much damage he might have done with his glib comments. "Just lovely."

Lonan seemed confused by his reaction.

"Yes," he replied. "She is."

"Salvage ship," Conrock noted when he entered the bridge. Looking at the exterior monitors, he added, "That explains a few things. I see you're playing the Checkmate Gambit with that oversized gun mounted on top. You know that will only be good for one shot, don't you?"

"The whole point of the gambit," Roy replied, "is to avoid having to take that first shot. What's my destination?"

"Phileas."

"Wait a minute. I thought people were trying to evacuate the Phileans from there, to save them from predation by treasure hunters? Why would they take one back there?"

"We're about to find out. How long until we catch up?"

"I don't know. What kind of ship are we chasing?"

"An Artomique Class Dreadnought. And we aren't chasing them. From what I saw, they're already there."

Roy shook his head.

"What exactly do you think a salvage ship can do against a Dreadnought?"

"Fortunately, they're running un-manned, on auto. Or at least one of them is."

Roy shifted uncomfortably in his seat. Because he obviously spent so much time in it, that took some effort to rearrange the deep indentations in the cushioning.

"I'm really not liking the sound of this," he said.

"Yeah… well, obviously we're going to have to be sneaky about it when we arrive,"

Conrock replied. "I'm getting the impression that's something your people already have some experience with. What I can't figure is how this collection came together. Obviously, it has something to do with Phaedra. She overheard me referring to her as a princess. I hope that's not something that will insult her."

"Not at all. Most of us refer to her as a goddess."

"Wait. What?"

"Give it some time; you'll see. And you're right. She's what brought us all together. So tell me about you and your friends."

"I wouldn't call them friends," Conrock replied, noticing how Lonan leaned in to listen to his answer. "We just met, and frankly, I'm not sure what to think of them myself. Up until a little while ago, I was certain that Mackstar might have had something to do with the disappearance of former President Bully Bravo."

Lonan laughed.

"Did I say something funny?"

Roy smiled.

"Yeah, you did," he replied. "We're probably the last people who saw President Bravo."

"Say what?"

"That's why this ship is *Gravedigger Deuce*," said Lonan.

"We loaned him the first *Gravedigger* so he could head out of the galaxy," Roy added.

"He was looking for some Wild Stars planet called New Atlantis," said Lonan.

"Yeah," said Roy, "we kissed that ship goodbye. But Phaedra bought us a new one."

"She... bought... you... a starship?" Conrock was incredulous. "What is she, rich or something?"

Lonan smiled and enthusiastically nodded his head as Roy replied.

"Beyond your wildest dreams. And I do mean the wildest."

"If she's so rich," Conrock asked, "what's she doing on a salvage ship?"

"You should see..." Lonan's next words were cut off by Roy's shaking head.

"We've already said too much. Any more will need to come from her."

As soon as he finished his last word, Phaedra's voice sounded over the inter-ship communicator, asking everyone to gather in the cargo hangar.

"I think she heard you," Conrock remarked.

In the hangar, he saw the Philean again, dressed in a blanket that covered her wings. Mackstar was trying to talk with her, but not having much luck, while Pam admonished him to leave her alone and give her some time.

Phaedra placed a hand on the Philean's shoulder and looked first at the gathered Brudwata, then slowly around to everyone else. She then nodded at Conrock.

"Our new friends here have brought concerning information about the people we've been looking for. It seems that they are in league not just with the Black Star Reavers, but also a Dire Grief."

The Brudwata all shifted nervously, instinctively gripping the handles of their weapons.

"Roy, neither you, Pam, nor Lonan have probably ever heard of them," she said, "but as you can tell by the reaction of our Brudwata friends, they are exceptionally dangerous. It's particularly distressing to hear that they've moved from Miri out into the stars."

"There was a valley near our home," said Carmdall. "It was a valley of death from the time we first arrived on Miri. Then one day, it was abandoned. We wondered where they had gone."

"Because of this," said Phaedra, "I've decided to abandon all efforts to contact the Five-Thousand Fingered Hand. We've gone to great lengths to stay hidden in the stars, and our new friends have saved us from making a terrible mistake."

There was something about the tone of her voice and the way her hand tightened on the Philean's shoulder that made Conrock nervous.

"I've also spent some time with the Philean," she paused, "and while she looks humanoid, I have to admit that she's really more reptilian."

"Excuse me?" Conrock interrupted.

"I've seen inside her mind…"

"She can do that," Lonan leaned in and whispered.

"…and I have to say there was not much awareness there. Pam and Mackstar have told me she has the capability of some speech, but I'm afraid that is more mimicry than anything else. But worse, from everything I've been told and could learn from her, she may be the last of her kind—a species that has recently been hunted to ex-

tinction."

Roy grabbed Conrock's arm to restrain him, sensing the same thing that Conrock feared was coming next.

"Because of that, we're going to change course. We're not going to Phileas."

"But what about the other Philean?" Conrock asked.

"You don't understand," said Mackstar, "that other Philean isn't really a Philean. She's my sister! She can shape-shift. She did it to hide from the people chasing us."

His words surprised Phaedra, and it was an experience that she was clearly unaccustomed to. She shook her head.

"If she's still in the form of a Philean, then she's probably already dead." She looked at Conrock. "I've seen that in your head. The people who took her have already arrived where they're going. By the time we get there, it will already be far too late. Hoping will not change what you already know."

Carmdall stood up and looked around at the other Brudwata.

"That does not matter," he said. "The man who did bad things to Phaedra is there. We must deal with him."

"No," Phaedra replied, "I was tempted when I first learned it was him, but he's too dangerous for us to deal with. We can't risk everything for petty revenge."

"When an animal is dangerous," Carmdall argued, "you put it down before it can do more harm."

"I'm with the big guy," Conrock said. "Going up against these people isn't something you'd do in a toe-to-toe fight. We don't stand a chance at that. But even if it's just Mackstar and me—and don't get me wrong, we'll take any help we can get—we have to go about this covertly. At the very least, we can find out what the situation is. If it's a lost cause, we'll bug out. I'm not suggesting anyone commit suicide. Just get us there, and the rest of you leave if you need to."

"I can't let you endanger my friends," Phaedra replied. "Not for me. Not for anybody."

"On Miri," Carmdall shook his head, "if you run away and hide, you will still die, just a little slower and much more painfully. Only if you face the danger do you have a chance to survive."

"He's right!" Lonan stepped forward, drawing immediate protest from Pam. "Count me in."

"Listen, kid," Conrock could tell the young man had a wiry, athletic build, but he did not carry himself in the manner of someone who would be good in a fight, "I know I said that I'd take any help that I could get…"

"No. And you, too, Pam. No." Lonan shook his fists for emphasis. "I decided a while back that I would never again run from a fight, and I meant it. I ran from my cousin's assassins, I ran from a saurocat…"

"You faced a saurocat?" Conrock was surprised.

"I ran then, and I'm not running ever again. And… I can help."

Before Conrock could speak the question of "How?" that was forming on his lips, Roy spoke up.

"He can unlock just about any door there is. Haven't found a place yet that could keep him out."

Pam shot Roy a sideways look of displeasure and ran her fingers in a zipper motion across her lips.

Conrock shrugged in acceptance, and all eyes turned toward Phaedra.

Chapter Twelve
Phileas

"Wait." Phaedra pulled Conrock away from Mackstar, Lonan, and the Philean when the *Gravedigger II's* hangar bay upper and lower doors opened and a ramp descended to the ground. "Put down the bag, I have something for you."

Her expression was one of displeasure, but Conrock could not hide his smile when Roy and Pam Kirk opened a locker cabinet and handed him a sniper rifle with the latest scope technology and a pair of plasma pistols. They all looked brand new.

"Thank you," Conrock nodded his head in satisfaction. "I certainly didn't expect this. I mean, you're flying around in a salvage ship with a personal guard dressed in animal skins and carrying a mix of antique and modern blades—and you've got something like this stored away? I've spent the last few days scrambling to stay armed with anything and everything I could find, and I've got to say that this is a more than pleasant surprise."

As he sighted the scope at the dense jungle surrounding the clearing where they had landed, Phaedra put a hand on the barrel and pushed it down.

"This Januman you're hunting," she said. "The only way you can hurt him is to take him by complete surprise; best if he's distracted by something. And you have to make certain that you kill him with the first shot. Not only won't you get a second, but he'll do whatever it takes to make certain you never existed."

Conrock found her statement odd, but considering what he had seen of Januman's abilities, he did not take it lightly, unlike the heavy duffle bag he strained to hoist to one shoulder.

"I need a guarantee from you," she said.

"We'll get him," Conrock assured.

"I have no expectations about that," she replied. "I want you to guarantee to me that you'll make sure that Carmdall comes back safe. He's the leader of his people, and he's too important to lose."

Conrock nodded. The four Brudwater already in the clearing were Carmdall and his son, along with Fistal and his daughter. The rest of the Warlords had elected to remain with Phaedra.

"I'll do my best, so long as he doesn't try to eat me."

"If something happens to him," she replied, "find your own way off this planet."

As he stepped off the ramp, he was joined by Mackstar, who noticed the new gear and tapped his own well-worn weapons.

"Want to trade?" he asked.

"Not on your life," Conrock replied. "But I've got some things for you that Roy helped me with."

Just before the group headed into the thick of the woods, following a dried-up wa-terbed that they hoped would lead them out of the valley and to the high ground, Conrock stopped to take one last look behind.

Phaedra stood motionless like a Greek statue, her eyes glued on the group as the breeze from the closing doors whipped what little clothing she wore. She was a remarkable woman whom he could simply not figure out.

Pam Kirk waved as she finished closing the door, while several Brudwata crowded near and sniffed at the last wisps of fresh air. When the ship did not immediately launch as he expected, he figured they were giving the expedition time to clear the area first.

"At least they got us this far," Mackstar commented.

When they had first arrived at Phileas, they stayed in deep orbit, reconnoitering the planet. There were indeed two Artomique Dreadnoughts in orbit, the *Merciless* and the *Godspeed*, but rather than stationing themselves where they could survey the entirety of the planet's upper atmosphere, they had positioned themselves side by side—guarding a specific area below. Conrock knew that was where they needed to go.

But before they made a move, Roy noticed heavy hauler hoppers making repeated runs between the planet and the *Merciless*, all coming from the same area where a long-range topographical image revealed a single large, manmade structure.

To avoid detection, the *Gravedigger II* approached from the far side of the planet at a low altitude, but they had to land even further away than planned when they detected groups of pirates fanning out in a search pattern around the area the Dreadnoughts guarded.

Conrock surprised everyone when he suggested that they land as close as possible to one of those groups. The *Gravedigger II* would then return to high orbit and await their signal.

"So what's your plan," Mackstar asked, his hand briefly holding that of the Philean.

"Why did you bring her along?" Conrock asked. "I can't believe Phaedra agreed to it."

"She wanted to come," Mackstar replied. "It's her world, after all. She might be able to help us."

Conrock disagreed with the logic, but with Lonan bracketing the Philean on the other side, she was as protected as she could be.

"We decided to call her Sundown," Lonan announced.

"Let's go hunt some pirates." Conrock shrugged. He was doubtful that the Philean was even capable of making her own decisions, but he was unwilling to get into an argument over it. "Wait. Quiet."

He suddenly realized that the Brudwata had disappeared into the surrounding green without making a sound. There was no sight of them or evidence of them moving through the woods, which was startling given their bulk.

"Brudwata?" He called out to no response, the only sounds came from him and the constantly chattering insects. "I hope you can still hear me, because I need to warn you about what we're up against out here."

"The pirates?" Lonan asked.

"The wildlife," Conrock replied. "I was in such a hurry to get off that ship before Phaedra changed her mind—I thought we'd save time and discuss it while we walked."

"We've got a long walk," said Mackstar.

"Maybe," Conrock answered cryptically. "I did some research on the way, and there are very important reasons why this planet has never been colonized. The first planetary scout to explore it labeled it suitable for our biological requirements, but gave it his highest rating in hazardous lifeforms. The scout was Bully Bravo, who later became President, so you know if he took this place seriously, we should also."

He pulled a roll of duct tape out of his backpack and began sealing the sleeves and ankles of the flight suit Lonan had given him, and then passed it to him and Mackstar.

"This will help protect you against insects," he explained. "I really didn't want to do this in front of Phaedra, and I'm not sure what we can do for the girl."

She did not resist when he took one of her hands and closely examined the skin on her arms, running his fingers across the many fine silicatein stones in her pores, and began to understand the evolutionary drivers for this unique form of body armor and why she was able to dress so lightly in thin, nearly transparent weave. Conrock could only wonder what kind of creature had created the silky material.

He then noticed that the Philean had completely changed her demeanor once they entered the woods. Her head rose for the first time as her eyes danced while rapidly looking all around.

"Is this happy?" she asked with a smile.

"Kid," he replied, "I'm the wrong person to ask that question. But I'm glad you're feeling better." He nodded to Mackstar. "So I guess this confirms that she's the real Philean. She certainly seems to feel at home."

"Probably," Mackstar replied with an uncertain tone, "but Akarastar didn't just do a superficial physical transformation. She went into Sundown's mind—mirrored her—became her twin."

"Either way, we need to get moving," he pulled out matching lightweight helmets and put one on. He handed one to both Mackstar and Lonan, but the Philean recoiled at his offer.

Hauling the bag back onto his shoulder, he called out to the jungle.

"Brudwata! I've got some of these for you, too! Listen to me, so you'll understand that you need to come get these." He pointed at the tall, green trees that swayed over their heads. "These trees not only provide perfect cover and hidden aerial warrens for both the Phileans and the predators that hunt them, but they tend to shed their bark much like an Earth pine tree. The problem is that their bark tends to be far larger and thicker, shaped in the form of a V. They can come helicoptering down on us at any moment, and while the senses of the Phileans are probably fine-tuned enough to their

natural surroundings that they're not surprised, nearly every expedition after Bravo had reports of individuals being smacked in the head—often fatally. That's why this planet is considered a death world—a planet of peril."

"Roy and Pam got these for a Halloween visit to a space station," said Lonan. "They remind me of British Colonial Officers that I learned about when I was young—before everyone on Ansa died. On these long space flights you have a lot of time to remember the things you miss."

The helmets had a narrow brim in front and a very large one in the back, somewhat like the rear brim of a fireman's hat, except it dropped down to cover the entire neck. This was not a fashion statement but a necessity. He saw Mackstar give an odd look at the human face that was hand-painted there.

"That's for the predators," said Conrock. "Most like to attack from behind, and with these they'll always think you're looking at them."

"So, if I lose this," Lonan tossed his helmet in the air and caught it before putting it on, "I'd best keep turning around."

"Won't do you any good," said Mackstar. "Back where the Brudwata and I come from, once a predator triggers into attack mode, there's no changing its mind. What I don't understand is why this world is considered more dangerous. We had three types of Griefs, the hulking browns, the pack hunting red, and the terrible Dire. The Earth pioneers just kept coming—even after the Brothan arrived."

"A couple of things Akara's World had to its favor was the norshahani leather and the tree wood. Akaran is considered the best in the galaxy for both. This Phileas wood isn't even good for burning. Too much tar. And there are just so many different types of predators here, all the way down to the insects. There was nothing that made it worth the risk to come here—at least until Sundown's people were discovered."

Mackstar took the lead as they moved along, picking up several pieces of bark that he discovered worked well as a boomerang. After just a couple of tosses, he was able to hit whatever he aimed for.

The Philean laughed.

"You play like a child." She started to spread her wings.

"Stay with us." Conrock grabbed her arm again to discourage her from flying away. Then he noticed how Lonan was still without footwear, just like the Brudwata and the Philean. "How do you do that?"

"I grew up what you might call wild on the Ansa moon after the Terraformer colony was massacred," he said, tugging at the crotch of his flight suit. "Didn't talk to anyone for a long time, and I'm still trying to learn how to interact with people—and to wear this uncomfortable clothing."

"Tell me about it."

"But Pam insisted. So, how did things change when the Phileans were discovered?"

"They didn't so much at first," said Conrock. "A bunch of preachers tried to convert them to religion, but all they did was teach them some English and give them passage off-world, where the value of their organic gemstones was discovered. When gold started losing its value on the monetary exchanges, that's when the Artomiques launched their Gold Exigency."

"Their what?"

"They planned to recover their lost wealth by switching their monetary base to Philean gemstones. With a limited supply against growing demand, the value of the gemstones is guaranteed to continue to escalate—not devalue like gold has."

"Because there's so much of it now?"

"Exactly." Conrock noticed Lonan had become nervous. "Know anything about that?"

Mackstar reached the crest of the ridge and stopped. Crouching down, he gripped his rifle with both hands as he looked off to their right.

There was a sudden rustling in the treetops, and a terrible screech erupted from the ground below, accompanied by the frenzied sound of a fight and then something crashing through the trees on the slope, headed away from them. The jungle went completely quiet as even the insect life became silent.

Even Conrock's city senses told him that was not a good sign.

"Brudwata?" Conrock called out.

"Keep moving, little man," came the distant reply.

When Conrock and Sundown joined Mackstar on the ridge, Lonan summed up the sight that lay below.

"Wowie."

Chapter Thirteen
The Dead Pirate Returns

"Wowie?" Conrock asked as he took in the sight of what was once a primitive city carved into the rocks of the canyon walls. There were holes all along the walls going all the way up to the top of the valley, most of them completely inaccessible from the ground. They surrounded the empty bed of a dry lake with a shore that sparkled like it was covered in snow crystals.

"That's what Pam would have said," Lonan replied. "I'm still getting my language skills back after living all those years alone. How would you describe this?"

"You don't want to be talking like me," said Conrock. "I've been dialing my language back ever since I retired from the military, but it looks like the Phileans weren't as completely primitive as we've been told."

The dry riverbed they were following had split into the two canyons from the main body that led up to the top of the valley ridge. Mackstar led the way into the new canyon below.

"So," said Conrock, "I'm the only person here who grew up with a roof over his head?"

"We had a roof over our heads," Mackstar stopped and gave a long, lingering look at Sundown. "Our parents had a house they built out by an oasis well. It was pretty remote, so we didn't interact with much of the other people living there, like the Brudwata. Akarastar and I pretty much had to entertain ourselves."

Any hopes he had that Sundown might share some recognition of his memories were dashed when she simply smiled and blinked.

When they started to walk around the shore of the dry lake, Conrock scooped up a handful the sparkly dirt and was surprised to discover it was covered with silicatein crystals just like those on Sundown's skin.

"Phileans must shed these things!" he announced emphatically.

"Then why are they being skinned alive?" Lonan picked up a handful and then saw the same answer that Conrock discovered.

While the smoothness of their crystal surface was sufficient to reflect light, the crystals themselves were dull and colorless, completely unlike the vibrant crystal that Achilles Hister had displayed in the Chancellor's office.

"When they're skinned," said Conrock, "it turns the crystals blood red. There must be another process at work that gives them their clarity.

"Someone in there?" Sundown walked inquisitively toward the darkness of the nearest opening.

"Sorry, darling," Conrock noticed how Mackstar lifted his nose to the air, as if he was sensing something. "There's no one left here, but ..." he heard the sound of skippers in the next canyon over, headed their way, "maybe we should go inside ourselves."

Conrock stayed with Sundown while the others hid in other openings. They barely had time to get out of sight when a pair of weather-worn skippers landed on the shore of the dry lakebed, directly in front of them.

With each skipper capable of carrying

several passengers, Conrock considered it luck that they were empty except for the drivers—whose eclectic clothing and choice of weaponry identified them as pirates. When they exited their vehicles, Conrock hoped the others would follow his lead when he rushed out with his weapon drawn.

But, surprisingly, the pirates began laughing at his order to surrender and put their hands in the air. He glanced at his sides to see what had happened to his companions.

They were there, but both Mackstar and Lonan had been disarmed and taken prisoners by several other pirates who had also been hiding in the tunnel openings.

"You walked right into our trap," said a voice behind him.

Conrock turned to see a hulking pirate wearing an eyepatch and nearly the same size as the Brudwata. He had Sundown's arm in one hand and a plasma pistol in the other—pointed at Conrock.

"We heard you coming a mile away. Never dreamed you'd make this so easy for us."

"Sweetheart, I should have listened to you," Conrock apologized to Sundown when she was the first one manacled with heavy chains that kept her from flying away.

"Look at those faces," said the big pirate with an eyepatch that did not fully cover the damage. "Hardly a bug bite on them. They must have just arrived on planet."

The pirates' own faces and hands were extensively bumped with red spots. They were particularly impressed by the weapons they took from Conrock as they chained

him and shackled him with a combination lock—all except the big one. His attention was elsewhere.

"Leave that one be," he said when the others started to manacle Lonan.

"Slane Takeshak?" Lonan's question was confirmed by a nodding head. "I saw you die."

"You saw me fall," Takeshak corrected him. "I fell into those stinking peppermint monsters. The one that broke my fall took my eye with a pincer before it died." He snort-laughed at an internal joke. "I call the peppermints monsters, and they are, but you and your friends were the bigger monsters. Letting me fall right before I climbed back to safety. And that's not the worst of it. What *was* that weapon you used to blow up all of our ships when you escaped? We could never figure it out. It was the most diabolical thing I've ever seen."

"That was Pam," Lonan replied.

"The naked pole dancer?"

"Yes," he replied with a shake of the head to Conrock. "Different Pam. A Splendora sex-bot loaded with $E=MC^2$ triggers."

Conrock had heard rumors about a formula that could cause people to spontaneously combust at a set time, but it was obvious that Takeshak had not.

"Stop wasting my time with technobabble." He stamped a foot. "That bot was in the clubhouse your weapon destroyed."

He addressed the other pirates with a smile.

"He's just trying to distract me. We've got the prisoners Nefarimor wanted. Hell, we've probably captured the last Philean still loose in the wild. Remember this day, boys. It's the extinction of an entire species. Nefarimor is going to be pleased, and I'm certain she'll understand if I take my bonus in advance. Another thing everyone here will never forget"—he showed his hands to Lonan—"is me beating you to death with my bare hands—because I'm going to take my time doing it. This is going to be fun, and it's going to get very… *ugly!*"

Chapter Fourteen
Attack from Above

Carmdall and his son Horos took one side of the trail, while Fistal and his daughter Kaoz took the other.

"Our friends in the riverbed stomp so loudly in those boots they wear," said Horos in a low, quiet voice as they blended through the jungle foliage, barely allowing anything to touch them. "I wonder if their plan is to draw attention?"

"Maybe," Carmdall regularly checked the flickers of movements he glimpsed in the branches above their heads. "While we are alone, there is something we should discuss. You have been distracted during this quest—I can see something is bothering you."

"There is something I want to tell you," Horos replied with a downcast head, "but do not know how."

"I think I know what is on your mind," Carmdall replied. "I have seen you spending more and more time with Fistal and Kaoz."

They traveled some distance before Horos replied.

"You have? I have feelings for Kaoz, but…"

"But you should not pursue those feelings," Carmdall felt an emptiness in the pit of his stomach when he said the words, and relief at the same time for finally saying them.

Horos was dumbstruck.

The silence between the two was louder than the clatter caused by the little men as they jabbered and walked. Horos's head fell down and he was no longer as attentive to his surroundings as he should be. Carmdall tried to be alert enough for the both of them, but he was not prepared for his son's next words.

"You sound like mother," said Horos.

"Your mother?" Carmdall was surprised. He had been wrestling how to convince her, without explaining why.

"You both think Kaoz is wrong for me."

Now Carmdall had his own questions.

"Why did your mother think that?"

It was quite some time before Horos replied.

"She made me promise not to tell you."

"Tell me what?"

As they began to work their way along the upper slope and out of the canyon, Horos finally came to a stop.

"You tell me first," he said. "Explain why you object to me being with Kaoz, and I'll tell you what mother said."

Carmdall found himself with a downcast head as he wrestled with his shame. Realizing that his wife already knew his long-concealed secret, he decided to blurt it out.

"Because Kaoz is your sister," Carmdall confessed. "You are brother and sister. I am her father."

Carmdall barely had time to process the conflicting parade of emotions that crossed his son's face before he realized how inattentive they had both been. Horos had walked directly beneath a devourer of flesh hiding on a tree branch—one that crouched to strike.

When the avian predator descended, it extended its blade-claws and spread its black wings with a spotted underside that created the impression of giant eyes, evidently intended to freeze its targeted prey long enough to keep it from running until it was too late.

Carmdall had no hesitation, leaping forward to push Horos out of the way with one hand, while his other swung his long blade and lopped off one of the predator's clawed feet. The creature screeched in rage as Carmdall did not relent, slashing away repeatedly at its head and wings until it scrambled to hop away on one leg, howling in pain.

Carmdall watched it leave, his chest heaving more from panic at what might have happened than from the sudden burst of exertion. Then he heard a strange sound behind him.

From a distance, the voice of Conrock sounded in concern.

"Keep walking, little man," Carmdall shouted back.

Then he discovered that the strange sound was Horos laughing.

"Thank you for telling me that," he seemed overjoyed. "Now, there is no reason why Kaoz and I cannot be together."

"Did you not hear me?" Carmdall asked.

"I just told you that you are brother and sister."

"No," Horos replied, "we're not. The secret that mother did not want me to tell you is that you are not my father. Fistal is!"

It was at that very moment when both Fistal and Kaoz arrived, their weapons raised.

"We heard a fight," Kaoz said.

The look of concern on Fistal's face showed that he had also heard Horos's last statement.

"We are not brother and sister!" Horos shouted as he picked himself up off the ground. "Fistal is not your father. Carmdall is!"

The expression on Fistal's face changed completely as his eyes widened.

The two young lovers had taken a single step toward each other, when both Carmdall and Fistal rushed between them with their weapons swinging. Sparks flew from their frenzied clash.

"You slept with my wife?!" they each accused the other.

Horos and Kaoz immediately grappled with their parents, trying to separate and disarm them.

"Take my weapon," Carmdall finally conceded to take a backward step. "This is a matter that needs settled man to man!"

Fistal nodded his agreement and allowed Kaoz to pull his blade away. The two then crashed headlong into each other with fists flying and feet kicking.

There was no finesse or technique in how the Brudwata fought. It was an eruption of rage where they did not care if their blows were strategically placed, only how hard they landed. They grunted with the effort of each punch as they thumped powerfully on one another, closed to grapple, fell to the ground, and began rolling.

Chapter Fifteen
Eight Toes

"Don't try to run!" Slane Takeshak warned Lonan Mcguffin when he dodged the pirate's lumbering attack, nimbly dancing out of harm's way. The pirate pointed at Sundown. "Not only will we shoot you, we'll start taking her wings off in tiny pieces, all the way down to the roots—unless you stand and fight me."

When Takeshak charged him again, Lonan still dodged the punches but stayed in close enough to land a number of rabbit punches that seemed to have no effect.

As Takeshak roared his anger, Conrock knew it was only a matter of time until the pirate landed one good punch, and the fight would be over.

While the other pirates were distracted by the duel, Conrock finally found an opportunity to try to escape. The combination locks they had used on their shackles were an older type that the Constabulary had discarded because they had a flaw—a secret master code that could never be reset like the user code. That they would end up on the black market was not surprising, but that they would end up being used to restrain him was a stroke of good fortune.

As he worked his thumb over the wheels to a reset of straight sevens, he wished he had some way of communicating this to the others, and was surprised to see Mackstar emulating his every move. That Mackstar could possibly see the combination he was keying meant that he either had the most incredible eyesight of anyone he had ever met, or that there might yet be something sinister about him—he might be another Januman.

It was uncanny how Mackstar also wrapped the loosened chains around his fist, inching closer to the nearest pirate just as Conrock did. Then a loud noise came from the ridge at the edge of the canyon.

Takeshak took advantage of Lonan's momentary distraction to land a debilitating blow to his stomach. The pirate stood over him with his foot on Mcguffin's chest as he then, too, turned to see the source of the noise.

The bodies of Carmdall and Fistal came tumbling out of the trees and down the grassy slope into the canyon below, punching away at each other as they rolled directly toward the pirates.

Conrock had been expecting the Brudwata to assist at some point in their escape, but their technique was completely unexpected. However, it was effective, and the pirates allowed the tumbling pair to roll right into their midst.

"What the hell? Did we just discover a new species?" Takeshak began cursing. "I don't see nothing shiny. Shoot 'em and be done with it."

That was when Conrock and Mackstar struck, using their chains to knock the weapons from the hands of the pirates. Conrock reached his rifle before any of them could react; in an instant, the control of their situation had flipped.

"Get those off of her." He nodded for Mackstar to free Sundown of her chains while using his gun barrel to wave Takeshak off Lonan. "Get away from him."

Surprisingly, the Brudwata seemed dazed as they unlocked from their grapple and took a step back from each other, gasping for breath.

"Interesting tactic," Conrock commented as he noticed how frantically Horos and Kaoz ran to join them. "Unorthodox, but it worked."

It only dawned on Conrock that the intervention had not been by design when the young Brudwata positioned themselves between their parents, urging them to stop fighting when they tried to rejoin the fray.

"Stop it, you both!" Kaoz shouted.

"You both did the same thing!" Horos added.

The only response they received was grunts and snarls from the two men ready to start clawing at each other again.

"Okay," said Conrock, "I don't know and don't care what's happening here. It needs to stop. We can't afford a repeat of this kind of distraction."

His point was illustrated when Takeshak made a break for the skippers. Conrock stopped him with a shot at the feet that was a little too close, and the pirate left bloody footprints as he limped to a stop.

"As you can tell, I'm a little rusty with one of these, so nobody go pushing their luck. Brudwata, put aside whatever is going on with you and help Mackstar and Lonan secure the prisoners."

Carmdall and Fistal groused their animosity in words that the translator kept repeating as "Unknown" or "Not complimentary," mixed with "Little man," but they grudgingly complied with Conrock's instructions and those of their children, who made certain to stay between them at all times.

Mackstar held one of the combination locks with a questioning look on his face.

"If they'd known there was a default combination," Conrock whispered, "they wouldn't have used them." He then caught Mackstar's arm before he walked away. "And when we have a chance, you'll need to explain to me how you knew what to do."

Mackstar shrugged.

"Like you said," he replied, "default code. What are we going to do with the prisoners? We can't take them with us and can't leave them chained up out here. From what you told me about this place, they'll be eaten alive."

"After what they had planned for Sundown and Lonan, I'm tempted to do just that. But I've got an idea—after I have a conversation with Mister Nine Toes here." He walked over to Takeshak and pointed the rifle barrel at his other foot. "And if I don't like what I hear, your next new nickname is going to be Eight Toes."

Takeshak cursed Conrock, and when an instant rifle shot did exactly what the former constable had promised, the pirate's tough guy veneer crumbled.

Confirming that the Artomiques did still have a Philean prisoner that they had brought back with them raised Conrock's hopes, but when he then learned that the Artomiques were preparing to abandon the planet, he knew they did not have much time left. Nefarimor had sent out search parties to scour for any last possible Phileans they might have missed, adamant that they be made extinct. With all the animal life that lived in the jungle, this had required a slow, physical grid search that they felt was nearly complete.

Herding the chained pirates into one of the abandoned tunnels, Conrock parked a skipper in front of it, blocking them in and anything else out. He made certain that even if they could escape, they would not be able to use the skipper by removing its anti-gravity suspension units and adding them to the other skipper to help compensate for the added weight of the Brudwata. Part of the roof also had to be removed.

"Not bad for C.F.S. certified," Mackstar quipped once the work was done.

"Let's go get our girl," Conrock announced as the skipper struggled to rise into the air, even with the extra suspension. "They shouldn't suspect a thing when they see us coming, and once we reach their perimeter gates, it's time for Lonan to do his thing."

Chapter Sixteen
The Butcher Warehouse

"Look at that smile!" Achilles Hister caressed the side of the Philean's face in a downward stroke that continued down to her shoulder and along the arm. "Her skin ornamentation is so bright and clear—a complete turnaround from what she looked like when we first brought her home."

"Can I go outside now?" The Philean looked up at the ceiling that penned her in.

"Very soon," Achilles Hister replied. "But first, I think it's time we gave you that tour we promised you of our… home."

"Look at that smile," Nefarimor repeated his words. "You've won her complete trust."

"Good food, plenty of water, and no stress will do it," Achilles replied as they led her from the cushion-filled room with a spa and into a sterile, blank hallway that was lined with darkened doorways that ran the entire length to a closed door on the far end. On the other side, the sound of grinding metal could be heard.

"She's clearly quite fond of you," said Nefarimor. "And as dumb as a stick. I've been in that head, and there's not much there."

"Januman said he'd looked into both of them," Hister replied. "This was clearly the brighter of the two, and the one the Dire Grief favored."

"It shows the dangers of shape-shifting. She's gone so deep into becoming a Philean to hide from me, that she lost herself completely."

"We're packing up our home," Hister told the Philean, with a reassuring hand on her shoulder. "But there's something we want to show you before we go."

The sight revealed through the door confused the Philean at first.

Massive conveyor belts undergoing disassembly were scattered in pieces across the floor, while the ceiling was filled with hanging hooks attached to rolling wheels mounted on overhead metal beams. The hooks were all empty, but on the far side of the room, large compactor bins were slowly crushing piles of skinless bodies that were so mangled it took the Philean a moment to register what she was seeing.

"There it is," said Nefarimor when a look of horror began to twist across the Philean's face with the realization that the bodies were dead Phileans whose flesh had been stripped away.

Their amputated wings were piled on pallets and wrapped for shipping.

Nefarimor felt the Philean's own soft feathers as she gently stroked her wings.

"I'll keep these for myself."

Pirates in blood-spattered coveralls seized the Philean by the arms and tightened clamps onto her wrists. They were connected to a length of chain, which was tossed over a hook that hoisted her into the air."

Achilles reached up and gripped her stunned face in one hand.

"The mass production side of this operation has already been disassembled, so..." he paused when something bubbled and turned in his stomach, "...so you get processed personally."

When Nefarimor handed him a flaying knife from a rolling tool cart, his fingers felt numb, and his dexterity was gone. The blade clattered to the floor.

"I'll do it myself," Nefarimor ignored the blade on the floor and reached for a butcher's hatchet.

The Philean's screams echoed throughout the hollow building as her wings were violently amputated.

"There we go," Nefarimor handed the wings to the pirates. "String these together in a cloak for me—right now."

She then examined the Philean's body gems. "The fear and pain has her blood pumping. Look at the clear, bright red. Time to cut them free before they start to cloud up."

Nefarimor climbed onto a stool and started peeling the Philean's face away while the workers restrained her kicking legs.

"Don't you want to join in the fun?" Nefarimor asked Hister. "I thought this was your favorite part?"

"It is." He barely got the words out, feeling more and more unwell.

He started measuring the distance back to the room they had left and the nearby exit.

Chapter Seventeen
Taking Control of Everything

"I thought this was your thing?" Conrock complained when Lonan fumbled unsuccessfully with the Artomique gate.

Lonan finally held up his hands in frustration.

"Any gate built by Terraformers, I can unlock," he said. "They've all got my grandfather's genetic code built into them. But this... this was built by the Artomiques. There's nothing I can do with it. Why don't we just jump the fence in the skipper?"

"That will set off the alarm," Conrock started to examine the gate on the opposite side from the locks, wondering how he could break open the hinges.

Carmdall pushed past and grabbed the edge of the gate and began pulling mightily, ignoring the electrical shocks that coursed through him.

"This is your head," he groused to Fistal as he slowly bent the metal piping.

Fistal grabbed the metal framework next to that which Carmdall had pulled.

"And this is yours," he snarled back as he began to wrench and deform the metalwork.

There was a loud pop as the hinge fittings snapped, and the two men ripped the gate wide open.

"That will work," said Conrock. "I can't believe that didn't set off any alarms. The contact switches are all on the lock's side. Now, keep that rage channeled. We've got a job to do."

The Brudwata were not listening when they rushed through the opening without a backwards glance.

"Great," said Mackstar. "Now what are they doing?"

"Lonan, stay here with Sundown at the skipper," said Conrock. "Mackstar, you and I need to find the high ground and do some reconnoitering before those Brudwata actually do set off an alarm."

Once they were out of sight of the skipper, Conrock slowed his pace and fell behind.

"I want you to stay in front of me."

"You still don't trust me?" Mackstar saw the rifle pointed at him.

"I know you've been lying to me."

"You want to have this conversation now?" Mackstar sounded exasperated. "We don't have time!"

"I wanted to have it back at the junkyard. You want to save time, start being honest with me. Tell me what's really going on."

"Fine," Mackstar kept his hands spread well away from his weapons. "But we can keep walking, can't we?"

"So long as you don't walk me into some sort of trap."

Mackstar turned his back on Conrock and picked up the pace as he headed in the direction of the warehouse hidden in the heart of a jungle.

"Fine," said Mackstar. "And you're right, Akarastar and I are related to the fellow you called Januman, but in a very, very distant sort of way."

"Akarastar?"

"What you're wondering is right. Our aunt was who Akara's World was named after. And yes, I can read your mind. It's a skill some of Father's people have. It's how I know Sundown is not my sister, because I can't talk to her like I could to Akarastar even after she made the transformation to Sunset. She's not Sundown."

"Your father was Erlik, the man that Bully Bravo killed."

"I've already told you that Bravo had nothing to do with that."

"So, what other skills did Erlik give you? What other skills does that Januman have that I don't know about?"

"Everybody is different, just like with

your people. Apparently, my sister and I are unique in our ability to shape-shift. Our father did a fair bit of time traveling, like Januman apparently did. That's how they both manipulated future events by affecting the past."

"How so?"

"A bunch of bad fellows kidnapped his granddaughter, Akara's daughter. Once he got that sorted, he swore off time travel. But my grandfather never did. That Phaedra we met? Grandfather used to be in love with her, and he literally moved the heavens and a few stars to save her from this Januman that Carmdall is hunting right now. Januman used to call himself the God Father until all his children were killed.[1] It was thought he'd been killed too, but guys like him don't go down easy."

As they neared the warehouse, Mackstar led the way up a hill, looking for the highest vantage point.

"I've noticed that," Conrock conceded. "Think he can dodge a sniper's bullet?"

"Back on Akara's world, there was the bull-headed, six-armed creature called a Brotan. A child of the Brothan's god Brotah. He was particularly hard to kill—had the gift of precognition. He did actually dodge a sniper's bullet." Mackstar slid along the ground and crawled the last few feet to a vantage point where he could look down at the warehouse. "But I don't think Januman has it. Had no clue about what was going to happen back at the junkyard, and... wait, do you hear screaming?"

"No," Conrock took a position far enough to the side of Mackstar that he might have time to react if surprised, then scanned the warehouse with the rifle scope. "I see guards all around that place—but they're not marines. Look like pirates to me. This explains a few things."

"What?" Mackstar asked.

"Hey, kid, you can read my mind. You tell me."

Mackstar hesitated.

"I was wondering the same thing as you—why the *Merciless* had no crew. It's because they needed it to evacuate the crew from this warehouse. They've been operating it as a pirate operation because they knew the Marines would never turn a blind eye to genocide."

"Still, wiping out an entire race like they've done, it's still going to get noticed."

"So they used pirates who, even if they told..."

"They'd be discredited." Conrock noted how the only landing strip could accommodate nothing larger than a heavy-duty hauler. "So now they're wrapping up operations, bit by bit, and once they're done, they'll level this place and leave no trace behind."

A flash of movement caught Conrock's eye.

"Wait... Someone is coming out. It's Achilles Hister."

"He's a nasty piece of work," said Mackstar. "He's used Wild Stars cloning technology to survive the centuries. But now the Artomique have switched techniques..."

"You're saying that he's not Achilles

---

[1] *See Wild Stars IV: Wild Star Rising! – Ed.*

Hister's descendant?"

"He *is* Achilles Hister. The reason he looks so young is because he's been creating clone bodies of himself. Last time, he cloned a child and let him grow to adulthood before he changed consciousness with him—swapped bodies, with help from Nefarimor and the Five-Thousand Fingered Hand."

"You saw this happen?"

"Only the last part, when Nefarimor killed the old man's body with the clone in it."

"That's monstrous!" said Conrock. "It also explains why Genghis was so familiar with them back at the Madam's House."

"So you've finally realized that there is a Triumvirate consisting of the Artomiques, pirates, and the Five-Thousand Fingered Hand."

"And apparently now the Dire Griefs and Black Star Reavers."

"That last part only you, me, and Phaedra's people are privy to. The rest of the galaxy only knows that the young Achilles Hister married Nefarimor, and together they've taken control over..."

"Everything." Conrock cocked his rifle and sighted the crosshairs on Hister's head. "What's he doing?"

Chapter Eighteen
Whiplash

Achilles Hister burst out of the slaughterhouse's side exit.

Knowing that he was wild-eyed, seeing the uneasiness in the faces of the pirate guards when they looked at him, he could see that the latrine was too far away for him

to make it. So he dashed for the jungle's edge and past as many shrubs and trees as he could to get out of sight before he fell to his knees in a small clearing and began retching uncontrollably. Eventually, his heaving slowed enough that he could hear light footfalls following his path.

"Now I see why you enjoy watching the slaughter so much," said Nefarimor. "Seeing that girl's look of pure trust and innocence turn to terror the instant she realized what was happening—it was deliciously exhilarating! Every skin gem on her went bright red when the cutting started, and the stones we harvested all had perfect ten-point clarity. Our last day on Phileas was a profitable one."

Achilles pushed himself up onto his knees. When he turned and saw the severed white wings hanging from the Red Queen's shoulders, his stomach knotted and he began retching again, but his heaves were dry. He had already fully vacated his gut onto his hands and the ground.

"I don't understand... What's happening to me?" Achilles gasped when his stomach finally untwisted enough for him to speak. "I didn't flinch when my father first taught me to draw and quarter a man. Why am I having this reaction now? I've relished watching the Phileans' faces turn from trust to horror when they first realized they were going to be skinned alive."

"Everything on this planet is trying to eat flesh." Nefarimor scanned the intersecting tree branches in the surrounding jungle. "But they've never encountered anyone who wanted their flesh for the jewels that were intended to discourage predators. And the flush of betrayal makes for the brightest red if you cut fast enough."

He began heaving again.

"This isn't me," Achilles gasped.

"You're right," Nefarimor swatted at jungle detritus and biting insects hitting her in the face when a gush of wind swirled around them, "more than you know."

The wind intensified, soon drawing the tops of trees in as the bushes on the ground reached upward as they were sucked into a vortex developing right on top of the clearing. Then, in a flash, the wind was gone, leaving a man in tattered body armor standing shakily in front of them.

"Bullson?" Achilles questioned.

Covered in blood and his armor damaged in several places, Bullson looked exhausted, and he fell to his knees, facing Achilles eye to eye.

"I barely found you," he said between gulps of air. "Trying to travel from outside the galaxy must have made it extra difficult. It was like you were fading from my mind. I was barely able to key in on you, on our connection, when I made my escape."

"Escape from where?" Nefarimor demanded. "You were sent with a fleet of the latest Artomique Dreadnoughts to chase down your father, Bully Bravo, and that Wild Stars witch, Daestar."

"Last I heard," said Achilles, feebly trying but failing to stand, "the fleet had destroyed New Atlantis and was chasing the fugitives into the extragalactic space between the galaxies."

"We caught them"—Bullson nodded and then began shaking his head—"but they weren't alone. Found them in a giant gas cloud, on a runaway world filled with more people just like the Ancient Warrior."

"More immortals?" The Red Queen was incredulous. Her eyebrows knitted, and she looked back over her shoulder at the slaughter house, where a distant voice announced that he was coming. She then asked, "I thought we'd exterminated all the Wild Stars immortals?"

"I said in my last MagLink report that I thought the Ancient Warrior was still alive." Bullson started looking at his jungle surroundings, trying to figure out on what planet he had arrived. "Wait... this isn't Akara's World, or Ansa. Where are we?"

"A nothing, backwater world," Nefarimor snapped.

"What happened?" Achilles tried to demand and was shocked at how weak his tone of voice was. It reminded him of his late son, Whip, whenever he had feebly attempted to assert command.

"There was nothing anyone could do," said Bullson. "The minute we arrived, we saw them turn on the fugitives we were following. Last I saw on the monitors, my father and Daestar were running for their Wild Stars scout ship. The Ancient Warrior stopped to face his people."

"How do you know that they were *his* people?" Nefarimor demanded.

"Because the next thing I knew, some of them were on the command deck of our ship! We were powerless to stop them. They took over the command crew's minds as easy as," he snapped his fingers. "But they couldn't control me. I don't know if it's because of my mother's heritage or my link with you, but they decided to deal with me the old fashion way. I was losing, and I've never lost a fight, but those two Extragalactics that came after me had skills like nothing I've ever seen. They fought in tandem, like a pair of dancers who've trained their whole lives together. I knew I was doomed, so I reached my mind out to you. You were the only thing I could think of, the only thing I could connect with, and somehow the Wild Stars teleportation system worked. I found you here. But almost didn't make it. You started receding, getting farther away when I got closer. It... you..."

Bullson shook his head as if rattling his eyes to clear them.

"I've never seen you kneel before," said Bullson.

"Get used to it," Nefarimor quipped.

"What am I doing here?" Bullson's expression changed to a look of horror similar to Achilles' expression. "What have I done? What have you made me do?"

Shaking his head even more demonstratively as he stood, the whirlwinds returned and Bullson vanished.

"Did he teleport..." Nefarimor seemingly asked herself, "or time travel?"

"I need to teach that to you," Januman approached from behind Nefarimor and put a hand on her shoulder. "Someday."

"Help me," Achilles implored with an extended hand.

"God Father," Nefarimor acknowledged him with a bob of her head.

"Those feathers look good on you." Januman ran his fingers over the soft quills. "It's only appropriate that God's Angel should have wings. You're a White Queen now?"

"What?" Hister's world swirled in vertigo.

"You never suspected that she was my daughter?" The God Father's expression of incredulity was mixed with humor. "You really believed that she was the Pirate Queen's twin sister?"

He patted Nefarimor on the back.

"Well done, girl. You can change back now, to your real appearance."

"We're not done yet," she countered. "Still a couple more tricks to play."

"Fine, just don't lose yourself in there."

"No chance of that," she replied. "I only absorbed the Red Queen's likeness based on the memories of others—not a complete identity duplication like that fool Akarastar lost herself in. I'll always be me underneath what I pretend. I was lucky that we were already so much alike."

Januman turned his attention back to Achilles.

"You know the great thing about how you built your... no, not industry... your *kindustry*, a monolithic family empire with you sitting all alone at the top? It made it so easy to take it all away."

The God Father seized Hister's head with one hand as though it was a melon, and squeezed once. The images that seeped out of Achilles's brain made the immortal instantly release him and stagger back a step.

"Why didn't you tell me that Bully Bravo has an immortal son? That was him that just left?"

"I thought he was one of your Purple Order," Hister replied, "just without the white hair."

"He's not one of mine. If you knew who the father was already, what would make you even think that?" Januman's frown became a glower that steadily intensified with anger.

"So Bullson's mother isn't one of your daughters?" asked Achilles. "Was she an early vanguard of the invasion by Extragalactics?"

The first part of Achilles's statement seemed to strike the God Father like a physical blow. It was obviously something that he was reluctant to consider. The second part also caught his attention.

"This is the second time I've heard about an invasion by Extragalactics," said Januman. "Do you know what this means?"

"No!" The Red Queen leaned and took a close look at Achilles's eyes, which barely saw her as though he was underwater that she floated in the air above, and growing ever more distant. "We waited too long to gloat. His personality is almost completely faded."

"Guess it's time to put Whip back in his place," said the God Father.

Chapter Nineteen
Remembering a Guarantee

"We've got problems," Mackstar pointed where Conrock should aim his scope. "Not only has Januman shown up, but…"

Conrock saw that the Brudwata were stealthily sneaking nearer to the warehouse and the clearing. They would soon be close enough to attack Januman.

"Still no sign of the other Philean," said Mackstar.

"Yes," said Conrock, "there is."

He made a gesture of trust by handing his rifle to Mackstar so he could use the telescope.

"Look at the cloak Nefarimor is wearing."

When Mackstar did, his head dropped away from the scope, and the rifle fell from his hands. But his jaw tightened quickly; he reached to grab the rifle back, but Conrock had already pulled it away.

"I'm going to kill them all," Mackstar vowed.

"I'm only going to get one shot here."

"Nefarimor," said Mackstar. "Or Hister? I don't care because no matter who falls first, the others will join them soon. But if the Brudwata reach Januman, you know he'll kill Carmdall."

"Januman saved our lives from the Saturnian," Conrock hesitated.

"And, to use his own words," Mackstar replied, "he spent them the first chance he had. He left us to die. Don't forget about what Phaedra said he did to her."

"I'm not forgetting Phaedra," Conrock grumbled, "or what she made me guarantee. Even so, I'm not sure I can do this."

"Have you never killed a man before?"

"Not without looking him in the eye first."

"Then give me the rifle," said Mackstar,

"and I'll jump right in the middle of them. It doesn't matter if I live or die as long as I take them with me."

Chapter Twenty
What Happens Next

One minute Whip had been standing inside the Red Queen's Scarlet Citadel, watching the flash from the gun muzzle as it discharged in his face, and the next he was kneeling on soggy ground in the jungle. In complete disorientation, he looked at his vomit-covered hands and the ground. Then he saw the pirate, the Red Queen, standing over him, wearing a winged cloak of feathers as white as the hair of the old man standing next to her.

"You really thought I put all of you in Hister's old body?" she taunted. "I only switched your conscious selves. I left both of your subconscious selves in place, letting you do the work of slowly taking control of your body back. And that fool thought the Five-Thousand Fingered Hand was helping him. That was why you were so troublesome when you occupied his body."

Whip saw how the backs of his hands were once again young, and his body felt vital, alive—, and more than a little nauseous.

"I pulled your consciousness out the instant before I pulled that trigger," she tapped a finger to her head, "and kept you locked away until your Daddy's hold over your body finally slipped."

The white-haired man smiled and nodded in agreement.

"What?" Whip asked. "Why?"

"Because I wanted you to remember me killing you. That way, you'll always remember your place and do whatever your wife tells you."

"Wife?"

"You're all mine."

"Play with your new toy later," said the white-haired man, "we've got other problems."

"What do you mean, God Father?"

"This shouldn't be happening," he replied. "Everything was going perfectly according to the future I'd planned. The Marzanti are a part of every future scenario, but because they're adapted to a limited environment, they can be dealt with as long as you understand how. The Grimgrip are nothing compared to the trouble the Stone Men will ultimately cause. But Extragalactics appearing from out of the void? I never anticipated an invasion by other immortals whose minds are twisted from extreme periods of isolation. This... this is something new. Something has changed."

"I don't understand."

"Anything is possible now," said the God Father. "The immortal mother of my Purple Order disappeared some time before our magnificent children were all killed. After that, I wanted nothing to do with the inferior children born from a mortal mother."

"Why not?" the Red Queen countered. "The Ancient Warrior's son and his offspring are what killed your Purple Order, and they were born of mortal mothers."

The God Father paid no attention to the pirate queen's words. His mind seemed to have already moved on to other considerations.

"Now things make sense. Only she has the ability and desire to do this. She is the most evil creature who ever lived."

"What are you telling me?" asked the Red Queen.

"All my work has been undone. I have no idea what is going to happen next."

The Red Queen screamed when the God Father's head exploded and sprayed across her white wings, followed instantly by the echo of a gunshot.

As a young boy, Michael Tierney watched live when Neil Armstrong took "one giant leap for mankind." He thought about how the stars had become the next frontier of exploration—like the Wild West had once been—and his work on the Wild Stars has continued ever since.

Out Now!

Children of Summer

By LOUISE SORENSEN

A scouting party has gone missing! Can Aedyn and Kerry find them in the bug-infested post-apocalyptic wastes, or will they too become food for giant insects?!

The snaps of Aedyn's shirt pinged as he ripped it open. "Check me for ticks."

He turned around and bared his back. His muscles stood out as he flexed. I scanned up, down, left, right...

"Turn around... Arms up..."

He raised his arms and turned slowly. He was muscular, in good shape. Better than that, he had a sharp mind and reflexes quick as a cat. A good man to have beside you in a pinch.

I checked every inch of his chest and back. He had a few red bites from days earlier, but nothing to be worried about and no new clinging ticks. Thankfully, tick season was waning. "All clear."

He put his shirt back on and sighed.

I hadn't been out of the house yet. Having checked for ticks the night before, I was pretty sure I was clear. After a few bites from spring bugs like mosquitoes or black flies, your skin got super sensitive and any little itch you'd investigate immediately, not knowing if it was a tick or a tickle. Sweat on the bites made them sting like hell, making spring an even more miserable affair. As Aedyn was always out and about the compound before anyone else, looking in on the livestock, testing the current in the fences, checking for intruders, he was a prime target for any ticks that got past the possums we kept near the house.

Our compound was in the part of Canada they used to call Ontario. Near the Great Lake, in a large sweep of farmland that had escaped most of the devastation of the Burning, when all the forests were afire. The young trees that had sprung up since then were healthy and big enough now to harvest for building or heat, but the land was still littered with blackened tree stumps.

"It'll be grand when winter returns," Aedyn said, giving his arm a gentle scratch.

"A seven-week holiday from heat and bugs. Hurrah." I went into the hall and inspected my armor. It had a few dings but would do for the day's work. "I'll be glad to go outside in plain clothes for a change. No armor. Light as a feather. And cool. I'd die for some cool. Aedyn. Aedyn?"

No response. Aedyn was ruminating. He'd wandered in from the burned zone a couple of years ago and joined us. We never turned anyone away, but he had been especially good company and become an instant hit with everyone for his high energy and great sense of humor. But his past, like everyone else's, sometimes haunted him, and he would get moody and dwell on things.

One of our teams hadn't returned from a hunt the day before. This made everyone introspective, but now was not the time to mourn. If we found them, dead or alive, then we could celebrate or mourn. Normally the house rang with Aedyn's laughter, and I missed his cheery optimism. I tried to divert his mind to a different track. "Eh? Plain clothes for a change?"

He startled, looking towards me. Yawned. "Sure. Absolutely. We're out of coffee."

That, on top of everything else. "Damn. We'll have to make a trip to the village." Good. He'd snapped out of it.

He shook his head. "We're doing enough today. Someone else can make a run when they finally drag themselves out of bed."

He'd turned moody again. Moving slowly. Tired. Our morning's work would have been better with caffeine, but when we returned, someone in the house *would* share their stash. Avoiding talk of yesterday's loss, we donned our armor, homemade, museum-raided, and cobbled together. Breast plates, kneepads, leg guards, steel-toed boots. Aedyn got the museum close helmet. It could be worn open but had a metal faceplate that could be dropped down to cover the whole face. I got the motorcycle helmet with full plastic faceplate. We took turns with the helmets because the close helmet got so hot. When we were finished dressing, we checked each other for loose straps and gaps. All good. Made a last stop at the door to pick up swords and sprayers, buckled them on, and went out. The gear was hot and heavy and, despite our best efforts to muffle it, occasionally clanked.

There'd been a long drought lately that had us worried for the crops, but we'd got some rain the night before, and the air was fresh. The plants around the house had perked up. It bode well for the livestock and harvest, but there was no telling what it had done for the bugs.

We kept our hands on our swords as we toured the grounds around the house. The apples and grapes were coming along, and the scent of roses was strong as we passed by. Their heady perfume would soon attract bees. We'd heard that in the old days, like most everything else, bees were little fellows. They'd become big buggers in our day—big as your hand. If you left them alone, they didn't bother you and went about their business of making honey. We were probably both thinking it was a damn good thing it wasn't time to collect honey. Nobody wanted to think about that.

Unable to put it off any longer, we went to the perimeter. Carefully pulling the connecting wooden handles off the electric fence, we slipped through and reattached them behind us. We were pretty sure nothing would have been able to enter the yard in the short time the current was broken. If something did sneak through, others at the house would have to deal with it. Our territory required constant surveillance due to danger from mutated wildlife and possible fires, and it was the team that went out to check everything yesterday that hadn't come home for supper.

Last night, no one would volunteer to look for them today, so the stronger among us pulled straws. Aedyn and I picked the short straws to try to find the team and whatever had befallen them. We were not confident about finding them, though. When a team didn't make it home for supper and didn't call for help on the talkie, they were likely dead and gone without a trace. I shivered. A goose had just walked over my grave. Not a great start.

Doing our duty, we struck out for the cultivated fields and the wildwood beyond the protected zone.

It wasn't long before we came upon a swarm of ticks that covered an area two feet by three. The individuals were tiny but numerous, blanketing the grass and bush in black.

We pulled our filter masks from under our helmets up over our mouths and noses, flipped on our sprayers, and drowned the ticks in a mountain of poison foam. I'm sure we were both screaming, "Die, you buggers, die," in our heads. I know I was, but of course, we didn't yell it out loud. The stench of the foam and even the faint hiss of the sprayers were enough to attract something in for a closer look.

A single tick was bad enough. Mostly they led solitary lives and would crawl up your leg from the grass, or land on your neck from a tree. As they gave serious bites and carried deadly diseases, they were to be seriously avoided. A single tick was bad enough. But when they got together with their friends, it was something else.

After blasting them, we expected the mass to fall apart and die. Instead, white with foam, it shuddered. A ripple passed through it. Then it rose, tall as a man, and formed a head, two arms and two legs. A mockery of a human. We'd known them to capture prey by imitating their shape to get close, until it was too late for escape. Then they'd feast, leaving only a bloodless corpse. We'd seen this previously, but only on a small scale. We'd never come across a colony of ticks this large.

We stepped back.

The creature shook itself. Thick clots of foam fell from it. The fumes, carried to us on the breeze, made our eyes water, and we moved out of the way.

The poison was taking a while to work.

Long.

Too long.

The creature shook again, throwing off the rest of the foam. The sun sparkled off the shells of each tiny tick, clinging together to make one giant glistening entity. Straightening up, it took a hesitant step. Its foot slithered through the grass with barely a rustle.

We held our ground.

It took another step, picking up speed. It was shambling towards us, closing the distance. One of its 'arms' molded into the exact shape of a hand, arm, and sprayer. Its head changed until it clearly had a human face, framed by long hair. Its face and way of moving were familiar to me, but I couldn't quite place it.

We stepped back. And back again. We backed up faster, careful of the footing.

Hoping the ticks hadn't built up a resistance to our poison and that it would still do the job.

Dreading the day when it didn't.

Wondering if this was the day.

It was too warm to run far in full armor. We'd have to ditch it. Then we'd be vulnerable to anything else we met.

I was giving the idea serious consideration. Looking at Aedyn, I reached for the buckle of my breastplate.

Before I could undo it, a tangle of grass caught my heel, and I lost my balance.

Quick as lightning, Aedyn grabbed me, murmuring, "Steady on," keeping me on my feet.

The abomination continued its advance, but it was slowing. It gave a shiver and stopped. Stood weaving. Fighting to stay on its feet, like a dying man.

I almost felt sorry for it... almost.

It was facing us. Moving its head up and down as if to scan us. As if it could see us. Raising its hands, palms up. Was it going to throw some of itself at us in a last-ditch effort to feed? Was it pretending to be spent so we'd come closer? Or was it pleading for its life?

It bent its knees and crouched. Preparing to leap at us? I stepped back. The breeze died. The sun was baking me. Sweat stung my eyes. I didn't dare look away or open my helmet to wipe them. The heat should have accelerated the effect of the poison, but the creature was still alive.

We waited. Aedyn swayed but kept to his feet. The heat and fumes were making me dizzy too.

I looked at the creature. It gazed back. Was there intelligence behind its gaze? Its face ran like liquid and reformed, reminding me of someone. Many someones. People I'd loved and lost.

It wasn't right to poison a creature like that. It needed help.

I took a step towards it.

Then I glanced at Aedyn. Would he help too? His faceplate was open, his mask down. He was standing still, scowling at it, hands fisted, jaw working but no words coming out.

When I looked back at it, the creature had moved closer and was almost near enough for me to touch. I thought about what to do. Reached out. Fumbled for my canteen. I would need to rinse it. It might need bandages.

Aedyn gave a strangled cry. "Kerry!"

I looked towards him. He was pointing and gasping. I looked at the creature. Suddenly, I noticed the acrid smell of the fumes and heard the rustle of its many parts. It had flowed forward and was almost upon me. Aedyn jerked me back.

The creature stopped and then continued staggering towards us. Instead of weakening, it seemed to gather strength and picked up speed.

Holding tight to each other, we retreated. Thinking this was the day. This was the day we wouldn't come back. Thinking about why it was us out here, with the sun shining and the sky so so blue and the wind sighing through the trees. Us. Facing the same fate as yesterday's team.

Something like this had gotten them. We

hadn't come across their bodies yet and likely wouldn't.

The creature slowed.

Stopped.

And then, mercifully, it collapsed.

Oh! My legs were shaking. We looked at each other. We waited a good long while before going near it, partly to let the fumes dissipate, partly to make sure the creature wasn't faking. When we were close enough I dragged my sword through the mass and broke it apart. Nothing moved. It was well and truly dead.

I opened my helmet and pulled my mask down. Aedyn did the same and looked shocked when he found his helm already open. The creature had gotten to him too. We took out our canteens, had a drink and doused our heads with water. Loosened our breastplates. A cool breeze started drying our sweat. Then, good little hunters that we were, we closed everything up again. High-fived, and plodded on.

The air was clear, the morning glorious. We could see every leaf on every tree. The birds were singing and getting down to the job of reproduction, and not a one was swooping down trying to kill us. We spotted a troop of squirrels observing us from the branches of a big oak. Not wanting to attract attention any more than *we* did, they were frozen in mid-motion, silent, watching our every move, but didn't attack, for which we were grateful. They're good eating, but vicious fighters, and we were vastly outnumbered. We made a note of their location so a larger hunting party could come by later and thin them out. Teach them a

little respect for humans. Squirrels these days were not averse to the taste of meat, and we glanced back many times to make sure they weren't sneaking up on us. We were highly relieved when finally out of their sight.

We followed the road to the north. The hay fields were greening up well for the second cut, and the corn had sprouted. So great was its response to the rain, it was growing visibly taller as we watched. We scouted around the cornfield carefully, lest the knife-sharp leaves cut us. If the wind whipped them up, they'd shred man or beast to bits. A couple of generations ago, in the time before the Change, the elders spoke of life as completely different from the way it is now, but since then, like many of the animals and plants in our world, corn had developed a defense mechanism all on its own. In this case, razor-sharp leaves. With everything in our world practicing eat or be eaten, it was the only way the plant could survive predation long enough to produce seed. But it'd be tame enough after the ears ripened, and because it was eager to spread its seed then, safe for us to harvest.

With the leaves of corn rattling like sabres in the breeze, it was a while before we noticed the birds had gone quiet. Never a good sign. We put our hands on our swords, kept our eyes peeled, and hurried further north to another hay field to get away from the incessant clatter of the corn. The breeze changed direction and carried a rancid stench of something rotting in the hot sun. We strained our eyes, ears, and noses as we hunted for the source.

The wind kept changing direction, and the source was not to be found. But if our lost boys or whatever was left of them were anywhere close, we'd eventually find them, as we'd be following the same route they took. A prescribed route was the rule, and now we knew why.

Ever watchful, we continued our wander. A few birds piped up. Flights of great blue butterflies plied yellow wildflowers. We relaxed a bit. Our stomachs growled. We thought about breakfast, which we'd gone without. I said I wished we'd at least had coffee. Aedyn concurred. We spoke about the verdant growth and lack of serious danger beyond the one tick swarm. We hoped, and yet dreaded at the same time, that we would spot our brothers, or at least come upon something big, something worth killing. Hoping it wouldn't kill us instead. No one was sure why we always had to send out teams of only two when hunting bugs. On the one hand, two were quieter than twenty. Less apt to be noticed, and on the average, more apt to be successful. On the other hand, the bugs tended to go for easy targets. On the third hand, losing two wasn't considered such a big loss. I don't know what idiot made that argument, but in our settlement, due to an abundance of deadly wildlife, humans weren't numerous, and two was a staggering loss.

And if you were one of the next two sent out, tough. I felt like bait walking around out there.

And then the wind paused, and our world became silent. There was no call of crickets or chirp of birds or rustle of small beasties in the grass. I realized with a sinking heart that we'd gotten complacent, forgetting the cardinal rule. Never make a sound when you're on a bug hunt. Maybe our armor had clanked in too regular a pattern. Maybe we'd spoken a touch too loud. We might as well have been out there beating on drums. But sign language is awkward when you're all bundled up in heavy gloves and armor and swathe.

I'd just raised my faceplate for a closer listen and a breath of fresh air when a grasshopper the size of a horse came out of nowhere and slammed Aedyn in the chest.

They skidded back ten feet, and then it was upon him, going for his throat. He was lucky he'd closed his helmet, as it was protecting his face, and the hopper couldn't get through the metal spikes of his dog collar. Or his breastplate. But this creature was bigger than any we'd seen before, heavy, bristling with thorny barbs, and scrabbling at him with its hind legs hard enough to do damage if not stopped quickly.

I ran towards them, but with full armor in that heat, I was not as quick as I wished.

Satisfied it had subdued its prey enough, the hopper hunched its back and stabbed at Aedyn's belly with its ovipositor—it turned out to be a she. I'm not sure what her plans were exactly, but the girls always did love Aedyn.

He was doing his best not to scream, but he was losing the battle. I finally caught up to them, laid into the creature's back with my sword, which was sharp as a mother's tongue, and cut a wide wound. It turned its head (they have necks these days, you know) and gave me a disapproving look. I briefly considered turning to run, but that would leave my brother to the bug's nonexistent mercy. And with the wildlife currently scoring better than the humans, I was running out of brothers. I decided to stay.

And to be honest, running away was never an option.

It was me facing the bug now. It didn't attack right away; the wound must have weakened it. Grasshoppers spit when they're angry; at least ours do. This one was frothing at the mouth. Frothing mandibles.

I stepped back a few paces, giving Aedyn time to get up, mind, he looked a little knackered. Not that I had any fear of the beast or doubted I could take it myself, wounded as it was. There was a lot of fine eating there, and we wouldn't be going home without it. Brave words, but these days it's kill or be killed. Unfortunately for me, it was still looking right perky. It turned its head to track my moves and started towards me.

Aedyn sprang to his feet and unsheathed his sword. "Holy mother of god," he said, "would you look at the size of that thing!"

I flinched at his words, hoping the daft bugger hadn't drawn the creature back to him.

Crap and hellfire, he had. The hopper charged him. They don't have much speed when they scuttle, but it was fast enough. Aedyn sent it a chop to its neck, but it dodged in time to prevent the blade from cutting its shell.

"Did ya not sharpen your sword this morning?" I shouted, hoping to distract the bug. There was no point in quiet now. "Did ya remember to fuel up your flamethrower?"

"I did!" he yelled and reached for the handle. We hesitate to use flamethrowers except in dire need and because we don't want to burn down the farm or have our food pre-barbequed, but with the rain last night, it looked to be safe enough.

He shot the bug a gout of fire to the snout. It was injured and confused, and I moved in to put it out of its misery. It circled away from me and kept kicking out with those powerful hind legs. I kept dodging and hitting it. My attack was mostly a distraction. I was barely holding my own as its kicks almost knocked the sword out of my grip every time.

Aedyn had taken up his sword and was whacking it on the neck.

Its head refused to depart from its shoulders.

Its shell was more heavily armored than usual. It was one of them big buggers we sometimes spotted and always avoided. You'd have to be stark raving to go after one of these devils voluntarily. Aedyn was hitting it so hard I thought the meat would be bruised and ruined if we *did* succeed in killing it. He got in a quick jab at last and skewered it between the eyes. It reminded me immediately of a good shish kabob, and my mouth watered as the creature fell. I'd have to put in a request to whoever was on cook duty.

Bazz, the science guy, was going to shit himself. When we used to tell him we'd spotted a hopper as big as a horse, he'd say we were seeing things. Mistaking a deer for a grasshopper. As if we were that dense. He insisted that insects couldn't get that big because of the level of oxygen in our world and the length of their trachea. Or some such. He had no trouble believing they grew as big as turkeys because we'd brought home enough of those fellows for supper, but he couldn't make the jump in logic to horse size. Well, we finally had proof. And he was going to eat his words. With hot sauce.

We rang up the house and waited till a crew sped out with a truck to pack the carcass home. And though we were pushing our luck, we continued our search.

It wasn't long before I felt an attack of nerves coming on and had to stop. I tried to fight it. Studied the ground. Reminded myself to be quiet. Thought about blue butterflies, though for the life of me, I don't know why. Then it became all too much. Gasping and shaking, I covered my mouth and clutched my chest.

"You okay, Kerry?"

That gentle inquiry opened the dam. I burst out laughing.

Aedyn took one look at me and smiled. He tried to hold it in and then threw back his head and howled with laughter. We hugged each other, held each other up as we laughed, flushing the adrenaline and fear out of our systems.

I sobered up and thought of all the pointy ears and hungry mouths that might be in our vicinity, looking for an easy meal. "Hush, Aedyn. Shhh." I held a finger to my mouth and scanned for danger.

"Hush yourself. You started it."

For a while longer, we stood silent, shaking with laughter.

What else can you do?

We carried on. A shadow passed over us, and we ducked. It swept by. Two huge vultures rode the thermals for fifteen minutes as they circled above, wings held wide, rarely needing to flap. Vultures can lead you to dead bodies, and although a full search party was also an option in case we couldn't find them, it would save time if we could point the searchers to our lost boys. There was no help from that quarter though, with the birds losing interest and gliding away when they decided we weren't going to drop dead in our tracks any time soon.

A little while later, we had a few tense moments when we heard a couple of raccoons facing off and growl-screaming in the distance, but they were a long ways away and in the end didn't trouble us. And as we were hunting bugs anyway, we both agreed it was not our duty to pursue them.

All in a day's work. From All Hallow's Eve to Christmas, it's winter and cool, with snow sometimes and revelry and all, but most of the time, it's just one big bug hunt.

Our grandparents would never have believed it, but since the Change, that's our lot.

Death a constant companion.

Heat, sweat, and bugs.

It's a grand life, if you don't weaken.

Louise lives on a farm in eastern Ontario Canada with her husband and critters. She writes SciFi, Fantasy, and Horror, and is working on a novel and a short story anthology. She can be found on Twitter as @louise3anne and her short stories can be found on her author page on Amazon.com.

Metamorphoses at the Gate

By LYSANDER ARDEN

There is nothing quite like a Summer friendship! However, Kaz is a stranger friend than most, especially since the local cult seems to have a keen interest in him!

1. Summer of Discovery

I never expected my story to end in overcoming—in transformation, but I must tell you that I have no regrets. Perhaps if I had been able to cling to my sanity a bit longer, I would have chosen a different path, but there certainly is no going back now. Let's start at the beginning.

Staying with my father in that desolate village up in the Catskills for the summer, life had quickly become tedious. There was little to do up in the mountains, and the glorious world filled with wild, unbounded adventure that I had anticipated was turning out to be an illusion. Until I met Kaz, that is. I discovered him by the creek. I had been exploring there for a few days alone, so I was startled but delighted to see someone my age squatting there on one of the large stones, fascinated by something in the clear water. As I approached, the slight figure with the pale face and hair the color of the cosmos did not stir.

"Hey!" I shouted across the creek.

"Hello," a quiet voice replied. He didn't look up.

"Do you live in town? What's your name?"

"Yes. Near the village. I'm Kaz."

"I'm here for the summer. Staying with my father. Can I play here, too?"

"No one's going to stop you." Eyes like dusk turned towards me. A sudden breeze sent the surrounding leaves in a whirlwind, and my soul stirred. Despite the aloof response, he then smiled, and I felt welcome in that fantastic world exploding with lush greenery and unexplored vastness.

There weren't many children in town. Maybe that's why I didn't realize, at first, how peculiar Kaz was. I thought he was shy, introverted. Awkward, owing to the fact that he grew up in a backward town of reticent villagers, wary hermits, and a sprinkling of elusive cult members.

It took time for me to acclimate to the pacing of life in the mountains. I wanted to go, to move. He wanted to sit and ruminate, observing the world around us. Sights and sounds I had never noticed when alone, I noticed when I was with Kaz. He calmed the disquiet in me, and one afternoon spent with him could have been one hour or one year. His laughter, clear and wild, startled the birds from the trees and made my heart sing.

Kaz took great interest in me. He absorbed every bit of information, from the descriptions of the Manhattan shops I frequented to stories about my fifth-grade classmates. I began to feel that he was analyzing me like some sort of specimen. But his expression, focused in rapt attention, was so charming that I never minded his questions. By the end of summer, he knew everything about me.

But despite Kaz's incessant queries, he never showed any interest in coming to visit. He insisted that his overprotective hawk of a mother would never let him leave the village, even for a weekend. A cloud of mystery surrounded Kaz's family, and I was given the impression that it was best not to pry into their business.

"Do you have any brothers or sisters?" I asked him one day.

"No. It's just me and my mother."

"Oh. Your parents are divorced, too?"

"Not exactly. My father doesn't live here," he replied, plucking small yellow and white blossoms from an overgrown bush. Their fragrance was intoxicating.

"Do you see him much?"

"I haven't met him." He handed me a flower. "You can eat the nectar, you know." I pulled off the petals one by one and got nothing.

"No. Like this." He held a flower, pure white, inches from my face and slowly pulled out the stem. One drop of nectar glis-

tened, and I stood, captivated. "Success," he said, and put the whole stem in my mouth. It was the sweetest thing I had ever tasted.

And just like that, my attention was averted. That's how it was. I never felt he was deliberately being mysterious. Some kids try to be strange like that. To make up for insecurities. Kaz didn't seem to have any insecurities. He resembled his mother. Her clear white skin and delicate features turned the heads of even the most withdrawn villagers. However, Kaz must have acquired his dark hair and eyes from his father. I guessed he was from somewhere far away, but never asked.

Then one day, I finally met his mother, the formidable mystery. Kaz had been wanting to invite me to his house. She usually forbade outsiders in their home, but owing to Kaz's deft persuasiveness, she soon conceded, and I was allowed to enter the small house in the woods. Old and weather-worn, but well-kept, it looked much like the other log cabins sporadically placed throughout the outskirts of town.

Passing through a spotless kitchen drenched in sunlight, we entered the living room. The light of the single floor lamp was losing a battle against a darkness emanating from within the house. Heavy drapes covered both windows, so not a trace of light could enter. Stifling. Kaz and I sat side by side on the couch for a while, sipping chai tea and making polite conversation with his mother. She addressed him as Kazemde and looked at him at times over-protective but, in the next moment, near reverential. Her attitude towards me was detached.

Decor was absent with the exception of a lone sculpture on a table against the wall. The dark wooden figure was not large, yet its shadow loomed tall. I went to get a closer look at the object, and a sense of dread washed over me. The long robe of the hooded figure was meticulously detailed, with strange symbols etched into its surface. It was obviously a male figure, yet something about it was not altogether human. I couldn't discern its face.

Suddenly, I wanted nothing more than to escape. A pervasive silence crept in; a chill pierced the air. A heavy gloom seemed to surround me, along with an acute sense of isolation. For a moment, I was the only living person in the world.

Something was not right in that room. When his mother finally told us to go entertain ourselves upstairs, a heavy burden was lifted.

Kaz's bedroom was cluttered with various strange accoutrements. Several cloudy glass bottles lined a wooden shelf. I could not ascertain their contents. A large metal box with coiling wires sprouting this way and that sat on a desk. Old books were stacked on the floor. He said these things belonged to his parents. There were no children's toys in the room at all. There were a few board games on the desk, which had yet to be opened. I tried to imagine Kaz in my bedroom, filled with all the trinkets and playthings of the average American child. Somehow, I couldn't picture it.

Something had been on my mind since meeting Kaz's mother. My father had warned me that several of the townspeople were involved in a local cult. The members called it a religion, but my father was unable to provide any details on exactly who or what they worshiped. Their beliefs were as old as the town itself, perhaps much older, and were a mystery to outsiders. For years, they had used the dilapidated Victorian church downtown as a meeting place, but the locked iron gate made it clear that new members were not welcome. The windows were kept boarded shut, and the immense door was always closed. I tried not to look at the place whenever I walked by, as it made me uneasy.

"Kaz, I've been wondering. Is your mother a member of that local religion? My dad said there was a cult. And I was thinking..."

He laughed at my question, and I was relieved that he was not offended. "Hm? You mean the church downtown? Yes, she's a member. She's friends with Pastor Evans. They're quite close. She goes there every Saturday night, but I usually stay home. It's not a *cult*, by the way."

Pastor Evans, I had seen around town. If I had to surmise his profession, religious leader would have been my last guess. There was something downright eerie about the stooped man in black attire. The mountain summers were never scorching, but his dark wool suit was out of place among the more appropriately dressed townspeople. Looking out from under a worn and out-of-fashion hat, he would glare at passersby on the street as he dashed about his business in town. Luckily he spent most days inside the old church.

Days later, when I was invited back to Kaz's house, he suddenly asked me, "Who do you think you resemble—your mother or your father?"

The question took me by surprise, considering he never talked about family. He was holding one of his father's bizarre objects in his hands and turning it over and over. There was something horrifying about the thing when in his delicate grasp. I had never seen anything like it. A metal box with crude etchings on each side. As mysterious as it was to me, he seemed quite dexterous when dealing with it. He kept it latched shut. I felt an overwhelming urge to grab the thing and hurl it away from him. Just looking at it filled me with a vague sense of hopelessness, as if the glorious summer thriving outside was a great distance away and childhood itself no longer existed. I told myself I should ask him more about it one day, but I never did.

"I think I'm like my mom. My dad is quiet and loves art, and he's always off painting by himself. My mom's really outgoing. She loves to travel, to try new things. I think I'm more like that," I said. Kaz nodded, pondering my reply. I asked him, "How about you?"

"I'm more like my mother, too. I look like her. I don't think I'm very much like my father at all. But they say I have a lot of his features in me as well. I've never met him, so I can't say for sure. I'd prefer to be like neither of them." He placed the device back on the shelf and stared at it for a mo-ment before turning to me. "But I guess that's not possible. We eventually become like our parents, right?" He didn't wait for my answer. "Let's go play at the creek," he said, taking my hand and pulling me downstairs and outside. Kaz was like that.

The end of summer rushed towards us. Days spent in sunlight so pure that everything it touched was enveloped by a nearly unbearable beauty, and nights spent under an indigo sky, pulsing with stars and life and all things amazing came to an end. I told Kaz I would write to him, and I did a few times, but after getting back to school and my friends, we quickly lost touch. I knew he would be there the next summer, waiting at the creek for me, and of course, he was.

2. Summer of Growth

Fiery orange bled into the blue sky, and the fading sunlight reflected in dusty shop windows as I made my way back to my father's house after a shopping excursion downtown. I had just arrived that morning. Clouded by thoughts of a long and dazzling summer ahead and unfocused on the present, Pastor Evans suddenly appeared, an ominous intrusion on my daydreams. Nearly bumping into him, I noticed we were now the same height. He smirked.

"Well, if it isn't the beloved friend of our very own Kazemde. Back in town for summer, I see?"

"Yes. We're friends. Is there a problem?" I asked, my tone perhaps more ostentatious than it should have been towards an adult. Pastor Evans had always unnerved me, but

I found his mention of Kaz irksome. The thought of my friend within sight of this man nauseated me.

"Not a problem at all. We welcome the advancement of his social skills." He forced a smile. "I mean to say, it is *fantastic* for him to have a playmate his own age."

As he began to walk away, I called, "What religion is it you're a pastor of? Who is the god you worship in your ceremonies in the woods? I heard about animal sacrifices."

"A god of brilliance and grandeur. Perhaps even the same god you worship." He turned away again and sauntered down the empty sidewalk.

"I don't worship any god," I shouted after him. I noticed a slight tremor in my voice. It did not come natural to speak in such an abrasive way, and this man was far more intimidating than most. But he did not turn back. Filled with an overwhelming gloom, I rushed home.

The weeks flew by, and with a few exceptions of outings with my father, Kaz and I spent every day together. Occasionally, we would spend the afternoon in town with his mother, following her as she did her shopping. Her expression less severe, perhaps she had come to accept me as a part of her son's life. Kaz, great at persuading her to buy this or that, always convinced her to get us ice cream before returning home. Even with her nearby, these days were carefree.

We spent most afternoons at the creek, just the two of us lost in our own world. A place of sunlight filtering through leaves onto crystal waters, the sounds of the stream in constant flow, and the fragrance of honeysuckle that came and went with the breeze. On the few days we spent in town, we wandered the streets, stopping at the drugstore for ice cream sodas and penny candy. That summer, we were inseparable.

"You'll come back every year, won't you?" Kaz asked me one day. He was lying on my bed, slender arms stretched in the air, examining his hands with great interest. The rain pounded on the roof and against the windows, nearly drowning out his voice.

"Of course," I told him.

"Do you think I've changed?" He sat up and stared at me. His thought process ran in some mystical way, floating from one seemingly random thought to the next.

"You mean from last year? No. I don't think so. Did you get any taller?"

He shook his head.

"You just look like you." My answer must have pleased him. His face contained all the radiance of the world and, suddenly overwhelmed, I didn't know where to look.

Filled with a vague but pervading sense of dread, I condemned the scent of autumn as the end of August drew near. The excitement of a new school year and reunion with old friends was overshadowed by the heartbreak of someone so treasured—delicate, yet as compelling as the universe itself—being torn from me. Again, we promised to write regularly, and this time we did.

3. Summer of Metamorphosis

Some nameless affliction had taken hold of Kaz while I was back in the city. I sensed it immediately upon my return to the mountains. A storm lurked behind eyes that had once shined with youthful curiosity. I was looking into something from another world when I looked into those eyes. He mentioned arguments with his mother, but never provided details.

Over the next few weeks, Kaz's condition worsened. Milk-white skin turned ashen, and bright eyes became dull and shadowed. We spent fewer days at the creek, instead opting for the comfort of my father's cabin. Kaz's focus on our conversations would sometimes falter, and he would stare grimly into a world only he could see. At times he spoke of strange things I couldn't understand, but I didn't dare interrupt him. He was not himself on those occasions. A few times he became so ill he couldn't leave his bed, and his ever-vigilant mother would not let me visit. Only fellow church members came and went, their faces somber.

Upon recovery, Kaz began to spend frequent nights with me in avoidance of his tyrannous mother. We talked of our life during the long winter or reminisced about the previous summer. Those sultry nights contained countless carefree hours amidst a slowly building rumble of chaos. To this day, I treasure them.

Around mid-summer, I had begun to insist on him letting me spend the night at *his* house. After his adamant refusal, I decided to appear at his cabin one Saturday night while his mother was at the church.

"What are you doing here? It's well after dark," Kaz asked. He stood in the shadowy doorway with his arms crossed. After some arguing in loud whispers, he reluctantly let me inside and upstairs. After tiring of the usual board games, we turned to his mother's chess set. We were not familiar with the rules, so we created our own. By the time she returned, we were lost in a world free of fear and worry and adulthood.

His mother was not alone. She had brought with her a small group of companions. From Kaz's room, I heard the muffled sound of voices downstairs. The guests stayed well into the night. Around midnight Kaz turned off the lamp, and we climbed into bed.

"Did you like any girls in your class this year?" Kaz asked suddenly. It was too dark to see his expression. I had to assume it was his default serious look.

"A few. One girl in my class was pretty cute," I said. There was something awkward about my answer. He would surely see through my lies. Actually, I was too involved with my studies to notice any of the girls in my class. My grades had fallen, and my mother's pressure to get high scores was enough to keep my mind on my books and off of distractions.

"How about you?"

"How about me, what?" Kaz asked.

"Any pretty girls in town?"

He paused. "No."

"Well...any boys?" He was making this conversation, a typical one among kids my age, more confusing than it should have been. Was I supposed to be boasting about something as my friends back home did? Or was I making him jealous? I had no way of knowing. Kaz paused again before offering another solid *no*.

"I didn't see any of them outside of school, though. The girls, I mean. I usually went straight home to do my homework. There was a lot this year," I said, rambling. That was the truth.

"I see." That was the first and last time Kaz ever delved into the topic of romance.

The voice of Pastor Evans slithered up to the second floor, along with others that I didn't recognize. A hideous concoction of feelings clouded my mind and kept me awake, restless. Kaz lay silent and incredibly still beside me. I asked if I could go down the hall to use the washroom, and he nodded. I used the bathroom quickly but stopped on my way back. Something in the voices downstairs had caught my attention. What I overheard made me regret going there that night.

"Why not his friend?" I heard the pastor say, followed by a sardonic laugh.

"No. Don't joke about that. He won't have it," his mother shot back.

"His father won't mind at all."

"You haven't a clue what his father will or will not mind," his mother replied, louder. Her voice was stern but tinged with panic.

"We can only guess," sighed an exasperated third voice. "But I do believe the Mills girl will be a better choice for *the key*. She will not be missed. Considering her absent father and her mother's love affair with whisky."

"Either way, we are agreed. The experiment is not working as planned." It was the condescending voice of the pastor again.

"But he was showing *so much potential* until this year," his mother said sorrowfully.

"You can always try again, my dear."

Her reply was a fury-filled tirade I will not repeat.

The third voice murmured, "...never was necessary...we'll find another way."

It was then that a fourth voice spouted forth. A sound. A deep bubbling. I could hear only a few words, but sensed an impatient and raw fury. "No time..." It was inhuman. The others quieted as the fluid grumbling commanded, "Prepare the gate." I rushed back to the bedroom.

Climbing into the bed, I squeezed next to my friend. In a panic, I gripped his arm as if to pull him far away but then, realizing the futility of the gesture, released him. He would think I was mad. As if sensing the hysteria threatening to detonate at any moment, he rested his head on my shoulder. His hair brushing against my face, the faint scent of vanilla ice cream and anise only added to my turmoil.

"What's wrong? Did someone see you?"

"No. Of course not," I answered. I didn't mention the voice. What could I have said? I tried to put the odd conversation and the gurgling monstrosity out of my mind. It was hours before I fell asleep. Even then, I could hear them downstairs, voices rising and quieting again well into the night, sometimes it seemed, in a heated argument.

The next day Kaz came to see me. He seemed unwell, and I feared for his health. Before we could finalize our rules for chess, he was sleeping by my side, his head on my shoulder. I put my arm around him in an attempt to ward off the unknown force consuming him. I felt powerless and small in a suddenly hostile world. It was near dark when he awoke with a start and broke out into a cold sweat. He would start to speak but then stop. The tea my father made did not calm the ceaseless shivering. After returning home that night, a high fever overtook him, and his mother said that he was too ill and once again did not allow visitors.

The first chill of autumn was in the wind when Kaz asked me to meet him at the creek. We hadn't been there for days, instead opting for my home or the lonely streets downtown. He was sitting on the same stone where I spied him for the first time. It seemed like eons had passed since then. Now, instead of the youthful visage peering into the water, a fine sheath of black hair obscured his eyes, and I could not see what he saw. He looked up, and I nearly gasped.

"I have to tell you some things."

I was startled. By what exactly, I still cannot say. Something not of this world was there inside the Kaz I had come to know and adore. It had been brewing from somewhere deep inside and was now on the verge of breaking free.

"When we first met, it wasn't a coincidence."

"What do you mean?" I asked.

Did his mother know he was there? Surely if she had seen him that morning, she would not have let him leave the house. It was then that I understood why she had kept him indoors. He was gravely unwell. For an instant, I suspected some terminal illness at hand. He was planning to tell me of imminent death. My chest tightened. I felt unsteady. I sat beside him, pulling at the thick green moss which clung to the rocks.

"I mean, my mother told me I could find you here. And that is why I came that day."

It seemed atypical of her to send her precious son off to make friends with an outsider, but I was grateful. I could no longer imagine my life without him.

"And..." He hesitated, turning to the shadowy forest. "I'll be leaving soon. I don't think you'll see me much more." Despite being so abrupt, I could see those words were hard for him to speak.

I sat in stunned silence, repeating his words in my head and trying to make sense of them. He never mentioned he and his mother leaving. So much were they a part of the town that the concept of them living anywhere else was ridiculous. The thought of a rare childhood disease pushed into my mind again.

"Well, stop being so vague and explain," I blurted out.

"I can't. I would, but it's not easy. I'm not...flourishing here. This environment. It's not good for me. The summer is coming to an end. You'll start school in two weeks."

"And I'll be back next summer. Just like always. You mean to say *you won't be here*?"

"Yes. I mean to say I won't be here. I'm sorry. This wasn't meant to happen." His tone was distant, but his eyes screamed despair. There was torment and miserable resignation there, along with a wall I could not penetrate. The bond I had thought unbreakable was now being lacerated by some abhorrent force.

"I've failed my mother and my father, and now I must do what I can. I'm not well, you know. They say things don't always go as planned. I *am* the plan gone wrong. I could not meet their expectations, and my purpose has gone askew." He gripped my hand and turned away. "I don't know why."

I didn't know what to say and did not press him further. Perhaps if I had been older, I would have. I would have interrogated him or begged him to stay. But at 13, I merely insisted that he visit my house the next day, and we quietly changed the subject.

The tragedy of the next day is forever burnt in my memory, a black stain on an already anguished summer. When Kaz did not appear at my doorstep, I hurried to the creek. He was not there. When I returned home, my father was sitting in the kitchen, his expression grim. A newspaper lay on the table in front of him.

"Sit down," he said, passing the Hudson Tribune to me.

The headline read, "Child Missing," and below it was printed a photo of a local girl, ten years old. Her name was Daria Mills. Police were investigating a site in the woods. A mysterious circle of stones. Burnt wood and ash. This was the infamous site of animal sacrifices. My father warned me to stay away from the church and to be home by sunset.

I ran to Kaz's house and banged my fist against the door for what felt like an eternity. There was no answer. I returned to the creek and, at last, the dreaded church. I crept through a narrow opening in the back gate and walked up to the wooden door. It was the closest I had ever been to the place. I knocked. A moment later, the door swung open. A strong odor hit me, and I was overcome by a wave of nausea. Musty incense vainly cloaked the sickening smell of rotting.

"Is there a problem, my young friend of Kaz?" Pastor Evans asked.

"Where is he?" I blurted out in a panic. I tried to look behind him, but could discern nothing at all that hinted at the building being a place of worship. All of the old regalia of the previously Christian facility had been removed right down to the pews and altar. The starkness of it sent a chill through my body. A gust of air from inside was cool on my sweaty skin. Perhaps I had expected candles and bizarre statues of the occult world, but there was nothing but the dim glow of an electric light bulb in a distant room. That and the thick, putrid odor contaminating the air.

"He is not with us now, as I'm sure you already know."

"Where is his mother? I have to talk to

her."

"She is well aware of the situation. I *strongly* suggest you not bother her."

"I'll go to the police." My throat burned, and tears threatened to flow at any moment.

"There's no reason to do that. Simply put, he's gone to live with his father. His mother has complied. Surely he told you that much. Surely you know this, *close* friend of Kaz."

"And the missing girl, Daria? What have you done with her?" Desperation was swiftly consuming me.

"I'm sorry. I'm not familiar with that name."

"I've heard you say her name before. I heard you say it," I said, my rising voice now tinged with madness.

"You must be mistaken. I know you are upset. It's unfortunate that our friend has left us, but I know nothing of this young lady. Was she your friend as well?" he asked.

In a frenzy, I blurted out, "I know everything!"

"You know nothing." Unfazed, he stepped inside the church, and the door slammed shut.

I turned and walked away, stopping only to vomit along the worn and dusty road, the lingering odor of the church inescapable. Fueled by a swiftly growing rage, I vowed to uncover the truth, no matter how appalling. But at that moment, I could only go home to my father and cry, inconsolable.

My investigation continued the next morning. I didn't have much time, as I was going to return home to my mother that evening. My father, concerned for my well-being, had arranged for me to leave a few days early. Avoiding the church, I went straight to the notorious site of sacrifices. As the newspaper had reported, a pile of wood and ash remained. Although a villager had mentioned late-night chanting, the police had found no evidence of the missing girl and could not connect the two incidents. The large pieces of wood were all thoroughly charred, and a faint, indiscernible smell lingered in the air. Something lay there, half-buried in ash. I kneeled down to examine my findings. A burned and viscous substance covered the smooth surface of a heavy oblong rock. Scraping away the thick film, I noticed several symbols I did not recognize intricately carved into the stone.

Kaz's mother stopped by our house in the late afternoon. I stepped outside, closing the door behind me.

"I'll never forgive you," I whispered.

"Kaz is not with us anymore, but I promise you, he is not dead. Is that what you think?"

"Where is he?"

"He was not meant for this place as I had hoped he would be. I truly had." Her voice expressed a deep sorrow. "I would never let anyone take him unless it was absolutely necessary. Just like you, I had come to love him. He was a part of me and our world as much as the other." Her arms were crossed to fend off the early autumn wind, her former proud and stern expression lost in the past. "Go back to the city. Let this all be forgotten. Nothing good will come of dwelling on it."

She turned and walked away, leaving me too exhausted to protest. I did not speak until it was time to say goodbye to my father at the train station.

4. Descent into Dreams

For the next several years, I buried my grief in my books. I graduated high school and was accepted into one of the east coast's most prestigious universities. Although eager to begin my anthropology courses, I never forgot Kaz and the incidents in the mountains and sometimes woke at night in a panic, chilled and soaked with sweat. I could not and did not want to remember the nightmares that haunted my subconscious.

A fresh beginning at my new school, I began to make friends and enjoy a quiet but contented social life. I found myself drawn to classes on the occult, ancient religions, and other such obscure facets of my chosen field of study. The description of classes such as *Modern Witchcraft, Obscure Religions,* and *Ancient Egypt* had sparked an interest that slowly blossomed into a full-blown obsession.

It was then that I began to dream much more vividly than before. In the first dream, I wandered that familiar path through the shade until I reached the creek. A dark moss-like plant had blanketed the stones. Slender tendrils stretched out from the thick mass, reaching towards the clear stream. No longer a timid child hunched over the water deep in thought, Kaz reclined there owning the universe. Golden bracelets chimed like bells when he lifted his arm, motioning for me to join him. I sat beside him, wary of the sprawling lifeform coating the rocks. He swept a curtain of black hair over his shoulder and blinked at me. Although now an adult, his essence was still very much the same. The contrast of the grotesque and the radiant made my head spin.

"I've missed you, Kaz."

"I miss you, too." A voice of liquid obsidian spoke, and I was seized.

"You look...healthy," I said. He laughed, eyes shining with a vitality so fierce I thought my heart and the whole world would shatter.

"I *am* healthy."

"I thought you were dead. For years, I tried to forget. I couldn't bear to remember."

"Hm? I should have told you more. But it was difficult for me. Everything was difficult for me then. I thrive here. But still, I wanted to see you."

He put his hand into the thick black-green moss with its tendrils stretching, crawling, and I trembled. This was not the Catskills.

"Can I see you again?" I asked.

"It's not so simple. I'm not the same. This will never be the same." He dipped slender fingers into the stream. The clear water teeming with life turned cloudy—a murky brown and then black. Tiny shimmering bodies of fish and insects bobbed to the surface, dead. Then they too, were sucked into the darkening miasma, disappearing completely. A thick vapor drew up from the water. The air was cold and wet. I drew my jacket up against the chill. As the horrific scene unfolded, I waited for him to continue.

"What you want from me, I cannot offer," he said. The winding creek was now completely black, as if nothing existed there at all. The surrounding fog grew thicker. Only that dreadful moss shone vividly, tendrils growing, curling and uncurling into the mist, reaching towards me.

"You don't know what I want, Kaz." I paused, trying to ignore the rising terror around me. "You never asked me."

He tilted his head and stared at me, in that same intense way he would look into the clear water as a child. His eyes were a starless sky. And then bitter darkness consumed me, and I awoke.

The next dream was less chilling. We met in the expansive old library of the university. Kaz's appearance was reassuringly normal. Leaning against a bookshelf, he was so well-suited to the environment that for a moment I could imagine we were students together.

"Can't stay away from me, can you?" I said, dropping my books on the table—*Rites and Symbols of Initiation, Primitive Religions,* and other familiar titles.

"I suppose not."

"How are you, Kaz?" I asked. I sat down and took out my notebook, avoiding his eyes.

"Doing very well. And you?" Joyous, his voice was the song of the first day of summer.

"I'm doing fine. Busy with my studies." My link with stability, with sanity, was being eaten away bit by bit. He gazed around the room as if seeing a library for the first time. I opened a book to a random page, pretending to search for something. My notebook was open to a clean, blank page. Stark white against the shadow of dreams.

"I once said that I was more like my mother. I am becoming like my father. I have already *become*. I told you we couldn't escape our parents."

"What are you talking about? And what does it matter?" I asked.

"Despite what I have become, when I see you, I wish things could be different."

"You're just you, Kaz. I can see it now. Still you." I sighed, closed my text, and looked up at him. "I will come for you if that's what you want." Despite the absurdity of my suggestion, I was resolute. He seemed startled by my offer but, for a brief moment, seemed possessed by a kind of mad pleasure.

"Come for me? You must know that if you come *here*, you can never go back. And if you could, you would not be the same."

The fact that he even acknowledged me going *there* brought about a creeping terror mingled with eager longing. I had meant what I said, but had yet to contemplate the steps it would take to physically retrieve my friend.

"I am unafraid," I said. His laughter rang out and echoed in the immense room. "The process...I'm sure it would be complicated. But you give me no choice, do you? This world is meaningless without you. I can't endure it."

Kaz shrugged but said nothing. Gazing at the rows of books, he raised his arm and pointed, the chime of bracelets carved in exotic symbols breaking the silence. I stood and took the heavy volume from the shelf, turning *Nearly Forgotten Rites of Rare Religions* by Theodore P. Ainsley over in my hand. I had never noticed this book before. What secrets did it hold?

Then he spoke. "I wait for you where the sun cannot reach and *they* reign in darkness."

I looked up, but he was gone.

Early the next morning, I rushed through breakfast alone in my room before heading to the library. I scoured the aisles on anthropology and religion, nearly giving up. What were the chances that this book existed in reality? A figment of my troubled subconscious. But there was one more option. I went to the librarian and asked if the facility had *Nearly Forgotten Rites of Rare Religions* in their rare books collection.

"Yes, we do have a copy of that. There are very few in existence, so we keep it in special collections."

"Are students allowed access?"

"Yes. Yes, of course. No one is allowed to take those books from the premises, but you can peruse it at your leisure in the back, if you'd like."

Settled into the dimly lit archives room, I opened the book. It was obviously an antique, much older than it had seemed in my dream, but the mysterious drawings on the cover were the same down to the exact detail. I carefully flipped through the pages. Something caught my attention. It was an image of a sculpture similar to the one I had seen at Kaz's house. A lanky figure cloaked in what looked like layers of heavy robes. Despite the great attention to detail in the carving, there was no discernable face. That was left completely blank.

I read about a "rare cult of Egypt that had spread small cabals throughout Europe and eventually to the United States." The groups of ten to twenty members did not proselytize. Few details were mentioned, but Ainsley provided a vague description of one of their rites. There was a photograph of a page from an ancient manuscript. Translating the rows of script and symbols, the author noted:

To open the gate, a key is required. For those who falter, those unstable of mind— success unlikely. Entry may be denied. All will be lost. Return not possible. Transformation inescapable.

It took time to understand the enigma of the ancient writings and the loathsome meaning of the key. Even then, it is a mystery I may not have solved on my own. I vaguely remember whispers in a dream. The speaker in the dark was not Kaz. Something else I cannot envision or even want to consider crept beside me. Those horrible instructions whispered not in words but in sounds and visions. For the sake of my sanity, I leave the obscure figure to my subconscious.

The final dream came one week later. I had given up my research. There was no other information on the mystery cult or their god to be found. No other information could have been of use at that point. Interest in classes and university life had waned to nothing. My friends sensed something was amiss, but had ceased to ask. They merely exchanged worried glances, occasionally inquiring about my well-being. Had something changed in my appearance? My demeanor? I could not tell. My anxiety at its peak, I needed an escape.

I drove down to the old cabin in the mountains. I could spend the week there alone, as my father had moved back to his hometown to spend his retirement. Upon arrival, I felt a great fatigue. After removing my shoes and jacket, I promptly fell asleep in my old bed.

When I opened my eyes, I stood in an alien place. The pure vastness of it was astonishing. A cool, thick substance seeped between my toes, but I dared not look down. A sinister sound gushed somewhere nearby, and odd structures stood far in the distance. Perhaps a mirage, they seemed translucent at times and solid at others. In the darkness, I squinted to see more clearly, but could not make out the forms. I had the feeling that I had left the planet entirely. Everything about the place, or non-place, was bizarre. And he stood before me.

"What are you waiting for?" His form changed. He was Kaz, and then he was not.

From something utterly non-human, then back to the visage familiar and dear. One face melting into another. Some darkly ambiguous, and others too hideous to describe.

"I don't know if I can do this." I looked into the void behind him. "I don't know what you want from me. Other than to completely destroy myself."

His face was a mass of tendrils, reaching and reaching. "I don't want your *destruction*. But it's cold here, you know, where the sun cannot shine," he said, a calm voice emanating from a grotesque body.

"If I survive, I'll surely go mad." I flinched as his form changed again and again, each one more horrible than the last. It was enough terror to make for a lifetime of nightmares. Then he was Kaz once more. Considering my words, he smiled.

"I'm coming undone. Unraveling," I told him, faltering as he transformed anew. It was dizzying.

"Exactly." He paused. "Or you can go back to school. You can turn to healthier interests. Focus on your future. Do as you want. But I cannot follow you there," he said. Was that derision? Or frustration? I could not tell. Even his voice was foreign to me now.

"You're callous." I looked into his eyes, pushing my fear aside.

"If you say I am. Either way, I cannot change who I am—what I have become."

The surging noise in the background grew, sometimes quite loud, and receded again. It sounded familiar, but too unnatural to be anything of earth. I thought I could make out words spoken deep within the low gurgle, but they were not of a language I understood. Kaz paid no mind to the noise, ignoring it completely.

"Do you understand? This is *me*. I was forced into this, but who I am now is *my choice* alone. Beyond an obstinate 'no' to them, I can scream 'yes' to something else entirely." There was desperation in his voice as it rose to a shout in a grasping effort to make me comprehend. "This is who I am. And I celebrate it."

I sighed. My choice had been made. I hadn't realized it at the time, but as surely as autumn came to the Catskills, there it loomed. Anxious yet exhilarated, I felt a dim glimmering of freedom.

"I am what *I* will." He spoke quietly but with resolve and awaited my reply. He was himself again, and I stood staring, helplessly enamored.

"And for that, I love you," I said.

Kaz's eyes widened, and he opened his mouth to speak but said nothing. He then shrugged and held out his hand. A smile—a flash of joy in that cold place—ever so brief, followed by darkness.

5. All Summers' End

A day spent in quiet contemplation within the darkened room. Calm. Reassured. Confidence overshadows anxiety. The subtle scent of damp and decay, more comforting than the painfully bright lights in town. Desire to visit the creek, now gone. Desperate for some unnamable thing, I doze on and off but do not dream. At last darkness falls over the village. I stand and walk to the door, determined.

And now I know what I must do.

And I must leave this place.

And I will go to the church and take the gate with the carved symbols, bringing it inside the circle of stones and placing it before the pyre.

And I will gather the key at the house of the pastor.

And as the flames reach into the sky, one may perhaps hear the sound of my laughter rising above the blaze, above the shrieks.

And I will shout, "Accept this offering, for it is the key. Welcome me beyond the gate."

There he waits for me.

Lysander Arden was born in the US and now lives in the Philippines. In addition to writing, they enjoy reading, drawing, and spending time with their cats. Lysander writes mainly dystopian and speculative romance. Their work can be found on Amazon.

The Chilling Account of the Wolf-Bann of Krallenburg

By J.E. Tabor

Krallenburg is beset by a werewolf! Can witchhunter Friedrich Rosch stop the monstrous curse before the town succumbs to siege by Protestant mercenaries!?

Translator's Note: This journal details the events of the Spring of 1610 in a remote village in the northwestern Holy Roman Empire. The manuscript has been translated into English from documents recovered from former Soviet archives in what is now the Republic of Latvia. I have sacrificed the accuracy of a literal translation in favor of retelling Fr. Rosch's story for modern audiences while retaining the essence of the original.

1 March, 1610

As I set out from the university, I wish to record my investigation into the recent werewolf attacks in Krallenburg, both for my own protection and so others may draw upon my experiences. I have grown to regret my part in the persecutions in Freiburg, but I hope some good can come of it yet. Krallenburg's lord has his own history with witch hysteria, and, though I cannot say so openly, I might leverage my reputation as witch-hunter to prevent a second horror in the village.

I offer all my efforts,

Ad maiorum Dei gloriam.

-Friedrich Rosch, S.J.

8 March, 1610

I arrived in the village of Krallenburg just before sunset on the day after the Feast of Thomas Aquinas. The village is built around an old castle atop a hill rising above the treetops of the dense surrounding forest. The castle was built during the Crusades, and I doubt it has been renovated since the Peasants' War. It is a relic of the past, and its interior reflects this. The walls are filled with the swords, shields, and regalia of the Teutonic Order. A century-old suit of armor greeted me at the threshold. I am told that the armor is no mere decoration: it belonged to the burgrave's own grandfather, though I doubt it has ever seen battle.

Burgrave Phillip Eigenstolz gave me a polite, if guarded, reception. The old man

103

sees enemies everywhere: satanists from within and Lutherans at the gates. Eigenstolz is convinced that there is a conspiracy against him and his family. The lord's first son, Conrad, was ripped to shreds on his way home from a grouse hunt over a year ago. Eigenstolz has shut himself in his castle ever since.

Conrad would have been the end of the Eigenstolz line, had it not been for little Matthias. The child, born just three months ago, is a biblical miracle. With a mother and father well into their fifties, Matthias is a living, breathing reminder that with God, all things are possible. His mother Lady Theresa Eigenstolz does not let the child out of her sight for a moment.

The magistrate already has a man in custody for the murder. A hermit named Franz Wulf is being held at what is known as the Witch House: a cellar Eigenstolz had specially repurposed for his witch trials. I asked to speak with the hermit at once.

9 March, 1610,
Feast of the Forty Holy Martyrs

The bars of Wulf's cell barely allow enough room to lie down in the straw blanketing the dirt floor. Flickering torchlight penetrates the darkness just enough to make out biblical passages scrawled on the grimy brick walls, warning of the Lord's judgment. This grim place is where I finally met the village magistrate.

Joseph Kramer is a fastidious and, dare I say, vain man. Not a strand of his long black hair was out of place, his beard and mustache meticulously combed. He is no

more than thirty by my eye. Kramer proudly wears a sword on his belt: an extravagant rapier with a silver guard and pommel. Blessed by the Pope himself, Kramer claims.

The magistrate recited his findings to me as if they were lines of poetry. He related various cruelties he inflicted: threats of sleep deprivation, thumb screws, iron boots, and general maiming. After his telling, the magistrate displayed a silver charm dangling from a leather cord. He called it Wulf's "demonic talisman."

I have seen such things in the hills of Bavaria. The pagan charm is known as a *wolfsangel*, not uncommon among peasants in the area. Its purpose is *protection* from wolf attacks. At worst, it is evidence that the hermit defrauds superstitious locals.

I told the magistrate as much, which only made him angry. Kramer countered that the hermit had already confessed to becoming a wolf and to eating men, women, and children. I politely asked the magistrate to give me the opportunity to interrogate the hermit alone, without threat of torture. If I am to get at the truth, Wulf's fear need be of God, not of me.

The prisoner was already ragged, his skin pale, and his unshaven cheeks gaunt. Wulf regarded me with the utmost skepticism when I suggested that his confession might be false. I dangled the silver wolfsangel charm so that it cast a twisted and spinning shadow atop of those of the prison bars. Only when I revealed that I recognized the charm and its purpose did Wulf say more.

He claims to be a *wolfssegner* protecting

the village with white magic. When I pointed out his apparent failure, he became pensive.

"There is a *wolf-bann* on Krallenburg," he whispered. "A curse."

Wulf explained that the werewolf does not control its transformations, only turning during the three-day period of the full moon. A review of the lunar charts confirms his theory. I asked Wulf some follow-up questions and admonished him to cease his practice of magic. Once I had heard the hermit's confession, I returned to the burgrave and magistrate above ground.

Kramer became furious when I asked that Wulf be released. I am well aware that my boldness puts me in danger. Objectors were among the first to be put to the fire, some by my own hand. I reminded Kramer of my reputation, that I am well-acquainted with the hallmarks of satanism. Franz Wulf bore none of them. The burgrave remained skeptical, but my status as a man of God won the day.

I was vindicated by a horrific revelation late this morning. The body of another boy was found in the woods, torn apart while Wulf sat in the Witch House. Martin Klein was twelve years old, butchered while watching his family's sheep.

"Destroy this monster," Martin's father told me when he learned of my purpose in Krallenburg. "Find the wicked monster that murdered my son, and burn it."

His anguished rage is all too familiar. The villagers will turn on one another if the attacks continue. I need to find the werewolf quickly, but I must not catch more innocents in my net.

Kramer and I investigated further rumors at the tavern that evening. Plenty of patrons crowded the tables, but I immediately noticed a rough-looking man at the far corner of the bar. He bore a great mane of blond hair and matching beard like that of a North American trapper.

Before I could question him, the wild-looking man stood up from his stool and called to us in a strong accent. "You are hunting *loups-garous*, no?

"Werewolves," he translated.

When I confirmed this, he announced himself as Henri Louvetier and offered us his services in exchange for a "modest" fee. (*Louvetier*, if I am not mistaken, means 'wolf hunter' in French, and is likely not the woodsman's true name.)

Kramer balked. He pointed out that he and I had overseen the execution of scores of witches and did not need the Frenchman's help. I note how quickly the magistrate has come to accept my partnership.

Louvetier was not impressed. "You are not hunting witches," he countered. "You cannot hunt the animal the way you hunt the man, *oui*? Cannot know you have the beast unless you have slain him in beast form."

I thought of the hermit Franz Wulf, how he might have burned at the stake had I not tempered Kramer's zeal. I accepted the Frenchman's offer before Kramer could argue. I must be certain we have the werewolf. I will not harm more innocents.

Louvetier has a plan. We will start at the site of the most recent attack and track the werewolf at night, while it is active. In other words, we will hunt the wolf as it hunts us. I am under no illusions about the danger this strategy poses, but I will not have Kramer finding werewolves in every vagrant and beggar in the village.

10 March, 1610

There were two attacks last night.

A child picking blackberries found Franz Wulf torn apart, his flesh gnawed to the bone. I almost feel guilty about taking his pagan charms from him, false as they were. I am grateful that I was able to absolve him of his sins before his end. Perhaps his soul was saved.

The second victim was a farmer, Werner Schmidt, murdered while standing guard over his stable. His sons heard his screams and rushed to his aid. Both were badly mauled and left to die. Somehow, they survive. The brothers are being treated at what passes for a sick house in this remote area. The one-room cottage sits at the edge of the forest just outside the village walls. It is run by Sister Katharina, tertiary of a holy order called the Forest Mothers.

I am impressed by this young woman's ministry. Katharina has the gentlest spirit, and I can see it in the way her patients respond to her. But the werewolf attacks have added to the hospital's burdens, and Sister Katharina's only aid comes from a shepherd boy named Hans, himself orphaned in the attacks. The boy cannot be more than fifteen, but he dutifully changes bandages and lifts the patients to clean their wounds.

Despite Katharina's efforts, the Schmidt brothers are in a pitiful state. Albert had not regained consciousness, and Eric has only barely. I could not take a proper confession, so I anointed them and left them in the sister's care. There is naught more for me to do but meet with Kramer and Louvetier this evening.

God willing, we will track the werewolf down and slay it.

11 March, 1610

My hands remain unsteady from last night's terror.

We waited until just before dusk. Louvetier armed us with lances and took a scrap of Werner Schmidt's shredded nightshirt to give the hounds the scent. We followed the trail on horses loaned to us by Lord Eigenstolz.

The dogs led us on a serpentine path, covering the narrow swath of forest between the ridge and river that formed the natural boundaries of the land. We followed the eager hounds bearing our oil lamps, otherwise engulfed by the darkness of the forest. I was sure we were lost, until one of the hounds let out a bellow and took off into the brush.

We quickly rode ahead to block the werewolf's escape. Eigenstolz's horses are trained warhorses, acclimated to the sounds and smells of battle. Nevertheless, they became impossible to control once downwind of the beast. They bucked and whinnied and refused to take a step toward the refrain of excited barks.

Those barks became snarls. There was a high-pitched yelp, and then another. The distant sound of whining dogs scattered like the wind. At that moment, the horse I was riding bolted from the scene. I had to cling to its mane to keep from being thrown as it galloped back towards its familiar pastures. The mare slowed to a canter only once it became exhausted. Kramer and Louvetier emerged from the tree line moments later, struggling with the reins of their own skittish mounts. Four of the dozen hounds were unaccounted for.

When we returned this morning, we found only the dogs' half-eaten remains and little else. It was the final full moon of the cycle. We will have to wait another month if we are to kill the beast in wolf form.

25 March, 1610, Annunciation of the Blessed Virgin

To add to the village's woes, the Lutherans have invaded Strasbourg. It won't be long before Krallenburg is in the path of the marauders. The burgrave's attention has so shifted. He is preparing the badly neglected castle defenses and is unwilling to lend his garrison to aid in our hunt. That means the village outside the walls is alone in dealing with the monster.

Tonight is the new moon, the halfway point. The next full moon falls during Holy Week. We will not remain idle in the meantime. Louvetier has another plan. We recruited a hunting party from among the villagers, and Louvetier is putting us through our paces with muskets lent from the burgrave's own armory.

It is hard to imagine, looking at the Frenchman in his furs and unruly mane, but Louvetier must have military training either in the service of King Henry or as a part of a mercenary company. With the burgrave's arms and the Frenchman's drills, our band of peasants has become almost recognizable as a fighting force.

7 April, 1610

We carry out the plan tonight. At sunset, we will draw out the werewolf with a lamb tied to a tree in the middle of its hunting grounds. Louvetier has revealed his secret weapon: a clutch of mechanical traps that will snap their iron jaws on whatever strays into their path. We will sow the ground with these modern traps, and our hunting party will lie in wait to cut the beast down when it springs the trap. I am optimistic that we will soon be rid of this curse.

8 April, 1610

God help us all. Nothing could have prepared us.

We followed Louvetier's plan to the letter. The woodsman grinned from ear to ear as he pried open the traps' iron jaws and set their springs. What he could not know is that he would be caught in equally vicious jaws before the night was through.

The burgrave's quartermaster distributed muskets, powder, and ammunition to our recently mustered militia. At sunset we took up a semicircle position on a ridge overlooking the defenseless lamb and waited for the moon to rise. Even in the dark of night, the full moonlight was bright enough to see the lamb's snow-white fleece clearly against the black and gnarly tree.

Every halt in the crickets' song set me on edge, but it was hours before an otherworldly howl wrapped its icy claw around my neck. The forest went silent. I held my breath until my chest burned.

Another howl echoed in the distance. And another. And another. The werewolf seemed to be calling on its pack, inviting them to share in its hunt.

There was a rustle in the trees, a metallic snap, and a shrill yelp. A gray shape struggled against the trap's iron jaws. There was a lightning flash, followed by a cacophony of deafening blasts. The shrill whistle in my ears muffled cries of alarm. Plumes of thick smoke billowed from the ridge like a chimney, stinging my eyes and obscuring the view of the grove. The pungent air was suffocating. I coughed and gagged on the black powder fumes. Blind, deaf, and unable to breathe, I fled in a panic from the noxious cloud.

I broke free of the smoke only to glimpse through my tears a beastly form circling the cloud. It darted past the curtain of smoke, and a chilling cry of terror pierced my still-ringing ears. I turned to run and met with a pair of yellow eyes glowing in the moonlight.

The wolf was bigger than any I had ever seen. Its muscles rippled under a shaggy coat of dark gray fur. It stood hunched over on hind legs, its foreclaws dangling little more than a foot off the ground, as if standing upright were unnatural for it. The creature bared its pale fangs at me, its saliva glistening in the moonlight, dripping from the corner of long canine jaws.

I was utterly frozen by fear. The monster crouched, readying to leap. When I finally brought down my musket to fire, it was too late. The wolf was upon me. Only the thick muzzle of the firearm pressed between its jaws protected me from its vicious bite.

The demonic beast snapped its jaws against the wood of the musket inches from my face. Flecks of spittle from its foaming mouth spattered my cheek. The weight of the creature pressed on my chest until there was an audible crack. A hot dagger thrust into my chest. Darkness closed around my vision.

The werewolf howled in pain, and the great weight was lifted from my chest before I could pass out from pain or suffocation. I rolled away to see Louvetier had pierced the creature's side with his lance. The werewolf recoiled and snapped at the spear shaft, splintering the wood like it was a branch of rotting pine. Louvetier fell onto the soft earth. The monster, spear still in its side, leapt onto the woodsman, burying its fangs into his jugular. I can still hear his ungodly screams as the monster chewed its way through his throat.

The smoke cleared. The militia had fled, many leaving their muskets in the dirt. In my senselessness and pain, I did little but gape at the pack of wolves feasting on the fallen. I felt a strong grasp on my shoulder and turned to find Kramer facing me with wild eyes, his rapier drawn.

Coming to my senses, I struggled to my feet and took to the forest like the prey animal I was. But every breath I drew was like a knife in the back, and I could not keep up with Kramer. I begged him to go on, but he would not leave my side. The young magistrate practically carried me to the village gates. It is only thanks to Louvetier, Kramer, and the Almighty that I survive to record this account.

Amazingly, Kramer had only suffered a minor wound to his hand in the struggle. Sister Katharina cleaned and wrapped it and sent him on his way.

I was not so lucky. One of my ribs is surely broken. Katharina has provided me a bed in the sick house, from which I now write. I must pray long and hard on what to do next. Krallenburg is plagued by not one, but a pack of werewolves.

9 April, 1610

I slept through yesterday's sunset, still haunted by nightmares. Now that I have finally awoken, I fear I will not sleep again for some time. The attacks will continue while I am stuck in this bed. Sister Katharina is nevertheless full of youthful cheer, shedding sunshine on my dour mood. I am not being figurative: she threw open the shutters to blind me with the morning light.

"You can't stay in the dark forever, Father," she told me.

She would be surprised how long I could manage. I was reminded of my darkest days in Freiburg.

I asked her about the rest of the hunting party. Her smile faded, and she placed a hand onto mine. Most of the men escaped, thank God. But Louvetier was killed outright, along with two of the militia. Katharina was able to save another man by the name of Lehman, but not his hand.

I quickly changed the subject, asking Katharina how she found her vocation. She laughed and said that nursing was in her family. Her mother was a midwife. And when her mother died several years ago, Katharina found her own calling. Without a formal church, much less a hospital, Krallenburg needed her.

This cursed place is in need of salvation, that is for certain. I asked Katharina if she were afraid of the beasts that prowl the woods, and she shamed me with her words.

"*Noli metuere, et noli timere,*" she replied. "Fear not, and be not dismayed."

She is right. I must have trust in God. I must remember that He is stronger than the forces of evil.

10 April, 1610

I am doing my best to emulate the forbearance of Blessed Ignatius. His leg was shattered by a cannonball. I merely have a few broken ribs.

Kramer visited me today, uncharacteristically disheveled. Wild strands strayed outward from his usually impeccably groomed head of hair. I could see the sympathy in his eyes when he saw my condition, but there was also defiance.

Lord Eigenstolz has requested my blessing for Kramer to take charge of the investigation. This darkens my mood considerably. Kramer will not wait for the full moon to be certain of the monster's identity. He wants to question the neighbors of the victims, as there are rumors of bad blood between them. But if the wolfssegner was right, this lycanthropy is a curse. The werewolves would be just as likely to prey on their friends and loved ones as their enemies. Perhaps even more likely.

I am going with Kramer. I had not even realized that tomorrow is Easter. It is as good a time as any to get out of this sick bed.

17 April, 1610,
Feast of St. Anicetus

Kramer is cleverer and more methodical than I gave him credit for. He didn't start with accusations, but basic questions of fact. Each answer was a brick that he used to build a wall around his suspect, from which they could not escape. That is when he would take them into custody, and the real questioning would begin. I can see Kramer building the pyres in his mind with each answer. He is already filling the Witch House with captives.

24 April, 1610

Kramer has levied allegations against dozens, and I have had to work day and night to ensure that no one has been convicted. I have denied Kramer access to his usual methods, but threats alone have gained him confessions from the most fearful of villagers. After much pleading, I convinced the magistrate to imprison the werewolves and to observe their transformations before we put anyone to the fire.

If I keep resisting him, his accusations will find their way to me. The Clergy were not immune in the witch trials in Trier, nor Freiburg. I hold no illusions that my cassock will protect me here in Krallenburg. I will not allow Kramer to intimidate me, but I must be wary.

30 April, 1610

As if werewolves are not bad enough, Krallenburg is in the path of Brandenburg's Protestant mercenaries. Eigenstolz has ordered the surrounding forest cleared and the construction of ramparts around the village to be completed at double pace. He has already placed guns and powder at strategic points along the walls and towers.

All the villagers have been commanded to pack what they can and take shelter within the walls. I cannot object. War in recent years has more often than not meant rape, pillage, and wanton slaughter of the peasantry.

Within these walls, the werewolves will not be able to strike from the shadows, only to slip back into the forest. They will have nowhere to run. Still, everyone knows that a wolf is most dangerous when cornered.

4 May, 1610,
Feast of St. Monica of Hippo

Any thought of escaping this cursed village has been foreclosed. The garrison and villagers cleared as much of the forest as they could, but the dense wood nonetheless concealed the mercenaries' approach. The marching columns could be heard before anyone caught glimpse of a soldier.

Hundreds of boots crushed grass and leaves and twigs underfoot. They emerged from the forest by the score, wearing mismatched uniforms, armed with pikes and muskets. The mercenaries made a show of the few cannons they had and paraded the whole of their force around the walls so that they could be seen from every vantage point. I hurried to the castle and found the burgrave in the library reading on the siege of Constantinople. He is unwilling to negotiate a surrender.

Lord Eigenstolz has made it clear that it is only for my benefit that he withholds judgment on the Witch House prisoners. He wants the pyres ready to burn the morning after the full moon. I have reluctantly agreed, though the werewolves may themselves be victims of the curse.

5 May, 1610

The cannons have not begun their barrage. Brandenburg still hopes to take the castle without a fight, but they do not know Eigenstolz. Even in the midst of the siege, Kramer has not let up on his interrogations. Despite his efforts, not one of them has confessed of werewolfery. The truth will come out tomorrow night, one way or the other.

6 May, 1610

I set out to hear the prisoners' confessions this morning. When I stepped foot inside what the villagers were now calling "the kennels," I was horrified. Kramer has packed the cells with more suspects since I last visited. There are at least two men to a cage, though we know of only a handful of werewolves. Most of these men are certain to be innocent. But if the monster is among them...

7 May, 1610

That treacherous devil. God forgive him, for I cannot. I stormed to Kramer's office and castigated him for putting innocent lives at risk. He protested, but I grabbed him by the arm and ordered him to bring his sword.

I sent the lone guard of the Witch House to go for reinforcements, and I dragged Kramer into the dungeon to witness the consequences of his recklessness.

"Have your sword ready," I ordered. "When the beast begins to change, pierce its heart before it can harm anyone."

The magistrate reluctantly drew his rapier at the ready. I thought I had seen actual fear in his eyes. The full moon edged its way into view in the prison window. I began to pray. After every completed recitation, I scrutinized the captives, looking for signs of the wolf.

Desperate cries rose from among the prisoners, but it was the clatter of Kramer's rapier against the floor that drew my attention. Kramer grinned at me with long canine teeth, his eyes now a solid yellow. His ears grew pointed, and dark gray fur sprouted from his exposed skin. He let out an inhuman cry as his jaw elongated into a canine snout. His widening shoulders ripped open his fine clothes, and claws extended from his fingers and toes.

I lunged for the rapier. The monster tore out of Kramer's rags and gave a low growl, ready to pounce. I struck at the lunging beast with all my might. The blade sunk into its flesh, its point protruding from its back. The werewolf howled in agony. It grabbed onto the steel coming out of its chest and bent it until it broke like a shard of brittle glass.

I stumbled backward, left with only a

jagged nub sprouting from the absurd ornate hilt. Furious, the monster lunged for me again. I struck at its face with the pommel, desperately bashing its snout and its eyes with the pathetic weapon. The werewolf recoiled, as if it had been burned with hot iron. With a final strike, I hit the monster square in the eye socket and drove the decorative hilt into its skull.

The blood and flesh around the wound sizzled like sausage in a pan. The creature unleashed a long, mournful howl and slumped to the floor. I backed into the wall and watched its shallow breathing slow until it exhaled its final breath. The fur, claws, snout, and fangs all receded into the form of the magistrate Joseph Kramer.

A pair of howls from across the village answered Kramer's dying call. The dozens of caged men looked in horror upon what Kramer was, what I had done. There had not been a werewolf among them.

I found the keys from Kramer's shredded belt and released every last one of the captives. Many are in poor shape, and I have asked Sister Katharina to convert the cellar into a hospital during the siege. The burgrave may object if he wishes.

Sister Katharina insisted on examining me thoroughly. She seemed almost disappointed to find I didn't have a scratch on me. She cannot know what I now believe to be true: the werewolf passes its curse through its bite. Kramer must have been bitten the night that Louvetier was killed. The coward hid his malady behind his zealous prosecution of innocents.

I burned Kramer's body on one of the pyres meant for those innocent men. I realize now what I held in my hand. The steel blade, blessed by the Pope himself, could not harm the monster. But the silver pommel killed it. We know how to slay the monsters. I reported my findings to Eigenstolz, and he has been gracious enough to donate thirty silver thaler coins to be melted down into musket balls. I have blessed each of them.

None of us can afford to let the beasts get close. The chance of passing the curse makes hunting werewolves in the confines of these walls especially dangerous. One wrong move could doom any of us. I need a way to draw the wolves into the open without the risk of being caught in their jaws.

I may have an idea that could work, if Lord Eigenstolz allows it.

8 May, 1610,
Feast of the Apparition of St. Michael

I cannot contain my joy, even in the midst of this siege. Eigenstolz reluctantly gave up his grandfather's suit of armor once I convinced him that it could be put to no better use than to end this evil.

I insisted on being the one to don it. I have approximately the right build, and I will not put anyone else at risk for the sake of my harebrained plan. You would be hard-pressed to find a man in Krallenburg trained in its use, anyway. Eigenstolz ordered all villagers to remain in their homes and lock their doors. Musketeers armed with the blessed silver ammunition took position on the roofs around the village square. I strode out in the clanking armor onto the streets of Krallenburg and under the light of the full moon.

The village was eerily silent. Every metallic step I took echoed down the narrow streets. I could hear my heart pounding inside the helmet and feel the sweat slicking the metal against my skin. I hobbled toward the village square, yelling and clapping my gauntlets together.

After several minutes of making a commotion, a howl sounded from the other side of the road. I could not help but lift my helmet's visor to look back. Two pairs of yellow eyes flashed from either side of the street, much too close for my comfort. I flipped the visor down and ran for my life.

Through the slits in the helmet, I could barely see Castle Krallenburg towering over the square, unobstructed by the village. I pushed myself to sprint as best I could in the armor, panting the entire way. The clamor of steel-on-steel became deafening inside my helmet.

One of the werewolves leapt onto my back. I lost my footing and slammed into the cobblestone street like a hammer striking an anvil. The concussion rang in my ears, and the full weight of the monster pressed the armor into my back. The creature panted hot breath on my neck, gnawing at the steel plate where my jugular would have been.

I splayed out on the road, unable to get up. Reaching for the nearest cobblestone in the road, I dragged myself forward, scraping the steel of the breastplate against stone. There was a sharp tug at my left arm and a searing pain in my shoulder.

The stone in my grasp came loose from the road. I gripped it tight and wrenched my dislocated arm from the werewolf's jaws. I rolled over and bashed the beast in the face with all my might, breaking the cobblestone against the monster's jaw.

It was unharmed but stunned, which was all I needed. I pressed up with my good right arm and scrambled to the center of the village square. When I reached my destination, I spun around only to find the two werewolves were mere steps behind.

A crack of thunder erupted. Both monsters were knocked to the ground, peppered with shot. At the same time, a piercing hot pain stabbed my leg. I was terrified that one of the beast's fangs had pierced the armor, but it was in fact a stray bullet from one of the musketeers on the roof.

My blood pooled on the street, but all I could feel was pure relief watching the smoking wolf corpses reverting to the forms of men. I must have lost consciousness because I woke up in the Witch House, now Sister Katharina's hospital. She could not contain her grief, for Hans had been one of the two final werewolves.

I am aggrieved about the boy. Such a good-hearted lad could not have deserved his fate. I will pray his soul finally finds peace, and that this curse is finally over. Time will tell. Tonight is the last night of the full moon, and I do not know how many monsters are left to fight.

9 May, 1610, Feast of St. Gregory Nanzianzus

No attacks. The wolf-bann is over. I can finally relax and recover from my injuries, thank God. The Protestants have not yet withdrawn their forces, but there is a cease-fire for the moment. Peace talks were set to begin on the first of March. Perhaps Krallenburg's hardships are coming to an end.

19 May, 1610,
Feast of St. Pudentiana

All the village's attention has turned to the war. They have nearly forgotten the horrors that took place less than a fortnight ago.

I have moved back into the castle, though I have not been sleeping. Nightmares of being mauled by wolves still haunt my dreams. It is as if my sleeping mind cannot accept that the threat is gone.

Little Matthias has not been sleeping, either. It seems he is teething, and the poor child is inconsolable. Lady Eigenstolz still nurses him to soothe the boy, but that has been understandably a precarious task. She complains of his little teeth breaking the skin, even, but would not hear of any suggestion of weaning the boy. That is an area I have no experience in and will not wade into now. In honesty, Lady Theresa has been a welcome companion in these lonely nights.

5 June, 1610

Matthias is finally sleeping, but I have not had the same fortune. Something has been bothering me, though I know not what. Tonight is the first of the full moon, and I hope to finally sleep once it has passed without event. For now, I spend my nights in the library writing by candlelight.

Lady Eigenstolz told me something puzzling this morning. Our conversation went to the miracle of little Matthias' birth, the answer to her prayers. The Lady went to Sister Katharina for advice in conceiving, as Katharina's mother had been a midwife.

Oddly, Sister Katharina directed that the parents should wait until the child has reached a full year of age before he is to be baptized. This is clearly incorrect theology. I will have to give the young sister some guidance. I cannot think of where she might have gotten this idea.

My mind has consistently been wandering to the curse and a question that vexes me still. If the werewolves had not voluntarily made a pact with the Devil, then someone else must have...

7 June, 1610

This will be my final journal entry.

The horrific realization came to me two nights ago. I dropped my pen in the middle of writing and rushed to the dining hall. There I snatched the first piece of fine silver cutlery I could find. Quickly and silently, I said a blessing over the knife as I rushed to the burgrave's bedchamber.

The shrieks of agony told me I was too late.

I rushed to the doorway to witness the scene. Crimson blood drenched the burgrave's white blankets as Lady Eigenstolz sunk her teeth into her husband's throat, pinning him helplessly to the bed. A lone guard followed after me, brandishing a spear at the she-wolf. The werewolf spun towards us, turning her fiery gaze to the crib in the corner of the bedchamber.

I rushed to intercept the monster as she bounded from the bed to devour the child, or so I thought. But I could not reach the werewolf before she plunged her jaws into the crib. To my horror, she pulled an infant wolf cub from the cradle.

This was no innocent creature of god, but a true abomination, its fiery eyes and needle-like fangs just as vicious as its mother's. I was too stunned to react. With her cub in mouth, the werewolf bounded to the doorway on all fours. She took off down the hallway, leaving a trail of bloody pawprints along the carpet. I gave chase.

I hoped to lock a door behind her and keep the monster from escaping, but the werewolf lowered her head and made an impossible leap through the window at the end of the hall. She burst through the glass and out onto the roof below. I rushed to the window to catch a glimpse, but she had disappeared into the darkness of the village streets.

I spent some amount of time in a panic, though I do not know how long. When my shock had finally worn off, I realized what had happened, and the person responsible. I caught the attention of a stunned guard captain and demanded a contingent of men accompany me. Despite his shock, or perhaps because of it, he complied. I marched these troops directly to the Witch House.

When the guards dragged Katharina out of bed in her nightgown, the young woman looked genuinely surprised. But the witch gave me the grimmest knowing smile when she saw my face. The guards tossed her into one of the cells for me to begin my interrogation.

In my time as inquisitor, I have learned a great many techniques to draw confessions from the lips of the accused. Katharina escaped none of them. Our sessions lasted through the night and into the morning. I learned everything.

Nearly two decades ago, Katharina's mother was caught up in Krallenburg's witch purges. A villager's daughter came stillborn, and the family wrongfully accused the midwife of witchcraft. Eigenstolz had her tortured. Although she was innocent, Katharina's mother confessed to all manner of heinous crimes. Eigenstolz burned her at the stake, one of so many innocents to die in the persecutions.

Just a girl at the time, Katharina fled. She swore to one day return and make the village, the burgrave, and his family pay for their crimes. Katharina deliberately sought the Devil's aid in exchange for her soul. She became the very witch the village thought her mother to be, and returned to the village in the guise of the sister of a false religious order.

Once she had established her fraudulent ministry, Katharina seduced Hans, the shepherd boy who would become her alpha werewolf. She confessed to performing foul carnal acts with the teen. She made him her pawn, bewitching him and afflicting him with lycanthropy. It was Hans that had butchered his family and orphaned himself. It was Hans who murdered Conrad, Lord Eigenstolz's first son.

After Conrad's death, Eigenstolz locked himself in the castle while the alpha werewolf terrorized the village, passing the curse to the poor souls he did not kill. When Lady Eigenstolz asked "Sister" Katharina's advice for conceiving another son, Katharina found her opportunity. With her black magic, she granted the lady's wish, sowing the seed of Eigenstolz's destruction. Katharina cursed Matthias with lycanthropy at his very conception. While his own curse lay dormant for months, he passed it on to his mother: the perfect assassin.

Once I had drawn out the truth, I demanded that Katharina reverse the curse. Even as long as I had worked on her, the cruel witch merely grinned at me with broken and bloody teeth. I continued my persuasions into the morning, but her hatred was too strong to be overcome. All I got from the witch were some mumblings of "Livonia," that war-torn realm on the Baltic Sea. Nothing more.

I took stock of my work. A wave of disgust washed over me. After all those years, I had reached back into my dark past, and I had nothing to show for it but "Livonia."

But if cruelty would not loosen her tongue, then perhaps grace would. I offered Christ's forgiveness, if only she would repent.

"It is much too late for that, Father," she laughed.

But that is not true. While we still breathe, it is never too late. Then I did something I never planned: I confessed my own sins to Katharina.

I laid bare all the cruelties I had inflicted on the innocent men, women, and children I had accused, humiliated, and tortured, leaving no painful detail unsaid. Katharina listened in silence. Once I had recited my litany of atrocities, I asked her for forgiveness for my part in the persecutions that drove her down her evil path. Katharina did not laugh. I believe she sensed the sincerity in my words. I doubt that anyone had ever expressed sorrow for the sins committed against her before that moment.

"After what you put me through, you want my forgiveness?"

"For persecuting the innocent, yes," I replied. "But you are not innocent, Katharina. That child is."

Katharina's expression hardened. But before she could respond, an old woman in bloody rags and holding an infant entered the cellar. I had not recognized the Lady Eigenstolz in her fallen state. In the passing hours, she had deduced Sister Katharina's crimes. She was there to question the witch who had murdered one of her sons and cursed the other.

Lady Eigenstolz handed me the baby Matthias, stepped inside Katharina's tiny cell and closed the gate behind her. The lady sat against the wall in the corner of the cell and spoke two sentences to Katharina: "My son has harmed no one. Please cure him."

Katharina glared at Lady Theresa with a fiery hatred that I have never before witnessed. "My mother harmed no one, yet you burned her alive," the witch spat back. "How will you cure her?"

The Lady Eigenstolz said nothing but did

not move from that corner of the cell. It was not until sunset that I understood what she meant to do. She fetched a burning torch from the wall and made me swear to care for Matthias.

"My Lady, there has to be another way," I protested.

But Lady Theresa's yellow eyes flickered in the torchlight, and I could see it was too late. The beast had taken hold, and she was beyond reason. I beheld the child in my arms, and I could not deny her.

The witch was stubborn in her hatred, even as full moon rose in the darkened sky. But as the lady set fire to the straw on the floor, the fear in Katharina's eyes was plain. She had been too proud to repent, and she knew she would spend eternity in torment because of it.

"It is not too late," I called to her above the werewolf's howl.

Bloody tears streamed down Katharina's face. "The Livonians," she sputtered. "They know of lycanthropy. They can help the child. Please, forgive me."

I whispered a few words of absolution. The crackling flames spread through the cell, obscuring the two women locked inside. There was nothing I could do but flee the prison under the rising moon, the carefully bound and swaddled child in my arms. A long and mournful howl carried through the night air, followed by a shriek of terror that was soon cut short.

It was not difficult to explain the fire that consumed the Witch House that night. Gunpowder is volatile, and the burgrave had stockpiles in every defensible site within the village walls.

I am left with my vow to Lady Theresa. My only clue to saving Matthias is that far-away land of Livonia. That is well enough. We cannot remain here. Matthias' age will not protect him. The Church would burn him if they knew the truth, and the Protestants would be no kinder.

I will make the journey to the Baltic. If I cannot save the child from his affliction, perhaps my guidance can yet save his soul.

Afterword

In 1692, eighty-two years after the events in Krallenburg, an elderly man went on trial for lycanthropy in Swedish Livonia. He claimed that, acting as the "Hound of God," he had regularly transformed into a werewolf to do battle with the Devil and the malevolent witches that plagued the area. His name was Thiess of Kaltenbrun, also known as "The Livonian Werewolf."

J.E. Tabor is the author of the planetary romance novella The Loki Exodus *and is a contributor to weird west anthology* A Fistful of Demons. *His debut novel* A Fool's Pursuit *comes out in 2024. J.E. lives with his wife and son in St. Louis, Missouri.*

The Angel Hanna

By RODICA BRETIN

Alix has always been a bit odd... but her past is even stranger! An orphan tells her strange tale of friendship and loss—a story of a girl who thought she was an angel!

Alix looked at me, then to the clear sky, dotted with stars. It was nighttime, and from the crenellated walls, the island resembled a ship sailing out to sea.

"Show me!"

I stretched my hands out to her, my fingers apart, as if I were pushing an unseen barrier, which thinned out and disappeared entirely when Alix pressed her palms against mine.

Suddenly, I had the acute sensation of someone who had woken up from a deep coma. Images, sounds, and smells exploded around me, like I was in the middle of a dizzying fireworks display. I could *hear* the light of the stars and each sounded different, like the instruments in an orchestra playing the sky symphony. I could distinguish the vibration of a pulsar, the cascading rumble of a black hole, followed by the overture in the crescendo of a supernova explosion. I could *see* through the sea all the way to the depths traversed by sharks, whales, dolphins, octopuses, and, farther still, into the watery abyss where strange silhouettes slid through the corals, antediluvian creatures dragged their tails through the sand in which cohorts of crabs marched

in formation, preparing for D-Day when they would invade the beaches of the world. I was *feeling* the smell of marijuana cigarettes two fishermen were smoking somewhere on a boat miles away, the scent of pine resin in a forest to the northwest, the stench of burned tires from a truck where a boy and a girl were making love, she for the first time, he...

And Alix, since when had she become translucent, like a crystal statue? I could see her bones and muscles, arteries and veins where blood pulsed in harmony with the eternal rhythms of nature. I heard the beating...of two hearts?!

Alix pulled her hands away, and my universe returned to the way it was, a pale, faded copy, a black-and-white representation of what Alix lived through, moment by moment. Alix, who...wasn't quite human. Some would name her *mortal goddess*—but they knew nothing! From the outside, she seemed always satisfied with herself and those around her, radiating balance and quiet acceptance, *an oasis of calm in a desert of madness.*

Alix heard my thought.

"Not really," she contradicted me without raising her voice. "Once, I was just like

118

you."

"You mean always angry about anything or anybody?"

She smiled, but her eyes remained focused into the dreary past.

"It's hard to not know *who* you are, but it's even harder to not know *what* you are. Until the age of nine, I thought I was *normal*. I never knew my parents, but there was nothing uncommon about that—in those days, many children in Stockholm, Copenhagen, and Oslo ended up like me, abandoned, begging on the streets, relying on the mercy of strangers. Do you remember *the girl with the matches*, who died frozen in the snow, while the rich and their families celebrated Christmas? A story that touched and struck a chord of sensitivity in generations of readers, or a fact of life recorded by Hans Christian Andersen with dramatic realism? Me, I was luckier than most. I ended up in a parish orphanage. I had a roof over my head, a bed with a mattress full of straw, a slimy blanket, and a place at the communal dinner table, where the daily delicacy was turnip stew.

"Everything was rationed. When we outgrew our clothes, we were given others, which were just as patched up and worn. As for shoes, we didn't have any. We had to be grateful for leftovers, rags, a piece of moldy bread, and a worm-eaten apple, because they didn't throw us outside, in the blizzard. We were a burden on the shoulders of the orphanage staff, the kitchen lady who every day was faced with a difficult decision; boiled or baked potatoes? We were suf-fering from hunger, from the cold; we were dirty and ragged, but it could be worse—and we kept hearing this until the other orphans and I started to believe it.

"But not Hanna.

"Hanna was my friend, the girl with golden hair and eyes of a blue so pale that they resembled two opals. Hanna spoke little and only with me, but not because she was shy, silent, or withdrawn.

"Hanna believed she was an angel.

"Her celestial parents were forced to leave her behind, but they hadn't abandoned her. Tomorrow, in a year, they would return and take her with them. Sometimes, she could hear them calling her by name, telling her not to lose patience, and hope. They had left for a while, but...

"'*Where did they go?*' I asked her one day.

"The next night, we sneaked through the attic window of the bedroom and stood together, gazing at the starlit sky from the roof.

"'*There!*' she said.

"She showed me a sparkle that was the same as thousands and thousands of others. But to Hanna, that star was a beacon, lighting her way back home. And, since then, we got out on the roof every night when the sky was clear. Once, she whispered another secret in my ear. '*I had sprouted invisible wings. If I opened them, I could soar over the houses, over the trees.*'

"'*And me?*' I asked her.

"'*I won't leave you, Alix. When my parents will come for me, we will go together.*'

"Forty girls lived in the attic bedroom. One of them—I never learned which—told the supervisor about our nightly escapades. In the orphanage, everything was scarce and portioned, food, heat, candle wax, everything except punishments.

"For the better part of two days, Hanna and I were forced to sit on our knees on crushed walnut shells. Then they gave us brushes, soap, and buckets of water to clean the blood off the floorboards. But the true punishment was yet to come. The headmistress had called a blacksmith to place iron bars on the attic windows.

"And on the night before the bedroom became a prison, Hanna came to my bed and put a finger on my lips. She didn't utter a word, but I understood her thought. These were our last moments of freedom. Why should we waste them?

"In the sky, the blackness covering the stars was beginning to fade. Earlier, it had rained, and the roof was wet and slippery. But so what? Hanna had wings, the stars were flashing between the ragged clouds, soon the firmament would be clear, and all ours.

"When the tiles slipped from under my feet, Hanna caught my arms, trying to stop me, but it didn't work. We both tumbled over the drainpipe and fell fourteen meters to the granite-paved courtyard.

"I woke up in the orphanage infirmary. The doctor told me Hanna was crushed and died instantly. It was a cruel lie, and I refused to believe it. Hanna had flown! She had opened her wings wide and was floating somewhere over the city. But why had she

left me there?

"Maybe she left me behind because all my bones were broken. No one in the orphanage believed I would survive till morning, and they waited and waited. At dawn, I still hadn't given my last breath, and by afternoon I had asked for a glass of water.

"Had a miracle happened?

"The doctor looked at me in horror and fright, like I was a three-headed calf—and so what? Hanna had escaped; she would come back to take me away from him, from all of them. That evening, my fever dropped, I could stand on my feet, and I got myself out of bed. The bathroom was on the other end of the corridor, and I had almost made it when I smelled a strange odor, like wilted flowers.

"I opened a door, then another. In the third room, I found Hanna, covered in a rust-stained sheet. But it was blood. I tore it off and I stared at the crushed body and the disfigured face of my friend. She had been a girl who dreamed she was a winged creature; now she was just an anonymous corpse, which the orphanage was about to sell to the Royal Clinique, as a teaching aid for Medical students.

"As for me, was I an angel, a demon, an abomination?

"They moved me from the common dormitory to a closet in the basement, passing me food through a slit in the door, as if I had leprosy, the plague, or some other infectious disease. The headmistress had called an exorcist, and the doctor informed his fellow anatomists to prepare the table and dissection instruments, but not before

running a few scientific experiments. Was I resistant to freezing water, fire, or sulfuric acid? Could they conserve me in formaldehyde?

"They called me *the girl with rubber bones*, who had fallen off a roof and had gotten up without a scratch. That's how urban legends are born. Was I lucky or a child of the devil?

"They didn't get to find out. The third day after the accident that brought me the unwanted fame, I ran away from the orphanage, leaving behind the town, then Sweden. I didn't linger for more than a couple of days in one place, still running although nobody was chasing me, with no other luggage except the memories. Up to you, Hanna was my only friend."

"A girl who thought she was an angel and another who fancied herself as a human," I said. "Both were wrong and right at the same time. But did you find out, finally, at the end of so many pathways, who are you, what are you?"

Alix tilted her head to one side and stared at me under her eyelashes.

"In the end...is it really so important?"

Rodica Bretin is the author of novels and story books in the domains of fantasy, science-fiction, paranormal, and medieval times. She published in magazines from her country, but also in Cirsova Magazine, Aphelion, Gracious Light *(SUA),* Teoria Omicron, Maquina Combinatoria *(Ecuador), and* Antares *(France).*

Trapped in the Loop

By JIM BREYFOGLE

Kat has a daring plan to trap Rhygir's forces, baiting them into a bend in the river where they themselves risk being cut off! Can Kat and Mangos hold their lines and catch Rhygir outside of Alness before his reinforcements are able to arrive?!

In the Current Time

Mangos stood on the small rise of grey schist at the neck of the Loop. The river All ran deep and swift around him. The field formed by the Loop was coarse sand and gravel, sometimes interrupted by sawgrass, sometimes by the underlying schist pushing upward. Makeshift scaffolds stood in the center of the field. A dozen bodies, or parts of bodies, hung from the scaffolds.

"Kill the birds if they won't give up their meal," Siln ordered from behind him. "Nasty things," he added, stopping beside Mangos and pointing to the carrion hawks perched on the bodies. "We never had them in Alness until Rhygir came. They're drawn by death and will fight to defend the food they claim." As the first soldiers of Kat's army approached the scaffolds, the hawks flapped their wings and squawked their indignation.

Mangos nodded his understanding as he and Siln surveyed the Loop. It was nice to have one of the few experienced Alnessi commanders so close. He was sure to be able to answer Mangos's questions.

The men fanned out across the field, pausing to look down. Now Mangos noticed the bones strewn about, as well as pieces of faded cloth and rusted iron: the bodies of Karn's Alnessi army and whatever wasn't worth looting.

Trees hedged the far banks, making a double barrier with the river. The only way in or out of the Loop was over the neck of land where Mangos stood.

It seemed crazy they wanted to fight a battle here when every fiber of his body screamed: "Trap!"

"The river cannot be crossed?" he asked, though he knew the answer. He could *see* the answer. Near the shore, the water foamed around rocks or fallen trees, but further out it ran dark and smooth. He could *feel* the answer, too; the wind that stirred across the field carried the tale of its coldness.

"There is a ford several miles east," Siln said.

The carpet of bones showed how helpful that was.

"How many of Karn's army survived going into the river?" Mangos asked.

"Damned few."

"Let's form up ranks," Mangos said.

"When the men are in position, I want markers laid for each squad. Each man must be able to find his place quickly. After that, form a detail and start to gather the dead."

The mounds of bones doubly disturbed Mangos. First, that they should be so large; they reached his waist, and when new bones were added, they clattered as they rolled down the sides. But secondly, thousands of men had followed Karn into this loop, and all that remained were these piles of bones that only came up to his waist.

A few hours' work, he thought, *will finish this task.*

He put his shoulder against one of the scaffolds and pushed. The post tipped, the end spraying sand as he ripped it loose. The whole scaffold twisted, the lashings broke, and it collapsed in a clatter of wood and bones.

"How do you deal with bodies in Alness?" he asked.

"Bury them, mostly," said Siln.

Mangos grunted. The land was too low here. If they dug graves, they'd hit water or schist, which they couldn't dig through anyway. "The Norfins consign them to the sacred river."

Siln grunted in turn. "That'd be easier, but it's never been the tradition. Nobody wants bodies fetching up on shore or cluttering up the bay."

The breeze picked up, turning the leaves on the trees. Mangos froze, straining to hear. For just a moment, he thought he heard a doleful moan, a mourning whistle as the wind whipped through the piles of bones.

What words would these dead wish to speak? Would they offer encouragement? Would they call for vengeance? Or would they shout warnings?

"The dead will favor us, buried or not," Siln murmured. "But this is a bad way to prepare for battle. It reminds the men how they died."

A soldier came forward with another armload of bones. He cradled them as a mother does her child. Arm and leg bones jutted out of the rib cage like bread loaves in a basket, and the skull balanced precariously on top. He lifted the skull with one hand as he gently lowered the rest of his burden onto the pile.

He stood looking at the skull, his face as expressionless as the one he held, but Mangos could almost read his mind. *Will this soon be me?*

The soldier set the skull atop the other bones. It wobbled and started to roll down the side. He steadied it, making sure it was stable before taking away his hand.

Satisfied, he turned and saw Mangos watching him. "When will the Rhygirians attack?" he asked.

"Soon," Mangos said. "They have scouts. They know we're here, and they think they know why. But not tonight."

The night air held just a hint of chill and carried enough moisture to tell Mangos there would be dew in the morning. The sky seemed abnormally black and the stars preternaturally bright. The sound of running water enveloped him, coming, as it did, from three sides.

He flipped a stone into the black water. The water claimed the stone, and the current erased both splash and waves. How many of Karn's men had thrown themselves into the river here, furthest from the neck of the loop?

"What are you doing?" Kat asked as she came up behind him.

"Making peace with how we came here in the noose of the river," he mused. "In case we should die."

"Is that what they're calling it?" Kat asked. "The noose of the river? It has a name, Cannai, but the noose is apt enough. Are you at peace with how you came here?"

"There are a few questions that trouble me," he said. "I agreed, but you chose the path."

Kat laughed. "Not such a bad analogy. If I were to say yes, I've been working toward this since the fall of Alness, would that answer your questions?"

Though he knew, Mangos was still amazed. He hadn't even suspected until recently, and there would be plans within plans that he didn't suspect even now.

"You might have told me," he said, though he wasn't really angry.

"Would you have helped? If I said every step I took was preparation to fight Rhygir?"

Mangos remembered first meeting Kat and how worn and dirty she looked. "I would have thought you mad."

"I had the resources I took away from Alness," Kat said. Her tone was mild, but

held a hint of steel.

She had escaped Alness with her dagger, her clothes, and her life. She didn't mean any of those things. "You had more skill than the average refugee," Mangos observed. "Yet no more fame."

"I'm a princess," Kat said as if that explained her skill. "But I would not be Queen; my older brother Kel was to inherit the throne. I was tutored and trained to represent Alness, not to rule it. But I have an aptitude even my teachers did not suspect."

"Why hide it?"

"It is important that the heir to the throne be the most suited to sitting on it," Kat said. She smiled, "Or at least thought to be. It didn't bother me, for Kel would have been a fine king. Only Father knew the truth."

The smile fell from her face as she continued. "That is why, when only we remained, he threw me into the canal and turned to face Rhygir so I might escape. I'd have taken Rhygir in with me and gladly drowned us both, but there would have been none to redeem Alness."

She moved, drawing his attention. "Let's see to the men."

"One last question," Mangos said, thinking of something that occasionally puzzled him. Something he never dared ask. "Why don't men desire you?"

"Spells were cast on me to protect my virtue, magic that turns aside men's lust. Before the fall, it was mostly a formality, but since then, it has helped avoid... distractions." She looked him in the eye. "Perhaps when this is over, we'll have the spell removed."

Mangos smiled, not sure why, only that he felt he should. He knew he should want the spell removed, but he didn't *feel* it. He let out a short, ironic laugh. Yes, the spell was working.

Gravel crunched as Kat shifted her weight. "I'd like to check the mood of the men."

Mangos nodded.

The encampment was quiet—quieter than one would expect of so many soldiers. The men were uneasy; Mangos could feel it. Too many mutterings; too much staring into the darkness, away from the fires, away from their comrades.

"They think of death," Kat said.

"Then we should remind them of victory."

"Victory is never further away than in the dark of night." She fell silent, and the two weaved among the fires, dropping smiles and greetings until Kat stopped next to a soldier silently staring into his fire.

He was a bit older, maybe in his middle thirties. Lines of grief were etched deeply into his face. His beard, though dark, had streaks of grey. His expression was bleak.

Kat stood next to him for a moment before asking, "Why do you fight?"

After a long pause, the man lifted his head so the firelight illuminated his face. "I fight," he said, "for Kat." He blinked. "Not you, Your Majesty, though I fight for you as well. My daughter Kat."

Mangos sharpened his ears to listen, as did the men around him. If the answer sur-

prised Kat, she didn't show it.

"She shared your birthday, so of course we named her after you," the man said. "You turned twelve the year she was born." He smiled, though it was clear he was looking back at better times. "To a father's eyes, she was every bit as beautiful as her namesake."

He blinked and his eyes focused on Kat's face. "I failed her, Your Majesty. I won't fail you."

Kat closed her eyes. "No," she whispered. "I never thought you would." After a second, she rested her hand on his shoulder. He bowed his head and reached up to grasp her hand.

Provisional Council, One Week Previous

Mangos could tell an outburst was coming. Sure enough, as soon as Kat stopped speaking, Trentor exploded. "Leading this army into the Loop is madness!"

Trentor might understand fighting Rhygir's mercenaries, but he didn't understand tact.

Drex, Captain of Kat's *Fedai*, raised his eyebrows at the words, his hands straying to his sword. Siln, the most senior of the Alnessi, may have frowned—it was hard to tell because of all the scars on his face—but the soft *tsk* conveyed his feelings effectively. Clearly, neither approved of Trentor's outburst.

Mangos smiled. He wasn't offended, for he, too, had a hard time remembering Kat should be given the respect of a monarch.

Only a thin wall of canvas separated them from Kat's army of slaves, refugees, and (Mangos suspected) bandits and thieves. The tent, sides glowing from the afternoon sun, felt warm, but the heat didn't excuse Trentor's lack of respect.

Undeterred, Trentor bulled on. "There is no escape from the Loop, and you'll be outnumbered. Not only that, but Rhygir's men are all experienced mercenaries. Half our men have no experience, and those who do have only experienced a massacre. They're veterans by survival, not skill. They certainly haven't tasted victory, and probably wouldn't know what to do if it came near."

"Don't demean the men, Commander," Kat said, resting her hand on the paper-strewn table in front of her. "They are survivors and better—fighters."

"Then wait and gather more men. But for the sake of your claim and your army, stay out of the Loop."

"We can't wait," Kat said. "The Bursa will prevent Bardor from sending his *Fedai* to help Rhygir, but that may change. Besides," she added, smoothing a map with her hand and placing a small stone on the corner, "we currently have food, but my money is limited, and Alness can't support an army in the field."

"The people support you," Siln pointed out.

"The food they give us leaves less for themselves. The fact is Alness can't feed itself. If we can convince the farmers to plant a crop, we may be able to get a harvest this year. That won't happen if the war drags on."

"Rhygir's bold, but he's not a fool, Your Majesty." Trentor shook his head. "He

didn't move against Karn until Bardor's *Fedai* arrived. He'll do the same thing now."

Kat smiled. "Not if we bait him."

"With respect. He's the sort to set traps, not fall into them." He didn't need to say, *that's how Karn fell.*

Drex snorted. All eyes turned to the stocky *Fedai*. He shifted and glanced down. "Your pardon, Your Majesty." As an officer, he still had his tongue, something the other *Fedai* lacked.

"Speak your mind," Kat said.

Drex looked up. "You can't have it both ways," he told Trentor. "Going into the Loop is suicide, but Rhygir will not recognize that? Her Majesty goes there to draw him away from the city walls."

"Rhygir won't be able to help himself," Kat agreed.

Mangos stirred, leaning forward. For years he had watched Kat's plans as they unfolded. He had never heard them beforehand, so never heard the note of absolute confidence that hers was the higher cunning.

If Kat said Rhygir would come to battle, Mangos believed her.

"He'll think we revisit the Loop to bury Karn's army," Kat said. "And once he knows we're there, he will act to serve us as he did Karn."

Siln ran a finger down one of the many scars on his face. "Perhaps this is not the best time, Your Majesty, but Karn was not a strong leader," he said.

"And what makes a strong leader?" Mangos asked. He wondered why Siln would bring this up, just before Kat was about to divulge her plans.

"The commander must help the men find peace and provide focus for the fighting. Battle plans mean little without the men's commitment."

Ah, Mangos thought. Questions of ability. But surely Siln did not question Kat.

Kat stared at Siln for a moment and then pointedly changed the subject. "What has happened in the Loop is past. This is what we will do in the future."

Siln cleared his throat.

Kat's eyes flashed. "Very well, Commander. You won't be diverted. Say your piece."

"You've worked a miracle gathering so many, and arming, and feeding them. From nothing, you have created hope. You have even recovered your father's crown."

"But—?" Kat asked, her voice even.

"There are men here who are not Alnessi."

Kat took a deep breath. "I see." She glanced at Mangos, flicked her eyes to Drex. "It's not Drex, is it?"

Mangos tightened, not consciously, but he felt all his muscles contract a little, and he realized he was frowning. They spoke of him! "Nothing has been said to me."

"Why should the men follow you?" Trentor burst out. "You're not Alnessi!"

"I am not Alnessi, either," Drex stated, in his deep, quiet voice.

"You do not command Alnessi," Trentor said. This was not true, for Kat had placed a battalion under his command in addition to his *Fedai*.

"The men follow well enough," Mangos said. "If *you* have a problem, I'm sure we can solve it." Fists, swords, or polybolos; any would be suitable, though he didn't say such aloud.

"It's not a question of nationality," said Siln. Trentor started to protest, but Siln talked over him. "Or really of ability, for you've done well." He cleared his throat. "I'm sorry, Your Highness, but this is a concern. Drex is a trained and experienced leader. Mangos is an adventurer. Will he know how to react when the unexpected happens, and he has men under his command?"

Mangos opened his mouth but realized nothing he said would matter. The decision was not his.

"He will do well," Kat said. "A man who keeps his head on dragonback will not lose it in battle. He cannot be 'just' a soldier. He is the Mongoose," she paused and gave her words a hint of irony with a smile. "He is famed for acts of reckless bravery, and the men admire him—whether you wish to admit it or not."

"As you say." He shot a look at Trentor that seemed to say, *I raised the point. Let it rest.*

Trentor looked ready to protest, but Siln frowned, and Kat glared at him. "Your concerns have been heard. Mangos will have the right wing," she said, her voice firm. "You will be with him, Siln. Make it work."

"Yes, Your Majesty." Siln's voice was respectful, not challenging. "Once Rhygir has us trapped in the Loop, how do you propose to kill him?"

"The Loop is wide enough to draw up lines of battle," Kat said, "like this." She ran her finger across the map.

The commanders leaned forward to read the markings.

"That's madness!" burst out Trentor. Drex looked troubled but remained silent.

"Your Majesty," Siln said. "The center must be strongest, for if it breaks, the army is divided and easily defeated."

"That's the way battles are traditionally fought," Kat agreed. Her eyes flashed anger and the muscles in her jaw flexed. "But we don't want to beat Rhygir, we want to *destroy* him. He can *not* be allowed to retreat into the city.

"So," she continued, "when Rhygir attacks, the center will retreat—not break." She held up a hand to forestall Trentor's comment. "Only the center will retreat. The flanks will swing in and encircle Rhygir's army."

The men stared for a moment. Siln chuckled. "That's clever," he said.

"Here now," protested Trentor. "That might work if the center only gives way. But if it breaks entirely instead of encircling the enemy, you'll have a stronger enemy between your divided forces.

"That's why I'll command the center," Kat said. "I'll have the *Fedai* on the left with support." She nodded to Drex, who nodded back. "And, of course, on the right, Mangos and Siln."

"It's a good plan," Siln allowed, "though I have misgivings." He flashed a meaningful look at Mangos but didn't raise that point again. "The chiefest is your insistence that Bardor will be unable to send his *Fedai* to assist Rhygir."

"I have the Bursa's word," Kat answered. "He owes me."

"He owes you a lot, including his life," Mangos said in a low voice.

"The men won't like it," Trentor said. "A few of them survived Karn's fall, and all of them know about it." He jabbed his finger at the Loop of land on the map. "That's cursed land. There's no guarantee you can defeat Rhygir anyway. And if he has five thousand *Fedai* reinforcements…"

"There have been no reports of Bardor's *Fedai* landing," Kat said. "I know Karn didn't know they had landed either. But we must seize this chance. We must trust the Bursa to keep the *Fedai* in Alomar."

"I like it," Siln said. "I was in the Loop with Karn, Your Majesty, and I'll follow you there, misgivings or no. Drex?" he asked. "What are your thoughts?"

"It's a good plan. I'd rather not fight in that trap, but the lure must be strong enough to draw Rhygir out of the city. We can't count on the Bursa forever."

"Not forever," Kat agreed. "But long enough to destroy Rhygir."

The men nodded. "I think we can count on the Bursa long enough for that," Siln said.

But so quietly that Mangos barely heard him, Trentor muttered, "Your father fell because one man failed him."

Back in the Current Time

A hunting horn blared, driving open Mangos's eyes and the sleep from his mind. An attack, and those were the inner pickets! He stumbled to his feet. The horn blared again, a short, truncated blast.

"Get up!" he shouted to the sleeping men around him. "Arm yourselves!" They weren't ready. An early attack could ruin Kat's plan.

Shouts of confusion and fear broke the morning twilight.

"Fall into your squads!" Mangos shouted. "Form ranks!"

Men rose from their rest and started to rush about. They were figures of grey in the half-light, hurrying in no specific direction, their movements marked by panic.

"Gods damn it!" snarled Siln, appearing from the confusion next to him. "This is why we had outer pickets, so we wouldn't be surprised like this!"

Mangos reached out and plucked up a man rushing past. "Form ranks!" he bellowed, throwing the man toward the line markers. "Form ranks!" he roared again, louder.

Here and there, men ran forward, taking their positions, facing the neck of the Loop and the forest beyond, which was still dark with the shadows of night.

Mangos grabbed another man and shook him loose from his panic. "Take a moment—arm yourself. Then take your position."

Men milled by the river, trapped by their fear and the swiftly moving water. Mangos pushed amongst them, shouting orders, yelling encouragement, shoving them away from the water.

"I hate fighting before breakfast!" he yelled. "And by the gods of Eastwarn, Rhygir will regret making me do it!"

Men cast incredulous looks at him.

"He's cost me a couple hours of sleep as well!" Mangos shouted. "And I'll take that price from his hide!"

The men started moving now, and Mangos risked going to the lines. They were thin, but more men came and filled in the holes. Drex's *Fedai* held their position on the left in solid lines, armed and waiting. Men rushed to the center—whatever Kat had done there worked.

Shouting Rhygirians burst from the forest.

"Hold the lines!" *Hold the lines while the rest of the men fall in*, he pleaded silently.

More and more yelling Rhygirians followed the first. The first flowed over the rise at the neck and into the Loop proper.

The foremost Rhygirian, a tall thin man whose feet kicked up small stones as he ran, outstripped the rest. He was the tip of the spear, screaming at them, and Mangos couldn't help but watch.

The Rhygirian neared the center of the Alnessi lines. He lifted his spear as he charged. But, at the last moment, a huge, shield-bearing Alnessi stepped forward, braced his feet, and drove the shield into the Rhygirian. The Rhygirian rebounded with a crash of metal. The Alnessi roared, and the rest of the Rhygirian attack struck home.

Mangos wiped sweat from his brow. The sun crested the trees to his right, the Alnessi line held, and the Rhygirians regrouped across the neck. "They'll not retreat," he said. "And a good thing."

"Why is that?" Siln asked.

"We can't kill them if they retreat."

Kat moved among the Alnessi, offering congratulations and thanks, words of encouragement or condolences as needed. When she reached Mangos she said, "I'm counting on you, Mangos."

"We're ready," he answered. He lowered his voice. "Can you hold the center?"

"We'll find out soon, won't we?" But she had a smile that eased his fears. "Be careful," she said and returned to the line.

The tone of the army had changed. They had survived the first onslaught. Their hatred ran cold and deep, but Mangos wanted it a roaring inferno.

He ambled forward, careful to keep his carriage relaxed. Very deliberately, he turned his back to the regrouping enemy.

"These men," he pitched his voice to carry and lifted his arm to point behind him toward the Rhygirians, "took your country. These men slew your King. These men stole your livestock and your money. They burned your homes! They," Mangos let his voice rise as he went on, "raped your wives and daughters! They killed your sons!"

He dropped his voice back down. "They're here to kill you. But!" And now he shouted, "Your Queen has given them to you instead! Soon you will not be asked to hold firm. Soon you will be asked to KILL!

"Ours is the easy task! Ours is the task for which you have prayed in the darkness of the night, for which you have lusted after each new indignity. They have seeded this ground with the bones of your kin—our task is to water it with their blood!"

The men lifted a cheer, and Mangos feared they would carry the fight to the Rhygirians. "Remember your orders, and the day shall be ours!"

"You've a knack for that," Siln said as the two looked over the army. Another roar rose, this time from the center of the line where Kat addressed the men there. "If only I hadn't seen so much death," Siln said, "I would feel better about this."

Mangos clapped him on the back. "Death's had his claws in you before, but you've always pulled free."

Siln chuckled without humor, running a finger down one of the scars on his face. "He left his marks, though."

At the neck of the Loop, Rhygir formed his troops. His silvecite armor flashed in the early morning sun. Teriz's white Kingsfisher armor almost seemed a shadow as the traitor of Alness helped Rhygir prepare for another assault.

No attacking pell-mell this time. The Rhygirians still outnumbered the Alnessi; by their lines, instead of a striking like a spear, they would hit like a hammer.

Rhygir shouted, and his men moved forward. They did not yell. They came forward for the grim purpose of killing, and the Alnessi waited with the same thing in mind.

Within minutes, the armies grappled with each other. The lines held as men hacked; pushing, stabbing, slashing at any exposed weakness. The wounded fell and were trampled and, with the dead, driven into the sandy soil.

The weight of numbers began to tell. The

Alnessi began to give ground.

"Hold!" Mangos bellowed. "For the love of Alness—hold!"

The men dug in; the right stopped falling back. Across the field, the left had done the same, but the center still retreated. The line began to stretch until it formed a 'U,' the men with their backs to the river.

"Hold!" Mangos shouted again.

The Rhygirians rushed the center, seeing the weakness, striving to break the line. Kat fought desperately; the men around her planted their feet and held their ground.

A horn call split the sounds of battle. Mangos's heart picked up. It called again, Kat signalling to spring the trap.

"Attack!" screamed Mangos, putting his words into action. He drove himself forward, clubbing a mercenary to the ground and thrusting his sword at the next. He didn't pause to see if the men followed; he could tell by their yells.

Like the boom of a drum, the word "KILL!" rang over the Loop. The left wing, led by Drex's *Fedai,* shattered the Rhygirians before them and swung out and around. Their chant rolled over the Loop, striking like another blow as they attacked.

"KILL!"

"Kill!" Mangos shouted, directing his men with his sword. They had momentum now. Men swarmed past, hacking and trampling the enemy, swinging wide and falling on the main body of Rhygirians from the rear.

Alnessi anger and hatred flowed like the Rhygirian's blood. Like carving meat, Mangos thought—mad butchers carving meat.

Panic rippled through Rhygir's ranks as they realized the Alnessi surrounded them. Rhygir kept pressure on the Alnessi center, but Teriz tried to turn the men, tried to face the new assault on their rear.

Mangos paused to survey the field. Kat held firm in the center though Rhygir pressed hard. Mangos couldn't see Drex, but the *Fedai* waded over piles of dead and dying Rhygirians. His own men pushed forward, leaving him behind the line. Once again, he found Siln next to him.

"That's someone worth killing!" Mangos pointed his bloody sword at Teriz. The Kingsfisher towered over the men around him, a bulwark amongst the beleaguered Rhygirians. Men rallied around him, his white armor drawing them like a banner.

"Not a simple task." Siln wiped blood from his face. "There's only two men in that scrum I fear, and he's one."

No need to ask of the other—Rhygir's silvecite armor was streaked with blood, but Mangos doubted it was his. Rhygir no longer pressed the Alnessi center; he had pulled his men back a few paces and was trying desperately to organize a defense. Teriz and Rhygir knew death; they knew it approached but would not go peacefully.

Siln clapped Mangos on the back and grinned. "A far cry from earlier, eh?" Their men exulted, years of frustration being swept away in brutal joy.

"By the gods of Eastwarn, yes!"

Siln threw his head back and laughed, a mad sound. "Kill them all!" he shouted. "Today, we reclaim Alness!" The nearest men roared approval. Somebody started singing, and more voices joined in. The song spread, and Kat's men slew to the sound of the Alnessi anthem.

The encirclement grew smaller, the Rhygirians more densely packed as the Alnessi kept attacking. The Alnessi outnumbered the Rhygirians now. Kat's plan had worked exactly as she promised.

Mangos started to move along the lines, his gaze fixed on Teriz. Everything would be better if the Traitor of Alness died.

Before he could attack Teriz, a hand grabbed Mangos from behind. He spun, sword raised. An Alnessi scout let go and stumbled back, shouting words that were lost in the din of battle.

Mangos started to turn back, but the scout made to grab him again. This time, the scout pointed while he shouted. Still unable to hear, Mangos followed the man a safe distance from the fighting.

"The *Fedai* are coming!" the scout shouted.

"What?" The words made no sense.

"The *Fedai* are coming!" the scout shouted again, pointing.

The words struck him like physical blows. Impossible, yet a glance west confirmed men marching along the river. Bardor had unleashed his death in the north. Again.

"By the gods of Eastwarn..." There was nothing else to say.

The words from the council echoed in his mind, *one man failed*. Then it had been Teriz, this time the Bursa.

I shouldn't have been fighting. The scout could have found me faster; we'd have more time if I weren't fighting.

He started to work, turning men, trying to organize squads, trying desperately to pull some order from the chaos the battle had become. Eventually he came to Siln and pulled the commander back, pointing to the ranks of *Fedai* rushing to Rhygir's rescue.

"Damn the Bursa!" Siln shouted.

Mangos shouted back. "We have to save the army!" Did Kat know? It was hard to tell.

Horns rang out from the woods. If she didn't know of the *Fedai* before, she did now. Hesitation rippled through the Alnessi forces.

The surviving Rhygirians cheered, and Rhygir immediately sprang forward. The *feel* of the air changed as momentum changed sides again.

"I'll take some men and try and keep part of the neck open," Mangos said. "You pull the men behind me and out of the Loop."

"What of the rest of the army?" Siln demanded. "We can't leave them!"

Mangos shook his head. The *Fedai* had reached the Loop and started to deploy across its neck. He needed to stop them. Already Kat's left flank was trapped and Rhygir again pressed the center. "We're not! We're opening an escape for as many as can make it!"

"Then I'll hold off the *Fedai*!"

"No!" Mangos shouted. He needed to act; the men had seen the *Fedai*, and Mangos could sense their fear. He couldn't let it overwhelm them. "Get as many men out as you can! Now!" He gathered men about him as he rushed to the east end of the Loop's neck.

The battle engulfed him as he crashed into the first ranks of the *Fedai*. "Stand firm for the Queen!" he shouted. "Every minute you stand is a comrade's life saved!"

He didn't know if any heard him, he didn't know how many lived. He didn't merely yell, not words of encouragement, not taunts, just a continuous yell that seemed to come not from his lungs, but from the movement of his body.

The *Fedai* fought fiercely. The battle pressed against him, pushing him back, pinching him away from the main action. For every lunge forward, he was driven two steps back until he found himself on the schist rise. While he had been fighting, the *Fedai* pushed past him and sealed the Loop—he was outside the lines and away from the fighting.

Few Rhygirians remained, but that didn't help the Alnessi. The *Fedai* owned the Loop and needed no other help imposing their will.

Some Alnessi had given up, had thrown down their arms and pleaded for mercy, but Rhygir and his remaining men butchered them where they knelt. The *Fedai* ground forward, slowed only by the need to kill the surrendering and wounded Alnessi.

Only at the river's edge did men still fight. Some of Kat's *Fedai* had drawn back from the left flank, and they mixed with the Alnessi to form a line with their backs to the river.

Where is Kat? Mangos rose onto the balls of his feet, craning to see better. *Please let her live.*

Bodies bobbed in the shallows, and the current swept more downstream. Alnessi threw themselves into the rushing water. Rhygir stationed men along the banks to push them back into the swift current if they tried to come ashore.

"I thought the *Fedai* wouldn't come north," said a voice at Mangos's side. He turned his head to see a dozen battered and bloody men who, like himself, the battle had temporarily forgotten.

"The gods hate us," said a bearded Alnessi, his voice hollow, shocked.

"Did she escape?" asked a third. "Is the Queen safe?"

There!

Kat stood knee-deep in the river All, mostly hidden by the men around her, fighting desperately to hold what remained of her army together. "She's alive," Mangos said.

"Do we die here?" asked the bearded man, and Mangos felt a wash of pride that they would stay and fight when escape lay open.

"Make your move," Mangos muttered under his breath. He would attack opposite her, mad as it seemed, and try to break the Rhygirian lines long enough for her to escape. "Show me where."

The lines of the Alnessi broke. A great roar went up from the throats of the Rhygirians and the *Fedai* as they poured amongst the defenders, cutting them down.

"No!" cried Mangos.

The river was pink with bloody foam and

black with bodies as more and more men sought to escape the slaughter on shore. Some sank, some swirled away.

"The rapids downstream will pound them to jelly," said a wiry little man. "Gods help them all."

Fedai pressed Kat. Her own *Fedai* died as Bardor's overwhelmed them, leaving her, for a moment, fighting alone. She retreated a step, her foot plunging into the deep channel of the river. She toppled backwards, vanishing into the dark water.

Mangos gasped and took an involuntary step forward. "No." He would deny it all in a single word, but it wouldn't help.

A cold feeling settled into his stomach as he turned away. "Go east," he ordered the men. "Find Siln and get away from the Loop. Get men downstream. The Queen can swim."

"You can only go into the water so many times," the bearded man said, letting his voice trail off, his implication clear.

Before you don't come out.

Don't miss the exciting conclusion to the Aventures of the Mongoose and Meerkat in our next issue... or in the collected Tales of the Mongoose and Meerkat Volume 3: The Redemption of Alness, out now from Cirsova Publishing!

135

Texas Goth

By MICHAEL TIERNEY with ABRAHAM STRONGJOHN

Jesus Dunn Jr. plans to do away with his abusive father... And there are no witnesses, except for the strange Goth girl who has started following him around!

"I'm going to carve that bastard like a Halloween pumpkin," he grumbled.

On that cold October night, the thoughts of hate and anger Jesus Dunn wrapped himself in kept him warmer than any blanket. Blood pounded in his ears each time he heard the giggles of the latest floozy his father had brought home. Her moans carried through the thin walls over the wafting strains of Simon and Garfunkel's April, Come She Will.

Earlier that day, Jesus had had a conversation with his priest. Though he'd not sought the absolution of confession, he'd confided the turmoil within his soul. Namely, his desire to leave home.

"We are commanded to honor our father and mother," the priest had said. "Though he may have provoked you in a discouraging way."

"Yeah, and those who trouble their family will inherit the wind; spare me, Father," Jesus had replied. "My pops has been nothing but trouble to me, and he ain't exactly been honoring my mother, either... You know that bastard's why she offed herself."

After a short volley of platitudes, Jesus had left none the more comforted, more resolute than ever that he should take some sort of action.

Something rapped on Jesus's window just as the "words of the prophet" were being "written on the subway walls." He ignored it at first, but the album had ended, though the other noises from his father's room had not. The rapping on his window repeated a second, third, then a fourth time.

It couldn't have been creaking or a knocking tree branch. It was too regular. Too deliberate. But what could it be?

Some asshole, at this hour, Jesus thought, the violent intentions that had been welling toward his father having found a new target in that moment.

Jesus threw off his blankets with an irritated grunt and kicked his legs in the air to swing himself out of bed with the momentum. The hardwood floor was cold under his feet, but his anger still simmered hot. He couldn't do anything about his dad right now, but he was ready to throw down with whatever jackass was bugging him.

There was nothing at his window. Only the scant silver light of the rising crescent moon. Calming a bit, Jesus pressed his face for a better look.

A dark-haired slip of a girl, dressed all in

136

black, was walking away.

Who the hell is she? Jesus thought.

The girl stopped and turned, offering Jesus an enigmatic smile and a quick wave. She shook her head and waved a finger, as if in warning. Though everything about her seemed enveloped in the shadows of evening, her scintillating black eyes clearly connected with his.

Jesus blinked but for a moment, but when he opened his eyes, she was gone.

"I'll be damned…" Jesus muttered, half-allured, half-bemused. He looked back at the vanishing moon. "Rogue moon, tomorrow night…"

"Quit raisin' that ruckus!" his father shouted from the other side of the wall. The woman who was with him giggled lewdly. "Get back to bed, boy, afore I tan yer hide!"

Jesus rubbed the bruise on his face; it was no idle threat.

"I'll get you, you damned bastard…" Jesus cursed quietly through gritted teeth. "I'll be damned if I let you touch me again…"

As dusk fell the following day, Jesus slipped out the back door and headed down the alleys and backstreets before circling back towards home. He leisurely sauntered down Main Street, wearing a jacket that hid his hoodie sweater beneath. He passed the police station, making certain that he was seen waving to a former classmate who had joined the fraternity of blue. As he did, a strange sight caught his eye.

Atop the police station was a gargoyle, similar to the one perched on the corner of the old cathedral he had visited just yesterday. He'd never given the one at the church any thought: cathedrals had gargoyles, that's just the way it was, right? This was the first time he'd noticed one down at the old precinct, however.

Silhouetted by the last crimson and gold rays of sunlight, the gargoyle's eyes seemed to follow him as he continued on his way.

"I'll bet that Goth chick digs you," Jesus said to himself with a wry laugh. "The old goobers who built this town probably loved putting creepy stuff all over the place."

Having completed the first part of his plan, Jesus went around the block and doubled back towards Stew Stu's Studio. He knew his father would eventually head there after his latest tryst. Jesus had hoped to wait in the nearby park to kill time, but the junkies and sodomites were already roaming the area in force. He'd have to find another spot. He eventually found some unoccupied bushes around a tree that wasn't too far from the Studio where he could wait but keep an eye out.

"And now, we wait for phase two," Jesus muttered, trying to sustain his wrathful determination to act.

"Phase two" involved a rather conspicuous baseball cap that he had nicked from a schoolmate. The two had constantly been at each other's throats and were ultimately expelled from school for fighting. Jesus didn't want to admit it, but they probably fought so much because they were so alike. They both had abusive asshole fathers, for one thing. The last fight they had happened because Jesus had stolen the hat. Fortuitously, Jesus had never given it back; the other kid's family had moved not long after they had both gotten expelled.

The hat itself was very distinctive. It had an openmouthed rattlesnake's head, frozen mid-hiss in lacquer, stitched to the brim. It wasn't the sort of thing you'd miss or forget if you saw it.

It was after midnight, in the Witching Hour, when Jesus finally caught a glimpse of his father driving past. He pulled his hoodie over his jacket and donned the garish hat, pulling the brim low over his eyes.

A fake ID flashed to the guy at the door who honestly couldn't care less got Jesus into Stew Stu's Studio. Jesus shuffled in with a side-to-side gait, fiddling with the foldout razor blade he'd tucked into his pocket, wondering if having crapped on it would really make any difference.

Keeping his head turned aside, Jesus shuffled past the sparsely populated dining area, where patrons were eating to sober up after having departed other establishments that were past their closing time. In the back was the bar where, over the din of music, he could hear his father bragging in his boisterous voice about his infidelities and dalliances with other men's wives.

This was it.

This was his moment.

Father and son bumped into each other in a fateful moment, one too drunk to realize what had just happened, the other keeping his head low and his face hidden.

"Watch it, punk!" Jesus's father shouted, adding several threats of bodily harm as Jesus retreated quickly across the club, hop-

ing to vanish into the crowd on the dance floor.

Jesus could hear, "Yeah, you better run!" but was not followed.

Then there she was.

Standing alone against the wall was the Goth girl who had been outside his window the night before. She looked so young, Jesus could not fathom how she had gotten past the door's security. Then again, he'd had no issue...

She was out of place. Not dancing, wrong fashion sense, for sure, and didn't have a cell phone glued to her hands. She was beautiful—striking, even—but she seemed to go completely unnoticed, even by the young men drinking at a table nearby.

She locked eyes with him, and again she gave him that taunting finger-wave of warning, a sly and knowing smile on her doll-like face.

Then everyone, including her, turned to the commotion back at the bar.

"Help me, I've been gutted!" Dunn Senior shouted as he staggered. He was clutching his intestines spilling through the blood-soaked gash in his shirt. Jesus had made the cut so clean that it had taken a moment before the muscles could no longer hold.

While every eye was transfixed on the grisly tableau, Jesus made for the door.

The smile on his face turned to shock. Somehow, the Goth girl had crossed the room in the blink of an eye and stood in front of him. She wore an expression of admonishment, but her eyes were aglow with excitement.

"You really did it," she said almost gleefully, her painted lips trembling.

"I..."

She put a finger to his lips, grabbed his hand, and pulled him towards the exit.

They were through the door and past the bouncer when someone shouted, "Stop that man!" but they were already bounding off into the night on long, sprinting strides.

When they reached the park, Jesus was panting from exertion. He shook his head and looked the Goth girl in the eyes.

"Who are you? Were you track team or something? You're not even..." he paused, having to catch his breath, "...breathing hard!"

"Fratricide is a sin," she taunted with a smile, wagging her finger once more, "but don't worry. I'm not going to tell anyone. Besides, he's not dead... yet. You're not mine until then."

"What the hell are you talking about?" Jesus dropped his head a moment, trying to catch another breath, but when he looked up, the girl was gone.

"Who are you!?" he shouted as he turned in a half-circle.

Even if he had seen which direction the girl had gone, Jesus did not have time to go after her. He had to get home before the inevitable visit later that night when the police would ask him his whereabouts and (if he was lucky) bring him to the hospital (and not an interrogation room).

Jesus ditched the blade, hat, and hoodie into a dumpster along the way.

J esus's luck had held, though it was strange luck indeed. He'd feigned surprise well enough that the deputies had taken him straight to the hospital without asking too many questions. Besides, it's not like a teenager would be out at an after-hours nightclub, right?

Outside his father's hospital room, he overheard frantic chatter from the nurses' station. The special trauma surgeon who had been called in had been in some kind of a hit-and-run accident on the way to the hospital. No one had seen the other car.

Eventually, another surgeon was brought in, but in the days that followed, Jesus's father developed sepsis from the feces that had been on the blade. They put him in a medically induced coma and hoped for the best.

Jesus was called in to the police station several times to speak with the detectives who had been assigned to his father's case.

They always wanted to know about the boy with the hat, how well he knew him, the past altercations, etc. The thing was, they knew who he was, and he certainly would've been a person of interest except for one thing: he was dead. By the time they had matched a name to the description that witnesses were able to give, the kid had already been killed. He'd been found with every bone in his body broken, as though he had been thrown off a building or even out of a plane. Except there weren't any buildings tall enough where he lived to do that kind of damage. And there weren't any flight paths over or anywhere near where they found his body—they'd checked.

They'd also checked all of the trashcans and dumpsters around Stew Stu's Studio, looking to see if the attacker had maybe ditched the weapon or his clothes. Nothing.

But Jesus played it cool. He'd had problems with his old man, sure, but even without a particularly great alibi, no one had ID'd him, not even the doofus who'd checked his fake ID at the bar. They had nothing on him, just a lot of weird circumstances. He hadn't lawyered up, either. Why would he? He didn't do it, and he'd be happy to see them find out who did. Too bad that their prime suspect would never face justice, but he sort of did, right?

Each time Jesus left the station, he'd look up and see the leering gargoyle perched atop the roof. It seemed to look with some kind of anticipation, as though it might come to life and leap upon its prey.

Finally, Jesus asked one of the officers, "How long has that thing been up there? It's creepy."

The officer just gave a shrug.

As the days turned into weeks, Jesus's fears melted into mere uneasiness. Day-to-day life took on a strange sense of normalcy as he waited for the other shoe to drop, if it ever would. He had a little money saved, and he did some work, but it would still be a while before he could finally skip town. Yet he was perpetually confounded by how the police had failed to find the discarded hat, hoodie, and blade. Even if they somehow never turned up, however, there was one thing that could betray him: the Goth girl.

Jesus searched through his high school yearbooks, hoping maybe to find some indi-cation of who she was. She was a runner. Fast. He looked at all of the pictures of the girls' track team, but none of them looked like her. He then went class by class, scouring every photo, but still he found nothing.

Maybe she was a transfer student?

He'd never graduated, so he didn't have a yearbook for his senior year. Determined to figure out just who this girl was, Jesus resolved to stop by the school secretary's office.

"I remember you, Jesus B. Dunn," the school secretary said, and not in a kind way, before handing him a copy of the previous year's yearbook. "This doesn't leave the room."

Jesus searched the pages under the secretary's watchful glare. Nothing. She wasn't in any of the photos for any of the classes.

"He's not in there, either," the secretary said with a sigh when Jesus handed her back the yearbook. She must have assumed he'd been looking for a photo of his father's assumed assailant.

"It's always a shame to lose a mother," she added, her mood seeming to soften. What could he say? He was a hardcase and not her responsibility anymore. "I'm so sorry to hear about your father. At least you had them both long enough to see you into adulthood. Now, the only person responsible for your choices... is you."

Jesus thanked the secretary and left the building. He did loiter for a while across the street until the end-of-day bell rang. He watched the students pour through the exits, into cars and buses, in their excited haste to be done with the school day at last, hoping to maybe catch a glimpse of the mystery girl. But after every car and bus had left, there was still no sign of the Goth girl in the thinning throngs. None of the girls looked or were dressed remotely like her. The Goth phase had long since passed through this southern town and seemed to leave no trace on today's student body.

"Damn!" he muttered as he turned away.

"That's right," came a muffled taunt, seemingly from right behind him.

Jesus spun around, but there was no one. He was becoming convinced that his conscience was beginning to play tricks on him.

Jesus sat alone in his room that night, the house strangely quiet and still. It seemed like only yesterday when the mystery girl had rapped on his window. He fiddled with a box knife, pushing the blade up and back in, brooding over her identity and the events of the past few weeks.

Jesus jumped with a start when the phone rang.

He'd begun to dread the phone. It was always a call for his father or about his father. Whether it was some girl, some girl's man, the cops, or a doctor, it was always about Jesus Dunn Sr. Would he ever be free of him?

Jesus let the phone ring two more times before going to pick it up.

"Hello?"

It was one of the doctors from the hospital, one particularly poor at the art of condolences.

"Jesus? We were about to call you back to the hospital," the doctor droned in a monotone voice, "but there wasn't time. It happened very quickly. Your father took a bad turn for the worse, and… I'm afraid he's passed."

"Thank you, Doctor," Jesus said with as sad a voice as he could muster. He set the phone down and looked around the home that was now his and his alone. He repeated in a jubilant shout, "Thank you, Doctor!"

Jesus's celebration was soon interrupted, however.

Tap tap tap…

"Aww, what the hell?"

It was coming from his bedroom.

Tap tap tap…

Someone was knocking on the glass window.

Jesus took hesitant steps back toward his room, slipping the box knife into his pocket. The knocking persisted, becoming more insistent.

Rather than go to his room, Jesus dashed through the house, out the backdoor and around the corner of his house.

The Goth girl was waiting for him. Over her lace and leathers, she was wearing his discarded hoodie and the ball cap with the lacquered rattlesnake head.

"What the hell?" Jesus said nearly shouting.

The girl smiled at him, almost innocently, then tapped the rattlesnake fangs with the end of a straight razor. The very razor Jesus had used to kill his father!

"What is this?" Jesus's hand slipped surreptitiously to the box knife in his pocket. "Some sort of blackmail?"

"No, silly!" the girl giggled. "I helped you escape! The laws of men, that is." Then she looked up at him from beneath the brim of the cap with shimmering black eyes that were untouched by her coy smile. "But there are some things you can't escape. I did try to warn you."

"Who the hell are you?"

"My name is Mary, but I'm no Saint. I cursed myself, just like you did." The girl made a strange courtesy, holding the corners of the hoodie, the straight razor still in her hand as she did. "I guess that's why we're attracted to each other!"

Jesus whipped out the box cutter.

"I'm gonna cut you, crazy bitch, and after tonight, you're not gonna attract nobody! And you're not telling anybody anything, neither!"

Jesus started to lunge, but then hesitated—the girl just stood there, smiling and unafraid.

"That's right, I'm not telling anyone anything."

Then the thought occurred: he might have some fun with her first.

The girl's eyes and face darkened as though a shroud had been cast over her.

"Heeeyyyy, Zeusssss…" she purred in a low voice, butchering his name and feigning coyness, "*there* you are, and here we go!"

The neighborhood woke to screaming. Whatever it had been was so awful that at least a few neighbors called the police. When the cops showed up, the missing hoodie, hat, and razorblade from the Jesus Dunn Sr. assault [now homicide] were found lying in a neat pile outside, beneath Jesus Dunn Jr.'s bedroom window.

Despite the BOLOs that were put out for him, Jesus Dunn Jr. was never seen or heard from again.

The local newspaper ran an article about his disappearance as well as the circumstances surrounding it, including that he was wanted for questioning as a suspect in the murder of his father.

In the same paper's local interest section, it was noted that the Cathedral had a surprising new addition: parishioners and clergy were stunned to find the gargoyle perched on one of the corners now had a mate. None could say exactly when or how the new gargoyle had been placed there. The article suggested it might be the work of a guerilla artist. What the article did not mention was the new gargoyle's horrified expression.

Michael Tierney is known for writing both non-fiction and fiction, the latter of which includes a variety of genres.

Abraham Strongjohn writes things every so often. When he does, they're usually published by Cirsova. His novelette, Maxus and the Lake of Blood, *is appearing in the Mighty Sons of Hercules anthology, along with Michael Tierney's* Battle of the Rages *and several other stories.*

Black Sky, White Knight

By MARK MELLON

Stranded in the woods without a mount, a Christian knight must make for Heilsberg Castle! Can he survive the trek through pagan territory and reach safety?!

Stark came to in the gathering twilight, longsword still clenched in one hand, left leg pinned under his dead horse. Corpses of men and animals lay scattered all around, grotesquely sprawled in their death agonies, the snow-dusted, frozen river ice stained with vermilion blotches, their lives' blood. Wolves plaintively howled nearby, drawn by the scent of gore, eager to scavenge dead, easy prey.

Stark cocked his right leg, put his foot on the high-cantled saddle, and pushed with all his strength. Slowly, agonizingly, he pulled his leg out from under the horse's weight. When he was finally free, he gasped for breath. Frigid air stabbed at his lungs. Once he'd recovered somewhat, Stark jabbed his sword point into the ice and used it for support as he heaved himself erect.

His left leg was unsteady, but still bore his weight. He was lucky; it wasn't broken. Stark removed his dragon-finned helm. Dirty blond hair poked out from beneath his mail cowl.

The Prussians had prepared their ambush well. The pagans had attacked while the knights were spread out on the River Alle, unable to charge on slick ice. An ash wood arrow had caught Stark's destrier in the chest and brought the big horse down. The knights' winter-*reysa* had ended in miserable defeat. He'd been left for dead with the other slain Germans. His only hope of rescue, Heilsberg Castle's log stockade, lay three leagues to the south, and he was on foot.

Stark sheathed his sword in its scabbard. He picked up the lozenge shield, slung it behind his back, and hung the helm from a hook on his belt. The ice was slippery under his leather boots, but he soon reached the riverbank and trod upon solid ground. The Northern night swiftly fell. Darkness was complete, with neither moon nor stars to guide him. Leafless trees stood straight and black all around Stark, beech, oak, maple, hazel, and rowan. The only light was the ghostly glow cast by heavy snow piled thick on the ground. A big crow landed overhead on a tree's branch and loudly cawed.

Already bone weary, body aching from the fall, he continued south, planted one foot after the other. His stomach rumbled from hunger. Stark ate a small handful of snow to kill his thirst. The wintry cold chainmail that encased him penetrated his thin linen undergarments, chilling him to the marrow.

144

Despite the pain and discomfort, Stark forged on, heedless of his misery. He was a knight sworn to Holy Mary's service, a monk-brother of the Order, accustomed to its hard, unbending discipline, sworn to a life of poverty and mortification, with no thought except to struggle for the Holy Virgin until death came with the promise of salvation and remission of all sins offered to worthy crusaders.

He tried to follow the track laid out by *strutere*, converted Prussians familiar with the *Wiltnisse* who acted as scouts for the Order. Yet it was hard to pick out hatchet-blazed trees in near total darkness. Stark soon realized he was lost. One wrong step and he'd fall into a ravine where he'd be trapped, easy prey for hostile pagans or wolves, certain to freeze to death before daybreak in any event. Stark's only hope was to orient himself by moss growing on trees' north sides and to continue south.

At a hill's crest, Stark spotted a red glimmer in the distance. A fire's light, undoubtedly a pagan camp where a hostile welcome awaited. Still, it was his sole hope for warmth and shelter. He could triumph over them or die in the attempt, the charge he'd accepted when he joined the Order. Stark headed toward the fire.

It took a long time. Stark struggled up and down rugged hills. At each crest, he looked for the crimson fire that steadily burned brighter as he drew nearer. At last, he looked down upon a narrow valley. A small, wooden, circular palisade stood at the bottom. The fire cast long shadows through gaps between the tall logs. Stark slipped and slid as he descended the steep slope. He hid behind a thick oak and carefully watched the palisade.

No guard stood watch. The gate was open. Inside the fire beckoned, promising warmth, salvation, and rescue. He donned his dragon-finned helm, took his shield in his left hand, and drew his sword.

"For Mary and in Jesus's Name!" he cried.

Stark advanced at a swift trot, ready to deal out death to whomever he encountered. He charged into the enclosure. It held a *maia*, a small, rude hut, and a wooden idol. Hewn from a single oaken tree, the idol towered thirty hands high. Four giant faces were carved into the gnarled wooden top, brightly stained with dyes from last summer's fruits and vegetables, the northern face sere white like winter snows, the southern black as mortified death, while the west burned blood red and the east shone mossy green. A great drinking horn rested in a lower branch, full of honey mead that gleamed golden in the firelight. A large white mare without blemish was tethered to the idol by a leathern bridle.

A young woman squatted by the fire on her haunches, tending an iron cauldron that hung over the fire from a tripod. Clad in a long deerskin tunic, more a girl than a woman, her long hair hung lank and flaxen. Freshly cooked barley cakes were piled beside her on a wooden trencher. She fished a cake from the cauldron with a slotted wooden spoon and laid it on the trencher.

The girl fixed Stark with pale blue eyes, her gaze indifferent, unafraid. "Why are you here?" she said in passable German. "You do not belong."

Stark stood tall in his white surcoat, emblazoned with a black cross on the chest. Face hidden by his dragon-finned helm, he raised his sword high to make his menacing intent plain.

"Sorceress. Prussian witch. I am Johann Ritter von Stark, a monk-brother of the Order of Saint Mary. I need food and drink and that horse. If you try to stop me from taking them, I'll slay you and not shed a tear."

The girl shrugged and laid another cake on the trencher. "I am the *Waidelinn* Erdwe, Sventovit's vestal. This is his food and drink; the horse is his sacred oracle. You cannot have them."

"No pagans' devil idol will stay me. The Lord commands me. I'll have what I must."

Stark strode over to the fire. He took off his helm, set it upon the ground, and crammed barley cakes into his mouth. Erdwe made no move to stop him. Stomach full, mouth dry, Stark went to the tree and took down the brimming horn of mead from the branch. He drank deeply of the mead. The potent alcoholic brew made the blood run hot in his veins, infused new vigor into him.

"Now you die, Christian," Erdwe said.

Stark laughed in scorn.

There was a deafening bass rumble from beyond the palisade. A huge, long-horned, shaggy black beast trotted into the enclosure, an aurochs, three times bigger than a domestic bull. Small eyes red with rage, he pawed the ground with a fore hoof and angrily shook long, curved horns.

Stark donned his helm. He took a solid stance, feet spread wide, guarded by his shield, sword ready to deal a killing blow.

"EEEEOOOOOOOOO," the aurochs lowed.

The great ox charged. He slammed into Stark's shield, knocked him flying through the air. Stark slammed into the palisade's logs with a sickening thud. He collapsed in a heap on the hard, frozen ground. Erdwe laughed to see his plight. Certain now of victory, the aurochs charged again, about to trample Stark and toss him about with his cruel horns until the life was thrashed out of him.

At the last second, Stark leaped to his feet, too tough to meekly submit even though every muscle in his body ached like a man on the rack. He neatly sidestepped the aurochs's second charge. With the precision and skill that only came from years of drill and practice, he brought his sword down in a low, swooping blow.

The heavy iron sword cut through the aurochs' right foreleg at the brisket. Leg neatly severed, the aurochs bellowed in inarticulate pain as he fell to the ground. The ox's eyes rolled around in his head. His long pink tongue jutted from his bristly muzzle. Red-black blood rhythmically pulsed from the amputated limb.

Stark ran to the aurochs. He plunged his sword deep into the heart girth. The great ox let out one last, sad sigh and died. Stark stood over the dead aurochs, shoulders hunched, panting as he recovered his breath.

"So, witch? Your champion failed you. Now I'll destroy your false, pagan idol before I leave."

Erdwe smiled cryptically and fished another cake from the cauldron. Stark snarled and spat at her. He raised the sword high to hack down the log idol. A huge black crow landed on the idol's top, loudly cawed, and flapped his obsidian wings. Wolves howled in the valley. Other packs took up their cries until numerous piercing wails loudly rang in Stark's ears, driving him to the point of madness.

Before Stark's unbelieving eyes, the idol's four faces contorted, stretched to life. Gnarled wooden folds twisted tight in broad grimaces of hatred and loathing, deeply inset eyes alive with wrath and foreboding. Despite himself, Stark trembled before the awful, portentous visages. He lowered his sword.

"Now your courage fails you, knight," Erdwe cried. "Sventovit is angry. Flee while you still can."

Stung by a woman's rebuke, Stark gathered up what remained of his courage. "May the good Lord damn you and your idol to hell, base witch!"

He raised his sword and severed the bridle knot that secured the mare to the idol. The white horse screamed. She reared up on her hind legs. Stark dropped his sword and shield. He grabbed the horse by the mane, neatly vaulted onto her, and took the reins up in his hands.

"*Vorwärts*, forward," he cried.

Stark repeatedly dug his heels into the mare's flanks. Maddened by the blows, the horse bolted from the enclosure at a full gallop. Stark rode away from the palisade, followed by the slowly diminishing strains of Erdwe's harsh, mocking laughter.

He snatched off his dragon-finned helm and threw it aside so he could see the way ahead. Surefooted even in the frozen night, the mare plunged on ahead as she tore over the hard-packed snow. A faint gleam from a nearby ridge heralded the eastern dawn. Sure of his direction now, Stark pulled hard on the bridle and kept the mare headed southward. He had a real chance to escape now, to reach Heilsberg Castle and safety. A rare smile creased his face.

The mare threw her head back and whinnied, a long, mournful cry as intelligible as human speech to Stark.

"Know your fate, Christian. Your next *reysa* means the end, brought low by a snare, hacked to pieces by women and children. Sventovit's doom will be mean and miserable."

Stark only clenched the horse's flanks more tightly. He slapped the mare's hindquarters with a hard, mailed hand to drive her on, grim face prematurely creased and wizened, the once blond hair now ashen white, but still determined as ever.

For he was a knight of the Order of Saint Mary, a monk-brother sworn to holy vows of privation and crusade, determined to give his life in the service of God in the sure certainty of relief from sin and instant ascent upon death to the Saints' company where he would sit at the Holy Virgin's foot, her servant in death as in life.

"So be it!" he cried.

The mare rode on through the endless Northern forest, a pure white steed in the endless white *Wiltnesse.*

Mark Mellon is a novelist who supports his family by working as an attorney. He has four novels and over eighty short stories published. Mark writes hardboiled, two-fisted, blood and guts pulp fiction. More information can be found at www.mellonowritesagain.com.

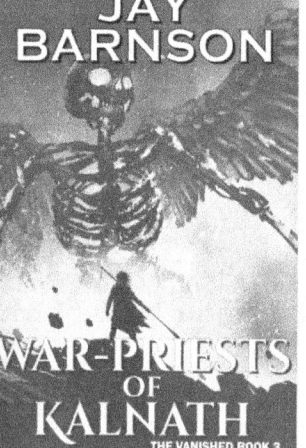

To a Dead Soul in Morbid Love

By MATTHEW PUNGITORE

In a ghoulish tale that drives to madness, the blasphemous corpse wizard Lord Tryphon, cheater of death, must make his grim way to the revelry of Dionysus!

(Manuscript found beside an unidentified male body in Cairo)

Angels sorrow and sphinxes stare amongst sulking rows of sarcophagi within that forsaken Egyptian tomb to which my ladylove had led me amidst the summer solstice gloom. That was a night of unforgettable loss, of unforeseeable doom. I remember how my mistress lit every forlorn candle and then knelt before an incredible statue of Osiris standing atop a pedestal engraved with hieroglyphs arcane and sensual.

Those symbols told a story of Lord Tryphon; it is one of the many myths surrounding that nefarious necromancer who is said to have died in 30 BC and risen again in AD 30.

I'll always remember how, after I had finished reading and translating those glyphs, my lover started giggling and moaning. And I shan't forget the weird voice from her mouth as she cried out in lust. Then she raised forth a knife and cut off several locks of her red hair.

My pretty lover pushed me away and plunged the dagger through her heart.

Nausea and horror mounted as I ran out of that sardonic sepulcher, my suicidal paramour's resounding laughter chasing me. What baleful cackling!

Bewitching presences, yawping revenants of yore, assaulted all rationality. Enchantment and mesmerism held sway with tenebrous gauntlets. Every thought in my skull took the image of Tryphon. Hypnotized by the hieroglyphs, which will no doubt haunt me forevermore, those words consuming every reason for living, I returned inside to the crypt and stood before Osiris, and I began rereading.

Three days or more passed in thirst and terror. Candlelight faded, slowly dying, until the light, too, abandoned me in total noxious darkness.

I'll never know what ultimately allowed me to regain control, but when I did break free of paralysis, I still wasn't myself. Perversity dominated. There's no justification for what happened next. After my unspeakable acts, I rushed screaming out of that frightening shrine.

The story on the pedestal has never vacated my thoughts. Its tail revolves behind my ears. The stench from its pictographs chokes my eyes. Each sense, a canopic jar of pain.

I must share the ancient narrative. Leave nothing of myself.

What follows is my translation of that legend engraved in black stone. An anguished memorial for the luscious corpse of my lady. This tale, which stole my lover's life and damned my soul, commands my hand, and starts thusly:

The African sky shrivels in a surreal sandstorm.

In a temple far below the surface, deep within an embrace of black earth, Lord Tryphon dreamed inside his sarcophagus.

Over the bubbling froth within his dreamscape, Stygian waves carried his astral form aloft to a floating nymphaeum wherein Gorgon shades shrouded their faces and ghostly nymphs tripped and pranced round a Lethean fountain.

Tryphon reached a stairway and ascended its twilit steps, whereupon he encountered somber-clad Persephone.

Before he awoke from this vision, he heard the goddess whisper a warning unto him.

"Condemnation's tide contaminates the realm of mortals, Lord Tryphon. Should you escape Hades and venture up into the living world above your palace pediment, hostility would harass you for your vanity and decadence."

The dream binding him to the nether-world was then done. He roared upon his unholy awakening in the earthly plane. Lord Tryphon had returned from death and blasphemed against sanctity with his new, undead existence. His profane metamorphosis had finished, and the immortality spell he had cast many years ago was now complete.

Removed was his flesh, exchanged for everlasting life. His will and bone remained. At present, Tryphon's body was a human-like skeleton. A vermeil cloak, his only covering.

Whilst he had been lying dead, his loyal servants had seen to it that his skull, fingers, toes, ribs, and teeth were encrusted with gold, red crystals, and precious yellow stones. Legs had transmuted into white jade; arms into orange sapphire and topaz. Infernal golden threads and unearthly clay united his bones, animated and made firm by chthonic influences.

Even his former senses had been replaced with artificial, otherworldly ones. Such faculties, although mimicking natural sensory abilities, were actually heightened, more in tune with dimensions above common understanding. Rich sensations!

Nitocris, the current servant maiden to Lord Tryphon, helped her master out of his pulsating coffin, which grotesque effigies decorated and spikes trimmed.

This was only her first night as Tryphon's living slave girl, and she had not drunk nor eaten anything since she took her vows of betrothal to him that morn. She would never be considered truly married to him until the moment of her physical death.

Many other lovely nymphs had come before her to protect the wizard lord while he slept, each starving themselves dead to maintain their purity, each becoming another one of his wives and joining his harem in the afterlife.

The skinny damsel's green eyes marveled at the hooded robe her master wore. Her soft jet-black fingers caressed its vermillion fabric made of the red hair of Tryphon's wives. Nitocris beamed euphoric, musing on how, at the hour of her death, her scarlet hair would be added to her lord's cloak also.

On Tryphon's awakening, Nitocris was allowed to eat and drink again. The magician's male priests brought her a small cup of honey, a plate of fresh grapes, and a thin jug of wine. While she ate in private, Tryphon spoke secretly with his ghoul clerics.

"An invitation to a festival in honor of Dionysus came for you, mighty lord," said a priest. "The revelry is at a grotto not very far from here, my sire. The gods knew that you would rise this night. It would be auspicious to show your power and majesty at the banquet now that you have come back to this sphere.

"If you do go, however, the trip might be perilous. There are many out there, in the land above, who abhor us, and they would try to harm you. Famine and plague have been tormenting the upper earth, and the mortals blame magic and the gods. Countless have turned to warlike doctrines and violent barbarism. Many of your followers and warriors have been killed by those barbarians and zealous rebels, who are banes to all diabolism and sorcery."

The undead sorcerer seethed. "Mortals have spilled the blood of my faithful people? I'll not be threatened by provincial savages. To the festival I embark, unguarded and undaunted, with only Nitocris beside me on the journey. We must take a chariot but no conventional contrivance, for my eldritch conjurations will perform sufficiently. The small-minded mortals will cower and bend to my noble beauty as I pass, and they shall know I fear naught of their caitiff sort. In blood and wine would I revel whilst those filthy knaves shrink in pestilent darkness!"

Spirits of the dead were summoned before Lord Tryphon in the amphitheater nestled betwixt the catacombs and the treasury. These lemures revealed the celebration's true location, and their prophecies foretold the destruction of Tryphon's shrine.

Those whom the ghosts marked as fated traitors were flayed alive. Devouring their flesh increased the warlock's strength. Their blood enhanced his spells of flame, necromancy, diablerie, spirit evocation, and item invocation. Tryphon practiced numerous esoteric crafts, including the art of materializing weapons and armor stowed in obscure ultramundane rifts.

Half the loyal cultists hid the treasure far from the temple; the other half stayed to defend the avernal labyrinth from the foreseen invasion.

Destiny be defied! If ruin were inevitable, the sorcerer reasoned, it would be fun to lounge on indulgence until the unavoidable end. Eternal splendor, he believed, would be reborn in him at that calamitous hour. Dionysus' party made a desirable distraction.

After preparations were done, the necromancer and his chaste hierodule left the underground fane to ascend upon the blighted land of humanity.

Their cadaverous horses, veiled in linen, could endure the sandstorm.

Nitocris pressed her waifish figure to revered Lord Tryphon, whose sylph minions shielded them both from any harmful effect of the hostile storm, while the quadriga raced across a wailing desert.

Malaise sweltered on the following morn. A sick Sun groped the shirtless sky. Its sandy cerements were torn off that ill Aether.

The duo drove past diseased tramps, decaying cannibals, coughing prostitutes, scabby cripples, leper doomsayers, self-mutilating lunatics, sermonizing outcasts, sordid beggars, bloodstained flagellants, brooding ruins, and burnt villages.

Crucified victims screamed as vultures and ravens were pecking at their bloody wounds.

The jeremiads of every prophet of doom, lecturing amongst tearstained congregations, forecasted Judgment Day.

Ominous mephitis fattened the maggot wind. A charnel stench, from numberless mass graves and corpse-heaps, shunned, stinking, impregnated the air with rot. Oh, vermin havoc!

Tryphon and Nitocris were progressing through this sorrowful wasteland with Olympian indifference. At dusk, their self-obsessed apathy turned to ire. A group of hostile chariots was now circling them in ambush.

Enemy javelins and arrows rained, but all in vain since Tryphon had summoned, with rapid incantation, a spectral aegis delivered by fiends of Tartarus. The shield instantly appeared and defended the magus and the maid thrall. Meanwhile, the wormy horses were essentially immune to those mundane thorns of bronze and iron.

Her red hair fluttering like cochineal curtains, Nitocris commanded the horses and sent them into the adversarial pack.

Swords and spears bit into the carnelian bones of the sorcerer, who was conjuring wraiths from the deep of Erebus.

As these emanations emerged, their hideousness maddened the ruffians. Bedlam flared. Those raiders and outlaws slashed and foined, deranged and hectic, yet striking themselves.

Fiery teeth and heart-stopping horror kindled a massacre.

When the conjurer's specters had completed their surge, the ambush now unquestionably quashed, netherworld shadows dragged the ghosts back to the chasm whence they came.

Without spending too much time, the repeated prayers of his earnest servant healed Tryphon's injuries.

Nearby air eidolons and dead plebeians drifting beside them were then overheard in grim conversation.

Nitocris, her face grief-twisted, wiped her tears. "They speak of our clan."

"Perished," said Tryphon.

"The wind says danger approaches," said

Nitocris. "An army."

Tryphon chortled. "A gang of brutes."

He started stroking her lustrous straight hair.

"Chariots carrying the severed heads of your priests, sire!"

"I'll honor those who loyally died for me."

"My lord, are you hearing what I do? A demi-giantess is with them. You can't!"

"Audacious arrogance, Nitocris, bare and brash, puts bite on even our bluntest blade."

By his command, they rested and waited for the threat to appear to them.

Nitocris, who had wanted to make haste for the party instead of loitering, trembled in the slender arms of the gaunt mage, whom she had adored above all else ever since she first began her lessons in the arts of mystic performance, demonic liturgy, infernal theologies, and funerary rites.

She feared what the spirits had just told her—a group of barbarians, commanded by a half-giant woman, was coming to hunt, to persecute.

Nitocris' earliest studies with the occult magisters had taught her to dread the tellurian giants of the torrid wastes: desert hybrids descending from the offspring of those Titans, behemoths, exiled humans, and dune apes who, in far more ancient times, had all mated with one another. For fun would those degenerate crossbreeds smash anything of magic or miracle, whether holy or not, and they would crush anything in their path that was enchanted by the gods, sorcery, or the dead.

The iconoclast ogres had further divided the mundane realm from the supernatural, the celestial, the infernal, and the divine. Those who had not wanted to see the death of magic slew many of these abominations. The surviving giants had avoided eradication by hiding themselves in the outskirts and wildlands, breeding with mortals who had wandered astray; thus, the true demi-giant race had begun.

One such creature, a chieftainess, part giant and part human, was presently stalking Nitocris and Tryphon. Anon, at the time of her arrival, she would bring with her a coterie of barbarians, wild humans hungering for combat and violence.

To fight distress, and to please the master, Nitocris removed her golden breastplate and began a dance. Her naked body moved with exotic, tantalizing physique and finesse. The loveliness of her floral breath cavorted on the breeze. Her supple legs drew graceful motions in the air. The passionate red of her hair kissed the sky. Her charming, dainty feet traced tiny scrolls in the sand.

A dance so alluring it attracted Satyrs, nymphs, and desert daemons. They came to dance along and play beside her.

The gambol did amuse Lord Tryphon, who was inconspicuously preparing a summoning trap for the battle to come.

When charioting barbarians emerged at daybreak, the dancing was through, and the happy divinities disappeared.

Berenice, the demi-giant commander of this gang, ordered her charioteers to halt before the skeleton wizard and his virgin slave.

This huge female, muscular and hairy, with her gray eyes did look daggers at the undead nobleman.

Berenice's words reeked venom. "The earth belongs to muscle and iron. Gods and demons are curses. Magic is plague. Faith brought catastrophe. I heard your awakening, devil. I've been slaying the supernatural for so long, I can smell it from great distances. I see the flies, toads, and worms moving between your bones; they prop you up, sorcerer. I toppled your unworldly temple, corrupt malefactor, and I'll crown those ruins with your sickening ashes."

Tryphon's concealed demons materialized at once and trampled into the barbarians. Javelins and arrows came down against the ghastly servants. Spears thrust into flying abyss fiends.

Boisterous, the gray Berenice fought howling.

Nitocris and her lord fled on their quadriga. The specter swarm assailed the enemy myrmidons. On an enormous war chariot, Berenice followed the two, and she attempted to ram them. Nonetheless, with Nitocris controlling the horses, her swift chariot dodged the heavy adversary's massive carriage.

Tryphon attacked the towering woman with his conjured sword, but she blocked with cowhide. The conjurer spent his fire exhalation upon Berenice's spear and shield. Clashing swords raged sanguine!

Deathly claws and basilisk breath vanquished the barbarians. After a hellish butchery, their corpses were taken as grisly trophies to the underworld.

In a furious spray of crimson, this vicious confrontation ended when Tryphon parried Berenice's swinging blade and pierced her heart with a radiant brand!

Berenice collapsed dead onto the road as Nitocris and Tryphon hurried to the party.

When they finally arrived, the grotto banquet welcomed them in with feasting, revelry, sacrifices, debauchery, and ritual suicides. Nitocris joined in the dancing upon a bloody floor. Amidst the festival, Tryphon tasted rapture, a wine of corruption, in the corpsy bed of a ghoulish coven.

Vice and vengeance victorious!

Thus concludes this tale of macabre spree. Lorn asp of love, slithering morbid lust undreamed of: narration's end, the open grave calling me.

Matthew Pungitore interviewed Alex of Cirsova Magazine (the interview appeared on the Castalia House blog). Matthew is the author of "Wychyrst Tower" (Cirsova, Winter 2021), The Report of Mr. Charles Aalmers and other stories, and more.

Notes

What a busy summer it's been!

Misha Burnett's Small Worlds is out the door, and Mighty Sons of Hercules has hopefully followed shortly after.

Our big fall project, of course, will be collecting **Wild Star 6: Orphan of the Shadowy Moon**, which we serialized last year.

We've got one installment left of **The Gold Exigency** and will be serializing **The Superior Griefs** in 2024. 2024…

We've got so much going on next year!

First, we'll be putting out an all new fantasy novel from Jim Breyfogle, **A Bad Case of Dead**, an action-packed fantastical romance about a young man who is struck with a curse of undeath which he must quest to remove so he can be united with his beloved.

Later in 2024, we're thrilled and humbled to be collecting SFF legend Adrian Cole's Dream Lords trilogy in a single omnibus collection along with a companion volume collecting the new Dream Lords stories he's been publishing since 2016.

We've also got an upcoming anthology of justice-dealing raygun-slinging action from JD Cowan.

I don't know what else we'll have on tap, aside from collecting **The Gold Exigency** in the fall, but suffice it to say, we're busy beyond believe here at Cirsova Publishing!

Finally, I'd like to specially thank Xavier, one of our copy editors, for all of the time and hard work he has put into making Cirsova Magazine what it is. This is the last issue of Cirsova Magazine that will have been edited by Xavier. We wish him all the luck in the world in his future endeavors!

Joining the team for our next issue will be Yakov Merkin. Author of the Galaxy Ascendant series, the Light Unto Another World series, and the forthcoming Amaranth Angels manga, Yakov has managed to find the time to squeeze in helping with Cirsova Magazine copy editing duties.

We hope you enjoyed this "gothic" issue. While a little bit outside of our usual fare, I think every story in here lived up to Cirsova's reputation for publishing the best in adventure, romance, and, yes, strange fiction!

Our next issue in December has some real doozies! You won't want to miss it. I know you probably can't tell because of our numbering, but the Winter 2023 issue will be the 30th issue of Cirsova Magazine! It's been a wild ride so far, and for the moment, we have no signs of slowing down.

"Alex" P. Alexander, Editor